Praise for the Aurora

"Plenty of charming characters, red herrings, labyrinthine twists and turns and brushes with death before you can even begin to guess whodunit. *Paint the Town Dead* is a cleverly crafted mystery full of secrets and intrigues that kept me guessing till the end."

– Connie Archer,
Author of the Soup Lover's Mystery Series

"Johnson paints characters with a folksy charm that makes them feel like family...Color me a fan!"

– Diane Vallere,
Author of *The Decorator Who Knew Too Much*

"Rory finds herself needing to uncover the truth of a friend's shocking death as everyone else seems satisfied with the easy answer. She's willing to risk friendships, and her own life, to chip away to reach the unvarnished truth."

– Christina Freeburn,
Author of *Masked to Death*

"The strength of the book, as in most good cozy mysteries, lies in the main character...The book really poses the question, within a well-written cozy, is nature or nurture more important in what a person becomes?...This underlying story makes this an interesting choice for book clubs to discuss."

– *Examiner.com*

"Johnson has penned a charming mystery filled with colorful characters, clever plot twists and unexpected surprises that will keep you guessing whodunit right until the end. A rewarding read and a refreshing debut."

—Hannah Dennison,
Author of the Vicky Hill Mysteries Mysteries

"With a smart, sympathetic protagonist, lots of colorful details, and even tips on creating trompe l'oeil paintings, *A Palette for Murder* is a work of art."

"Rory is definitely a quirky character; she has the ability to draw the readers in so that they want to follow her through her adventures."

"Johnson has crafted a clever mystery with a colorful protagonist. Set along the vibrant Southern California coast, this story resonates with a rich understanding of the artistic as well as the homeless communities. A smooth read!"

"Johnson has an assured, steady hand in creating complex plotlines in *Fatal Brushstroke*. Readers will definitely want to revisit Vista Beach in Aurora's next outing of investigating."

"A fun and fast-paced romp with plenty of suspense and intrigue, colorful characters, infidelity and family secrets. *Fatal Brushstroke* is sure to please cozy readers, especially those who love crafts mixed with murder."

"Enjoyable, fun and entertaining...Aurora is a strong character you immediately feel like you have known her a lifetime...I love books that keep you reading late into the night and for me this is one of them great books."

Designed for Haunting

Designed for Haunting

An Aurora Anderson Mystery

Sybil Johnson

HENERY PRESS

Copyright

DESIGNED FOR HAUNTING
An Aurora Anderson Mystery
Part of the Henery Press Mystery Collection

First Edition | October 2018

Henery Press, LLC
www.henerypress.com

Trade Paperback ISBN-13: 978-1-63511-402-7
Digital epub ISBN-13: 978-1-63511-403-4
Kindle ISBN-13: 978-1-63511-404-1
Hardcover ISBN-13: 978-1-63511-405-8

Printed in the United States of America

To libraries and librarians everywhere

ACKNOWLEDGMENTS

I've dedicated this book to libraries and librarians because of everything they've given to me over the years, for all the worlds they've introduced me to, real and imagined. Without them, I would not have discovered many wonderful books and authors or learned so many interesting things.

Thank you to everyone who has read my books. A special thanks goes to Pam Kuch for spreading the word about the adventures of Aurora Anderson and encouraging others to follow along.

To Maria Edwards, Meagan Smith, and everyone else at Henery Press, thanks for helping to make this book the best it can be. And to all of the hens in the Hen House, I've enjoyed talking with each and every one of you over the years.

To Diane Vallere and Bear Vallere, thank you for letting Bear do an "acting" gig in this book.

And, finally, to my husband, Steve, a big thank you for his continued support.

Chapter 1

Two weeks before Halloween, Rory Anderson received an email from Beyond The Grave.

Chills ran down her spine as she stared at the words on the computer screen.

"I think I have a stalker," the message read. "If you're reading this I'm either missing or dead. My life may depend on what you do. Please find out what happened to me. You're the only one I can trust." Below the startling words were Zelena Alvarez's social media and email accounts with their corresponding passwords.

Rory pushed her chair away from her desk and closed her eyes, taking several deep breaths to slow down her racing heart. Once the analytical side of her brain kicked in, she rolled the chair back to its place in front of her computer and stared at the screen once again. As she reread the unexpected message, looking for clues to its authenticity, a brown Abyssinian cat jumped up on her lap and butted her head against the sleeve of Rory's gray hoodie. She absently stroked the cat's fur. "What do you think, Sekhmet? You've met Zelena. Do you think she sent this?"

Sekhmet meowed, then curled up on Rory's lap and closed her eyes. Rory stroked the cat's fur a few more times before picking up her cell phone and dialing Zelena's number. When the call went to voicemail, she left a short message, then sat back in her chair and stared out the window in front of her desk at the street beyond. A delivery van drove down Seagull Lane past her single-story stucco house, stopping at a two-story Mediterranean three doors down. The driver hopped out, package in hand, and headed up a walkway lined with foam tombstones. Ghosts hanging from a tree in the yard across the street swayed in the ocean breeze.

As she watched the cluster of white sheets move back and forth, she thought back to the last time she'd seen her friend. Zelena had seemed fine at the decorative painting chapter meeting a few days before, but Rory had been so busy discussing the group's upcoming charity event and the changes everyone wanted her to make to the chapter's website, she might not have noticed a problem.

Rory swiveled her chair back and forth. Sekhmet opened one eye and stared at her in disapproval. When the movement didn't stop, the cat jumped off her lap and, tail held high, walked across the great room that spanned the front of the house, into the area set aside for the living room, and curled up on the sofa.

Pushing a strand of her shoulder length brown hair away from her eyes, Rory picked up her cell phone once again and dialed the number for her best friend and fellow painter, Elizabeth Dexter.

"Hi, Rory," Liz said in a cheerful voice. "Hold on a sec."

Rory could just make out voices speaking Japanese in the background.

"Sorry about that. What's up?" Liz said when she came back on the line.

"Are you with a client? Do you have time to talk?"

The click click of heels on a wood floor followed by the soft thud of a door closing came over the phone line. "I'm showing a house to cousins of my mother's." Liz lowered her voice. "Between you and me, they're driving me bonkers. I'm running out of places to show them in Vista Beach. They want to be close to LAX and my mom. I've suggested neighboring cities, but they insist on buying something here in town."

"Are these the same cousins you stayed with in Japan that one summer?"

"They're the ones. I'm leaving them alone to discuss the place in private. I have a few minutes. What did you want to talk about?"

"Have you heard from Zelena recently?"

"Not since the chapter meeting last weekend. Why?"

"I got the oddest email." Rory read its contents to her friend.

"Are you sure she sent it?"

"Technically it's from some company called Beyond The Grave."

"Creepy."

"Hold on. Let me see what I can find out about them." A few keystrokes later and Rory was staring at the search engine's results on the company. "Huh. Veronica wrote a piece about them for the paper," she said, referring to the reporter for the local newspaper, *The Vista Beach View*. "They're based here in town. It says here they send out emails...after you die."

Liz sucked in her breath. "You don't think...?"

"I hope not." Relief washed over Rory after she finished reading the article. "Apparently, they also store and send out information at a specified time. Maybe that's what happened here."

"Are you absolutely sure that's who the message came from?"

Rory leaned back in her chair. "You think it's a prank."

"There have been a lot of them around town in the last week or so."

"This doesn't seem the same kind of thing as changing the names of streets and egging houses. Those were obviously Halloween related."

"Maybe it was sent by accident then. Just a sec." Liz spoke in Japanese to someone on the other end of the line. "I've got to go. They're ready to talk business."

"I'm going to call Beyond The Grave to find out more about this email. Can you call some members of our painting chapter? The ones you think are the closest to Zelena. Maybe someone has heard from her since the meeting."

"I'll get on it right after I'm done here."

They hung up after promising to get back in touch as soon as they had any news to share.

Rory called the phone number for Beyond The Grave listed at the bottom of the disturbing email. After explaining about the message she received, she heard the tap tap tap of a keyboard over the phone. Finally, the woman on the other end of the line said, "That message came from us, all right. It was triggered when Ms. Alvarez didn't respond to three heartbeat messages in a row."

"How often do you send these heartbeat messages?"

"As often as the client specifies. Ms. Alvarez has her account set up so we send one to her each day. The client clicks on a link in the email and enters a password so we know she's okay. If three messages are ignored, the system automatically sends out the emails the client has put together."

Rory sat up straighter. "You can set up more than one message?"

"As many as you want, to whoever you want."

"Did Zelena send out more than one?"

"I'm afraid I can't give you that information without authorization from a supervisor."

"I understand." Rory drummed her fingers on her desk while she thought about everything the woman had told her. "What happens if someone's somewhere she can't receive email?"

"The event will be triggered unless she notifies us she'll be out of touch for a period of time." A few tap tap taps later, the woman said, "I don't see any pauses registered."

"And this message couldn't have been sent by accident? Some glitch in the software?"

"Certainly not. We take our job seriously."

"Of course. When was the last heartbeat message sent?"

"Tuesday...yesterday...at eight a.m."

"All the previous messages were sent around the same time of day?"

"That's right."

Rory did a quick calculation in her head. That meant something happened between the end of Saturday's meeting and eight a.m. Sunday morning.

The woman cleared her throat. "I hope that's all this is, Ms. Alvarez forgetting to notify us. Is there anything else I can do for you?"

"No, thank you for your time." After she hung up, Rory clutched at the hope Zelena had simply forgotten to register her absence with the company. She was deciding what to do next when Liz called back.

"I couldn't get hold of everyone, but none of the people I talked to have seen or heard from Zelena since Saturday's chapter meeting. Maybe she had to leave town suddenly on business."

"She's a kindergarten teacher. I don't think she goes out of town on business much."

"Some family thing, then."

"I don't know much about her family, but I got the impression she wasn't on speaking terms with them." Rory hit her forehead with the palm of her hand. "Of course. Vista Beach Elementary. Someone must have noticed she didn't show up for work."

"They're on break this week. Plumbing issues. Toilets overflowed in several of the bathrooms and flooded some areas, so school's out while they clean up and fix the problem. Do you think we should call the police?"

"Let's wait and see if we can find her first. I don't want to jump the gun."

Liz said in a hushed voice, "Do you think she's...dead?"

"I hope not, but I think we need to check her apartment. She might have had an accident and be unable to call for help."

"Right. The Dynamic Duo to the rescue! Meet you at her place in a bit."

Rory stuffed her cell phone in her pocket, grabbed her keys and headed out the door.

Ten minutes later, Rory pulled into a parking space in front of a tan stucco building in the eastern part of Vista Beach, a mile from the ocean. A driveway extended down one side of the triplex, a narrow walkway down the other. The small lawn that separated the sidewalk from the unit closest to the street butted up against hedges planted under the windows on either side of the front door. Two jack-o-lanterns grinned at her from opposite sides of the porch, the only Halloween decorations in sight.

As Rory stepped out of her car, she spotted a petite figure standing on tiptoe, leaning over the hedge to the left of the door. Dark brown hair fashioned in a pixie cut, the woman wore black dress pants and a long-sleeved blouse printed in a red and black pattern.

Rory crossed the lawn toward her. "Any luck?"

Liz turned around and shook her head. "I tried knocking, just in case the doorbell wasn't working. No response." She wrinkled her petite nose in worry and gestured toward the window she'd been trying to look into. "I'm too short to see inside. You're a lot taller. You try."

Rory leaned her six-foot frame over the hedge, her jeans brushing up against the foliage. With her face pressed against the glass, she cupped her hand around her eyes and peered inside. Partially drawn curtains revealed a living room that appeared to be deserted. No overturned chairs, no lamps lying on the floor, no signs of a struggle. "Everything looks okay. Let me look in the other window." She repeated the process on the other side of the door but the blinds were drawn, preventing her from making out anything inside. "Can't see anything over here." She stepped back and looked up at the second floor. For a moment, she thought she saw movement, but it was only a curtain fluttering in a light breeze that blew through the open window. "Doesn't look like she's home."

"I saw Zelena's car parked on the street. We need to get in there to make sure she's okay. Like you said on the phone, she might be inside, struggling to call for help." Liz glanced around before taking a slim case out of her purse and displaying its contents. "I brought my tools, just in case."

Rory raised an eyebrow. "When did you get lock picks? Are those even legal? And where do you—never mind, I don't want to know anything about them. We may not need them, anyway. Zelena told me once she keeps a spare key out here." She studied the foliage next to the doorstep before zeroing in on a cluster of plants. She parted some leaves and picked up a garden gnome, turning it over to reveal a key taped underneath it. "Got it."

"I'm never going to get any practice," Liz grumbled as Rory inserted the key in the front door.

Moments later, the two of them stood in the apartment's entryway facing a flight of stairs that led to the upper level.

Rory called out in her loudest voice, "Zelena, are you home?" and anxiously waited for a response.

An oppressive silence hung over them. They both strained to hear the faintest sound, but no answering call greeted them.

"You take the downstairs, I'll take the upstairs," Rory said.

Liz bobbed her head in agreement and headed into the room to the right of the door while Rory climbed the single flight of stairs to the upper level. She made her way down the hall, looking into each of the three rooms. Part of her hoped she'd find Zelena lying unconscious behind one of the doors, part of her hoped she'd find nothing. Rory knocked on each door before entering, calling out as she stepped inside.

Nothing stood out as unusual in the bedroom and bathroom. No evidence of a fight or a hurried departure. The bed was made and the towels hanging on the racks were bone dry as if they hadn't been used in days.

The final room held a home office. Rory's gaze swept the area, taking in the furniture as well as the movie and television show posters that decorated one wall.

A half dozen framed childrens' drawings hung above a desk, each one neatly labeled with the date and artist's name, one for every year Zelena had taught kindergarten at Vista Beach Elementary. Rory's gaze zeroed in on a laptop that sat in the center of the desk. She checked the few papers neatly piled beside it before she powered up the computer, crossing her fingers she would be able to view its contents. Luckily, Zelena hadn't found the need to password protect it so she was able to conduct a brief search, looking through the files on the desktop and scrolling through the browser's history. Nothing she saw explained her friend's sudden disappearance.

Liz walked in the door while Rory was turning off the laptop. "Everything looks okay downstairs. I found an empty suitcase in the hall closet. Unless she has another one, she didn't go on a trip. I didn't see her purse. Is it up here?"

"I haven't found it. There weren't any empty hangers in the bedroom, either. Other than that, it's hard to tell if there are any clothes missing. Did anything look out of place?"

"Not that I could see." Liz nodded toward the laptop. "Find anything on it?"

"Nothing obvious. Her browser history doesn't show any recent visits to travel websites. I'd have to look at it more closely to be absolutely sure, but I didn't see anything that indicates she planned on going anywhere or that would explain her disappearance."

"In her message, she said something about a stalker, didn't she?" Liz pointed to a framed poster for the television sitcom, *Mommy's Little Helper*. On it, a ten-year-old Zelena stood arms folded in front of her with an impish grin on her face. A brown Teddy bear leaned against her leg. "Maybe it has something to do with her time on *MLH*. She *was* really well-known."

"That show went off the air at least fifteen years ago."

"Some people still remember her. There's even a Facebook page dedicated to the show. People post on it all the time."

"I don't like to think she's being followed by a deranged fan."

"Neither do I, but it happens."

Rory's gaze swept the room one last time. "I guess we're done here. I don't see anything that'll help us find her." She led the way down the stairs to the front door. When she opened it, she found a uniformed officer standing on the doorstep, his hand raised as if to knock. A stout woman with gray hair hovered behind him, a yipping dog cradled in her arms.

The officer, who looked like he'd barely reached adulthood, lowered his hand and said loud enough he could be heard above the barking, "We got a report of a break in. Do either of you live here?"

Before they could say anything, the woman said, "That's not her. That's not Zelena. I don't know who those two are, but they don't belong here."

Chapter 2

The uniformed officer turned to look at the stout woman now standing directly behind him, her face inches away from his elbow. He motioned toward where Rory and Liz stood in the doorway of the apartment. "You're sure neither of them lives here?"

"Positive. I make a point of knowing all of my neighbors." Emboldened by the officer's presence, the woman stepped in front of him. "I bet you thought no one noticed you looking in the windows, making sure the coast was clear. In broad daylight too. Shame on you! This'll teach you."

Rory stepped forward, her hands held out in silent appeal. "We weren't—"

The woman clutched her dog tighter, bringing on another round of barking, and cowered behind the young officer. "Did you see that? Do something! She was going to attack me!"

"I wasn't, honest." Rory appealed to him with her eyes.

"Why don't you go back home, ma'am, and let me take care of this."

An older man with a bald spot on the top of his head peeked around the hedge between the triplex and the property next door. "Doreen!" he called out. "Come here. Let the officer do his job."

Doreen appeared ready to stand her ground, but when her husband called out again and the officer motioned with his hand, she gave in and headed toward the house next door.

An almost inaudible sigh escaped the officer's lips as he

watched her walk away. Once she'd disappeared into her own yard, he turned his attention back to Rory and Liz. "Can I see IDs, please?"

"This is all a big misunderstanding. We're friends of Zelena, the woman who lives here." Rory handed over her driver's license. "We were just checking on...something for her. We have a key, see?" She held up the key they had found taped underneath the gnome, hoping he wouldn't notice the speck of dirt still clinging to it.

"Uh-huh." He examined Liz's license first. When he looked at Rory's, a curious expression came over his face. He handed it back to her and said, "So, you're Green's girl, huh? I've heard a lot about you."

"We're dating, if that's what you mean," Rory said cautiously. His comment piqued her curiosity about what everyone at the police station was saying about her. She made a mental note to ask around and see what she could find out.

"You two wait here. Let me make a call." He stepped to one side of the yard, far enough away they couldn't hear the conversation. Positioning his body so he could keep an eye on them, he talked into the radio on his shoulder.

"What do you think he's saying?" Rory whispered.

"No idea, but I wish he'd hurry. I have to pee," Liz whispered back. She rocked from foot to foot, a distressed look on her face.

"Why don't you use the bathroom inside? I'm sure he'll understand. It's an emergency."

Liz waved to get the officer's attention, then mimed the need to use the bathroom and pointed at the door. After he blushed and nodded his head in agreement, she went inside. When she returned a short time later, Rory locked the front door of the apartment and pocketed the key, not wanting to place it back where they found it with the officer looking on.

After what seemed like hours, but was probably less than fifteen minutes, he walked over to them. "Okay, you can go. Just be more careful in the future." He drew Rory aside and said in a low voice, "Detective Green wanted me to tell you he'll meet you at your place." With a nod to the two of them, he headed toward the police cruiser parked in the driveway.

"Somebody's in trouble," Liz said in a sing-song voice as soon as he was out of earshot.

"You're in just as much trouble as I am."

"I'm not the one dating a police detective." Liz looked around as if making sure no one was watching and lowered her voice. "Guess what I found inside?" She took an amber prescription bottle out of her purse.

Rory examined the bottle, turning it over in her hands. The label was torn off, leaving only the corner that showed the pharmacy where the prescription had been filled. "So you're looking inside medicine cabinets now?"

"I was looking for some aspirin. I have a headache."

"Kind of odd there's no label."

"That's what I thought too." Liz tucked the bottle back in her purse. "Seemed out of place."

"Why do you have a headache, anyway?"

"My mother's driving me insane with this house for her cousins. I can't seem to find anything they like." She sighed. "Speaking of which, I need to get back to work. The sooner I find them a house, the happier my mother will be. When I have some time, I'll talk to a pharmacist I know and see what I can find out about this prescription. You go and deal with that boyfriend of yours." Liz headed toward her car, calling over her shoulder, "Say hi to Dashing D for me."

When Rory pulled into her driveway a short while later, she found a man with a muscular build wearing a suit and tie sitting on her front porch. Detective Martin Green's handsome face lit up as soon as he saw her. Her heart skipped a beat and she returned the smile. Even though they had only been dating for two months, she felt as if she'd known him for years.

Rory walked across the lawn and held up her hands, palms forward. "I wasn't doing anything illegal, honest. I was worried about a friend, that's all."

Martin patted the step next to him. "Tell me about it."

Rory settled down beside him so their shoulders touched. She sat there for a moment, enjoying his silent company.

He butted his shoulder against hers. "Okay, what's going on?"

She was gathering her thoughts, trying to figure out how best to describe the situation to him, when movement in her neighbor's yard captured her attention. She looked over to see Mrs. Griswold peeking around the wooden fence that separated the two properties.

Rory gave an almost imperceptible nod toward her inquisitive seventy-six-year-old neighbor. "Let's go inside."

Martin followed her gaze and nodded. While Rory unlocked the front door, he waved at Mrs. Griswold who ducked behind the fence as soon as she realized they had seen her.

Once inside, Rory took him by the hand and led him toward her work area.

"Why are you so concerned about your friend?" he said in his deep voice.

"It'll make more sense if I show you."

After they settled down in chairs in front of the computer, Sekhmet wandered into the room and brushed against the detective's leg. The cat dropped a ball of crushed paper on the wood floor and looked at him expectantly. He leaned down to scratch her behind the ear, then threw the paper ball across the room. Sekhmet skidded across the floor after it, returning to drop the ball beside him once again. The scenario played out half a dozen times before the cat appeared satisfied with the attention and, announcing her departure with a meow, headed back into the living room where she jumped onto the windowsill and studied the world outside.

Rory smiled at the game of fetch, then turned her attention back to the matter at hand. She explained about the email she'd received that morning and how that had led to visiting Zelena's apartment to check on her.

Martin raised an eyebrow.

"Don't worry, we didn't break in. I have a key." She took the key out of the pocket of her jeans and placed it on her desk.

"Let me see the message."

Rory brought it up on the screen. As Martin leaned forward to study it, she caught a whiff of his cologne, a subtle woodsy scent that sent her pulse racing. She closed her eyes and drank in the intoxicating smell. A gentle touch on her arm brought her back to reality.

"Where'd you go?" Martin asked, an amused note in his voice.

Rory felt her face heat up. "Nowhere in particular. I'm just tired and a little worried about Zelena."

He squeezed her arm. "Don't worry. We'll figure out what's going on. Let's take this one step at a time. When did you last see her?"

"At Saturday's chapter meeting. It ended around five."

"How did she seem? Nervous? Happy?"

Rory settled back in her chair and considered the question. "She seemed the same as usual to me, but I didn't spend a lot of time talking with her."

"How did she get home? Did she drive by herself or carpool with one of the other members?"

"I assume she drove by herself. If she did, she made it home since her car is parked by her apartment." Rory cast her mind back to Saturday's meeting. "You know, I think she walked. It wasn't that late and I remember someone asking if she wanted a ride."

"Was it unusual for her to walk home?"

"No. She walked whenever she could. It was her way of encouraging parents to let their kids walk or bike to school instead of driving them. She figured if she showed it was safe they'd be more open to it."

"I see." He studied her, curiosity written all over his face. "What do you do at those meetings, anyway?"

"Lots of different things. Sometimes a teacher comes in and we work on a painting project. Or we share what we've been working on at home. Saturday we mostly talked about our charity project, the Halloween Holiday Boutique."

In honor of Decorative Painting month, every October the chapter hosted a weeklong event where they sold projects painted by members.

"It's in that house you told me about, right?" He frowned as if trying to remember more. "A client of Liz's is letting you borrow it?"

"That's the one. They're hoping they'll get more offers with all of the people going through it. We're supposed to open this Saturday. Lots to do before then. Hopefully, we'll get the final details worked out at tomorrow's meeting."

"That escape room you told me about sounds interesting. That's new this year?"

Rory nodded. "Created by the guy who owns Escape Key, that escape room business in town."

"Tobias Worthington?"

"That's him. He's married to Penny, our chapter president."

"I'll definitely have to try it out then. He's gotten good reviews on Yelp. Now, where were we..." His brow furrowed in thought, Martin studied the message on the screen. "So she disappeared sometime after five on Saturday."

"That's right. And she wasn't around when Beyond The Grave sent the heartbeat message at eight the next morning. Or at least she wasn't reading her email. If she'd seen it, she would have responded and I wouldn't have gotten the message from BTG on Wednesday."

"That gives us a time frame to work with. Did you check to see if she actually received the messages from Beyond The Grave?"

"Not yet. I feel a little uncomfortable looking at her mail, but if it'll help us find her..." Rory directed the browser to the site Zelena used and typed in the username and password her friend had provided in her message. She scrolled through the contents of the inbox. "The heartbeat messages are all here. She didn't see them, though. They're all marked as unread."

"What about this stalker she mentioned? Did she talk to you

about her suspicions?"

"It's the first I've heard of it. Do you know if she reported the problem to the police?"

"Not that I know of, but I'll check on it when I get back to the station. Is there any particular reason she might be the target of one?"

"She was a child actress. Pretty well-known when she was on *Mommy's Little Helper*."

"The sitcom?"

Rory nodded. "I can't think of anything other than that."

"There doesn't have to be a reason. She could have just caught someone's attention. Or it could be an overly enthusiastic fan." He sat back in his chair and studied her. "Do you know if she sent out any other emails?"

"No idea. Beyond The Grave wouldn't tell me when I asked. Client confidentiality."

"Any idea why she sent it to you? Are you two particularly close?"

"We're good friends, but there are others she spends more time with." Rory stared out the window and thought about why Zelena had chosen her to receive the email. "She knows we're dating and that you're a police detective. Maybe she thought I was her best bet for finding out what happened to her. She probably figured I could always ask you for help."

"Makes sense. Check around and see if anyone's heard from her. If not, you should consider coming down to the station and filing a missing persons report." A faint beep sounded. Martin drew his cell phone out of his jacket pocket, glanced down at its screen and sighed. "I've got to go. I'll be glad when Halloween's over."

"Another prank?"

"This one's under the pier." He kissed her and stood up. "Don't worry too much. She probably just took a break and forgot about the messages."

After he left, Rory scrolled through the rest of Zelena's mail, but didn't see anything that would help them find the missing woman. Her mind kept drifting back to the prank Martin had left to check out. Finally, her curiosity got the better of her and she headed out the door to find out what was going on underneath the pier.

Chapter 3

A bony hand hung over the side of the rope hammock stretched between two concrete posts beneath the Vista Beach pier. Wires attached the hand to the rest of the skeleton that lay back in the hammock as if enjoying a fall day at the beach. A cool breeze wafted over the area. At the bottom of a short slope twenty feet away, waves gently washed onto the sand. A photographer took pictures while a uniformed officer guarded the scene, keeping the small group of curious onlookers away from the area.

Her feet sinking into the sand with each step, Rory joined the crowd observing the unusual police activity on the beach. She shaded her eyes from the glare off the water and stared at the skeleton. Sunglasses covered its eye sockets. A cardinal visor embroidered with a gold *USC* perched on top of its head. Shivers crept up her spine as she looked at the skull with its teeth bared in a permanent grin.

"The Provocative Prankster has struck again, I see," a voice behind her said. "Is it wearing *board shorts*?"

Rory turned and smiled at Liz who was picking her way across the sand in her bare feet, black pumps dangling from her fingertips. "I guess the grapevine's working. Who did you hear about it from?"

"Someone from the office was eating lunch nearby and saw the activity. I suppose Dashing D told you. I wonder where it came from."

"There's a toe tag." Rory moved closer to the skeleton and

tilted her head so she could better read the single word written on it. "It says 'Sid'."

Liz moved forward and pointed at a necklace draped across its shoulders. "That looks an awful lot like the one you painted for Zelena." Her hand flew to her mouth and her eyes widened. "You don't think that's...?"

"I'm pretty sure that skeleton's not real. It looks plastic to me." Rory leaned forward, her arms crossed in front of her, and stared at the necklace made of painted wooden pumpkins, tombstones and other Halloween figures strung together with tan cording. "That *does* look like the necklace I gave Zelena for her birthday." Her gaze rested on the witch at the center of the piece. "Lots of other people have painted that design, though. It's probably not mine."

"Only one way to find out." Liz glanced over at the uniformed officer who stood nearby. Preoccupied with the questions of a new arrival, he didn't notice her walk up to the hammock. She was reaching for the necklace when a deep voice said, "Stop right there."

Her hand hovered over the skeleton for a moment before Liz dropped her arm to her side and walked over to stand beside Rory.

Detective Green stepped between the two women and the hammock and folded his arms in front of his chest. "What are you two up to?" he said in a stern tone.

"We just wanted to get a closer look at the necklace." Rory pointed to the skeleton.

"Why?"

"I might have painted it."

"What?" He unfolded his arms and stared at her.

"It looks like something I made for Zelena. We were just going to turn it over and see." When a puzzled look came over his face, Rory added, "I always sign the back of my projects."

"Wait a moment." After consulting with the photographer to make sure all of the necessary photos had been taken, he motioned the two of them forward. With a gloved hand, he carefully removed the necklace from the skeleton and turned it over, angling it so they could see the back of the witch. Three tiny capital As painted in gold shone out on the black background.

Rory drew in her breath.

"Your work?" Martin said. "For Aurora Amelia Anderson?"

"That's right. I gave it to Zelena for her birthday a few weeks ago. There are earrings shaped like tombstones that go with it." Rory studied the skeleton and the area around it. "I don't see them anywhere. I wonder what happened to them."

"We'll keep a lookout for them." The detective placed the necklace in an evidence bag. "Did you see her wearing it recently? Or did she mention losing it?"

Rory screwed up her face in concentration. "I'm pretty sure she had it on at the meeting on Saturday. Or maybe that was when I saw her earlier in the week." She looked over at Liz. "What do you think? You always remember what people wear."

"She was definitely wearing it on Saturday. I remember how it complemented her forest green blouse. I'm sure of it."

"I'll see if we can pull some prints off it." Martin looked at Rory. "Have you filed that missing persons report yet? I think you should do it now."

"I'll go down to the station after I leave here."

The detective was about to walk away when a woman with a nose ring and a red stripe in her black hair thrust a miniature digital recorder in front of his face. "What's this about a missing person's report? Who's missing? And what does it have to do with the skeleton?" Veronica Justice, reporter for the *Vista Beach View*, said in a raspy voice. Wearing a long-sleeve crop top and skinny jeans that fell below her waist, exposing a tiny gold belly button ring, she stared intently at the detective and waited for a response.

"No comment at this time. We'll have a statement later. Now, if you could join the group over there and let us work." He motioned to the uniformed officer who guided the three of them away from the hammock.

Veronica clicked a button on the recorder and shoved it in the tote bag that served as her purse. She directed her attention to the other two women. "What's going on?"

For once, Rory was glad to see the reporter for the weekly newspaper. "We could use your help. A friend of ours is missing."

Veronica jotted down everything they told her about Zelena's disappearance in a small wire-bound notepad. "What does this have to do with the skeleton?"

"Not really sure at this point," Rory said. "Do you have any idea where it came from? The toe tag on it says 'Sid'."

"There's one missing from the high school. Someone broke in and took it out of one of the classrooms. Could be it. I'll find out for sure." Veronica wrote something down in her notepad. "I'll pitch the missing persons story to my editor and see what he says. Can't guarantee you the front page, but I should be able to get the article in tomorrow's paper."

"With her Hollywood background? That's front page material, for sure," Liz said. "A Hollywood connection, even if it's an old one, sells papers."

"Oh, she's *that* Zelena. I didn't realize she lived in town. That makes a big difference. Email me a recent picture of her if you have one. Who knows, maybe someone will come forward with some more information." Veronica exchanged her notepad for a camera. "I'll post about it on *VBC* as well," she said, referring to *Vista Beach Confidential*, the blog she maintained that covered happenings in and around the beach city. "A lot of people don't bother to read the newspaper anymore. I'll get on it as soon as I'm done here."

After thanking the woman, Rory and Liz walked across the sand toward the street, leaving the reporter taking pictures of the skeleton and the crowd around it.

"How's the house hunting going?" Rory said.

"Slo-o-o-owly. There's always something wrong with a place. My mom's cousins are really nice, but very picky. I'm at the end of my rope."

"Anything I can do?"

"No, we'll work it out. But I need a break from them. I'm going to see what I can find out about that prescription bottle before I go back to the office."

At the top of the hill leading down to the ocean, the two friends parted. Liz went on her errand while Rory walked toward the police station to file the missing persons report.

After her stop at the station, Rory headed to her mother's store a few blocks away to say hi. The bell over the front door tinkled when she stepped inside Arika's Scrap 'n Paint. A handful of customers browsed the racks of painting and scrapbooking supplies while classical music played softly in the background. Rory recognized Pachelbel's Canon, a particular favorite of her mother's.

As she closed the door behind her, Rory thought she heard her own name being mentioned. She directed her attention to the cash register where Arika Anderson, cropped hair speckled with gray, stood talking to a rosy-cheeked woman with shoulder length auburn hair in corkscrew curls.

Dressed in a light blue cardigan and matching shell over darker blue pants, Arika looked up and nodded toward her daughter. "You're in luck. Here she is now."

The chunky silver jewelry around the rosy-cheeked woman's neck rattled when she turned to face the front door. She wore a maroon sweater over black jeans and knee-high black boots.

Rory smiled at the two of them and headed across the floor. "Did I hear my name mentioned?"

Arika gestured toward the other woman. "This is Samantha Granger. She came by hoping to find you here. She'd like to speak with you if you have a few minutes."

There was something familiar about the name, but Rory couldn't immediately pinpoint where she'd heard it before.

"You may have heard Zelena talk about me," Samantha said. "I was her manager years ago when she was acting. Now I'm just a friend."

"Of course." Rory glanced over at the sitting area near the back of the store. The couch was empty and no customers browsed the nearby shelves. She gestured toward the area. "Why don't we sit over here. We'll have more privacy."

Once they settled down side by side on the sofa, Rory angled her body so she was facing the woman. "What can I do for you, Ms. Granger?"

"Please, call me Samantha. I feel like I know you, Zelena has told me so much about you and all of her other painting friends."

"Why did you want to see me?"

A worried look on her face, Samantha pushed strands of her curly hair behind one ear. "I'm afraid something has happened to her. We usually talk a few times a week."

"But...?"

"But I haven't heard from her since last Friday. I was out of town for a while. My phone suddenly died on me. I got it repaired as soon as I came home. I was expecting to find a message on my voicemail from her, but..."

"She didn't leave any."

Samantha nodded. "I called and went by her place, but she wasn't there. Then I remembered her talking about you and your mother's store. How much she enjoyed it here so..." She made a sweeping gesture with her arm. "...here I am."

Rory folded her hands on her lap and cleared her throat. "I'm afraid I have some bad news. I just filed a missing person's report on her."

Samantha sucked in her breath. "As bad as that? Tell me."

Rory explained about the email she'd received and how they had all become worried about Zelena's whereabouts.

The woman fingered her necklace as she took in the news. "I may have a way of tracking her."

"How?"

Samantha looked down at her hands. "I'm embarrassed to admit this, but a couple weeks ago I was worried about her so I installed a...tracking app on her phone. One of those hidden ones. Just in case. I felt bad about it as soon as I did it. Then everything seemed okay so I never used it. And I would never invade her privacy like that ever again, only..." She cleared her throat. "I never actually uninstalled the app."

Rory straightened up. "So you know where she is right now?"

"I haven't looked at the app yet. I didn't want to use it unless it was absolutely necessary. I'll check it now." She took her phone out of her purse and, a few screen taps later, she had a location.

Rory angled her head so she could see the screen. "That's not far from here."

Samantha's brow furrowed. "But that's a drugstore. What's she doing there?"

Rory stood up. "Let's go and find out."

The two headed out the door and walked the short distance to the address on the app. When they didn't spot Zelena anywhere inside the store, Rory dialed her friend's phone number.

A faint ringing sounded in the distance. Rory stopped in the middle of an aisle to orient herself. "I think it's coming from the front of the store."

The two hurried forward until they found themselves beside a row of recycling bins for electrical cords, spent printer ink cartridges and electronic devices. Rory pointed to the bin marked *MP3 | Cellphone | Ink.* "Sounds like it's coming from in there."

She took a plastic bag from the next bin and groped around inside the one with the cell phone picture on it until she unearthed a ringing phone. "This must be Zelena's."

As soon as Rory hung up the call, the phone from the bin stopped ringing, confirming her belief.

"But what's it doing here?" Samantha said.

"I don't know." Rory carefully set the cell she'd unearthed on top of one of the bins and dialed a number on her own phone. "But I think it's time to call the police."

Chapter 4

With gloved hands, Martin Green placed the cell phone in an evidence bag before addressing the two women standing nearby. "Tell me, in detail this time, how you found the phone."

Rory and Samantha exchanged glances. The older woman cocked her head, indicating Rory should take the lead. She explained how they used Samantha's phone to pinpoint the location of Zelena's. To Rory's surprise, the detective didn't comment, but merely raised an eyebrow when she got to the part about the hidden app. She was just finishing up when a slender man with a name tag that indicated he was the manager of the drugstore walked over to them.

"Wait a moment. I might have some more questions," Martin said to the two women before turning his attention to the manager. "Anything?"

The man shook his head. "No one remembers anyone dropping off a phone, but I didn't really expect they would. We ignore these bins until it's time to empty them."

"What about security footage?"

"None of the cameras point this direction. The best I can give you is footage of the entrances and the pharmacy area."

Martin Green nodded in understanding. "Give me what you've got."

"How far back?"

"It must have been dropped off fairly recently," Rory said.

"The battery was still partially charged."

Martin looked at her and nodded. "I want everything since Saturday morning, just to be safe." He took out his cell phone and showed a picture of Zelena to the manager. "Have you seen her around in the last few days?"

The man shrugged. "Maybe. I couldn't really say."

After the manager went off to take care of the request, Martin turned back to the two women. "I think that's all I need from you two for now." He handed his business card to Samantha. "If you think of anything else, let me know."

Rory and Samantha were walking toward the exit when a whirlwind in red and black headed toward them. "What's going on?" Liz said when she came to a halt in front of them.

"We found Zelena's phone," Rory said in a quiet voice.

"Where?"

She nodded toward the recycling bins.

"That doesn't sound good." Liz stuck out her hand and said to Samantha, "Hi, I'm Liz."

After Samantha introduced herself, Rory said to Liz, "What about you? What are you doing here? Have you been in the store long? I don't remember seeing you come in."

"I was out in the alley talking to someone. I'm looking into that thing we talked about earlier. Just came in the back door to buy some aspirin."

"What thing?"

"You know, *that* thing."

"I have no idea what you're talking about."

Liz unzipped her purse, pulling out a pill bottle far enough so the top peeked out, then quickly shoved it back inside.

"Oh, *that* thing." Rory eyed the detective who was now talking with another store employee. She lowered her voice. "We shouldn't talk about it here." In a louder voice, she said, "Have you had lunch? I'm starving. Let's all go to the diner down the street."

When they entered Buddy's Rockin' Diner, they were swept back into the '50s. With the Everly Brothers' "Wake Up Little Susie" playing in the background, the three walked across the black and white checkered floor toward a red vinyl booth in the back corner. Rory slid into the seat next to Liz while Samantha sat on the other side of the laminated table.

After they'd ordered, Rory turned to Liz. "What did you find out?"

"I'm not sure how much it'll help." Liz paused and looked questioningly at Samantha.

"You can talk in front of her," Rory said.

"Okay." Liz placed the pill bottle she'd found in Zelena's apartment on the table. "The pills are Valium, but my pharmacist friend couldn't tell me anything else. There's not enough of the label left on the bottle and lots of people get prescriptions for it."

"Where did you get those?" Samantha stared at the bottle and her face turned pale.

"Zelena's apartment," Liz said.

"Are you okay? I'm sorry, I should have realized how hard this would be for you." Rory pushed the pill bottle across the table toward Liz who put it back in her purse.

"That's not it," Samantha finally said.

"Wait, do you know something about them?" Rory asked.

"I...I gave them to Zelena. She wanted something to calm her nerves. Wouldn't say why."

Rory and Liz looked at each other. "When was this?" Rory finally said.

Samantha screwed up her face in thought. "A couple weeks ago. Not long before I went out of town."

"Is that why you put the app on her phone? Because of the Valium?"

Samantha nodded.

"How many pills did you give her?" Rory asked.

"I don't know. I didn't count them. Just gave her the rest of an old prescription of mine. I don't remember how full the bottle was." She looked down at her hands and said softly, "I can't help wondering if this is all my fault."

"Why do you say that?" Rory asked.

"Maybe she found the hidden app I put on her phone and thought it was her stalker who put it there. She might have ditched her phone, thinking it was compromised. If she hadn't done that, we might be able to find her."

Rory gave her a reassuring smile. "I suppose that's possible, but I think it's more likely that someone else put it in the bin. Maybe we'll learn more when the police look over the footage they get from the drugstore."

"Do you think Zelena's parents might know what's going on?" Liz directed her attention to Samantha. "You've known her for a long time, right? Can you call them and ask?"

"I'm positive they wouldn't know anything. She hasn't seen or talked to them in years. I'm not even sure they know where she lives."

The waitress delivered their food, temporarily cutting off further conversation. The three quietly ate their lunch and, by unspoken agreement, avoided any further talk of the missing woman.

For the rest of the day, worry over Zelena's whereabouts was Rory's constant companion. While she went about her daily routine, working on code and fielding calls from clients about software projects, thoughts about Zelena were always in the back of her mind.

She periodically found herself staring out the window, wondering if she'd done enough to find her friend. Finally, she gave up on work and turned to Zelena's email and social media accounts, looking for clues about where she might be. Rory sifted through post after post and message after message, but nothing significant leapt out at her. After a couple hours, she returned to her work, convinced she'd done everything she could for the moment. She hoped the police would have better luck and find her friend soon, safe and sound.

After dinner, she updated the painting chapter's website in preparation for the next day's board meeting, then headed to bed.

Sekhmet curled up on top of the covers next to her, leaning against Rory's legs. But even with the cat's comforting presence, Rory couldn't settle down enough to fall asleep.

She finally got up around midnight, making her way through the house in the dark, letting the light that filtered through the windows from outside illuminate her path. She was in the kitchen, getting a glass of water, when the outside lights on her next-door neighbor's house winked out.

Rory set down her glass and peered out the window that faced Mrs. Griswold's property.

Odd. As the Neighborhood Watch block captain, Mrs. Griswold encouraged everyone on Seagull Lane to keep their exterior lights on at night. Rory waited for them to turn on again. When they didn't, she made sure her own lights still worked, inside and out, then peeked out the front window. None of the other houses on the block seemed to have been affected.

Rory put on a robe, grabbed her keys and headed next door to check on her neighbor. She was almost at the edge of her own property when a silver sedan backed out of the driveway next door. When the car passed under a newly installed street light, she glimpsed Mrs. Griswold in the driver's seat. After midnight seemed an odd time to be leaving, Rory thought. She'd never noticed her neighbor going anywhere at this time before. As far as she knew, the woman hated driving in the dark.

Rory hugged her robe to her chest and headed back inside, puzzled and a little concerned by Mrs. Griswold's unusual behavior.

Chapter 5

At noon the next day, Rory headed downtown to Arika's Scrap 'n Paint for the painting chapter board meeting. The bell over the front door tinkled as she hurried into the store. Arika and a six-foot tall broad-shouldered woman with salt and pepper hair, wearing a brightly colored top over black pants, stood next to the cash register, deep in conversation. Towering over Rory's much shorter mother, the Bea Arthur look-alike spoke in a strident tone of voice.

Arika frowned. "That wasn't the deal last time."

Jeanne Cayce poked her finger at her own chest and stepped forward until she was mere inches away from the store owner. "Zelena's not in charge now, I am."

Arika stared up into the other woman's eyes and raised an eyebrow. "Really? I think I'll talk to Penny about it. She's still the president of the chapter, right?"

Jeanne frowned. "If you must." She glanced over at Rory and nodded before heading into the classroom next door.

With a worried look on her face, Rory walked over to her mother. "What was that about?"

"Nothing." Arika patted her arm. "Don't worry, we'll work it out. Go on into your meeting."

Rory nodded and headed into the classroom next to the sales floor for the lunchtime meeting. She slipped into a seat next to Liz. "Did I miss anything?" she whispered.

"Not unless you count the Overbearing One getting all huffy

about something." Liz nodded to where Jeanne now sat at the opposite end of the table, arms folded in front of her chest, a dour look on her face.

Rory glanced around the room. Six women sat around one of the two eight-foot tables in the classroom, chatting among themselves as they patiently waited for the meeting to begin. Disappointment washed over her. Rory had half hoped Zelena would be there, laughing away everyone's concerns, explaining how she'd left town for a few days, lost her phone and forgotten about the messages from Beyond The Grave.

"Ladies, ladies." A tall blonde, hair styled in an ultra-short crop with sweeping bangs, stood up and rapped her knuckles against the table. Conversations gradually died down and all eyes turned toward Penny Worthington, president of the painting chapter.

As soon as she had everyone's attention, Penny continued. "Before we start, I want to thank Arika for letting us have our meeting here in her store."

Arika bobbed her head in acknowledgement from her position in the doorway. "Delighted to have you. I'll let you get down to business. I'll be out front if you need anything." She smiled at them and headed out onto the sales floor.

"I see everyone's not here yet, but we have to get started. We have less than two days before the house opens and we still have a lot to do. We'll begin with the department reports."

Jeanne stood up. "My department is doing well, of course. Best—"

Penny waved her hand in the air, cutting her off. "We'll get to you in a bit, Jeanne. Please sit down."

Jeanne harumphed and sat back in her chair.

Penny perched reading glasses on the tip of her nose and gazed down at the piece of paper she held in front of her. "The website is up first. Rory?"

"I made the changes you wanted last night. Everything's up and running smoothly."

"No problems with the online ticket sales?"

"None that I know of." Rory turned to Liz who was in charge of keeping track of sales. "People are signing up, aren't they?"

"Lots of signups. No one's reported any problems. We're doing way better than last year at this time," Liz said.

Penny nodded her head in satisfaction. "Can you give us more details?"

She looked over her glasses at Liz who consulted a piece of paper before answering. "So far we've sold fifty-five advance tickets for entry into the house. Twenty have paid the additional fee for the escape room experience. I refunded two tickets to people who were unexpectedly called out of town and convinced two others to donate their unused tickets to the cause." All of the proceeds from the house went to a charity that provided money for art supplies and instruction in schools.

"Very good. Keep me posted on the advance sales." Penny checked off something on her paper. "What about the escape room? Are the time slots filling up?"

"There are only a few left for this Saturday and the other days are already half full," Liz said.

"Toby will be pleased to hear that. He put so much time into creating it," Penny said.

"It's not like he was being altruistic," Jeanne said in a loud voice. "Your husband's own escape room business is bound to be helped."

"Weren't you the one who suggested he do it in the first place?" Penny asked.

Jeanne mumbled something Rory couldn't quite catch.

Penny eyed the disgruntled woman for a moment, then continued, "Speaking of the escape room, Toby's putting it together now. I need two volunteers to try it out tomorrow. One to be a customer and the other to supervise and hand out clues."

Rory raised her hand. "I'll be the customer."

Liz waved her arm enthusiastically and bounced up and down in her chair. "Oh, oh. I'll give her the clues. It'll give Madame

Elizabeth a chance to practice."

"Madame Elizabeth?" Rory said.

"That's my psychic persona. I've got this great outfit all planned and—"

Penny consulted her watch and waved her hand to cut off the flow of words. "I'm sure it'll be wonderful as always, but let's continue. We don't have much time left."

"It's going to be great," Liz said softly.

Rory smiled sympathetically at her friend. "I'm looking forward to it," she whispered back.

Penny was consulting her agenda when a woman dressed in a suit raced in waving a copy of *The Vista Beach View.* "Did you see...?"

"If you're not going to get here on time, why bother coming?" Jeanne said.

Teresa Mut pushed her glasses up her nose. "I was working with a bride. You can't rush clients, especially brides-to-be. You know how the wedding planning business is. I got here as soon as I could. I told you I might be late." She settled down into an empty seat and placed the paper on the table in front of her.

Jeanne raised an eyebrow and looked pointedly at the newspaper. "You obviously had time to get a copy of the *View* and read it."

"Speaking of that—" Teresa pointed at an article on the bottom of the front page.

She opened her mouth to say more, but Penny waved her hand in dismissal. "Let's get back to business. You can show us the article after the end of the meeting. Since you're here, Teresa, can you give us a report on finances?"

Teresa distributed copies of her treasurer's report to the group around the table. While they all studied it, she said, "As you can see, our expenses are well below those for last year's event and revenue is higher than expected for this time. I think it's going to be a banner year."

Jeanne smirked. "I told you my way was better."

"And you are to be commended for that, but let's continue. Next is the volunteers chair." Penny consulted her notes, looked around the room and frowned. "Where's Zelena?"

"That's what I was trying to tell you. There's an article about her in the *View*." Teresa poked a finger at the paper lying on the table. "She's missing. No one's seen her for days."

Penny's eyes opened wide. "Missing? What do you mean, missing? We all saw her on Saturday."

"Good thing she's not in charge of the event this time around or we'd be scrambling," Jeanne said.

"That's cold," Liz whispered to Rory who nodded her head in agreement.

Rory held her phone in her lap and texted Liz, *You didn't tell Penny?*

Liz gave an almost imperceptible shake of her head, then texted back, *Couldn't get hold of her or Jeanne. Figured we would talk to them after the meeting.*

Rory looked around the table. "Has anyone seen Zelena since Saturday?"

Everyone looked a question at each other, a troubled look in their eyes. One by one they all shook their heads.

"What does the article say?" Penny nodded at the paper.

As Teresa recounted what she'd read, Rory skimmed the article herself. It talked about how the kindergarten teacher hadn't been heard from in several days and appealed for information about her whereabouts, giving the number of a police tip line. Rory had been quoted as well as Edgar Geller, the CEO of Beyond The Grave who said he was happy to cooperate with the police. He added that, without the services of his company, no one might have noticed there was anything wrong.

Rory pushed the *View* across the table toward Liz who read the article and frowned.

"We'll have to deal with the volunteer stuff another time. The last report is the painting donations. Jeanne, how are we doing on those?"

Jeanne stood up, a smug look on her face. "As I was trying to say earlier, this is the best year yet. We have more than enough painted pieces to sell. I'm working with Liz on how to place them around the house. We'll be doing the setup tomorrow so those of you who haven't given your pieces to me yet, make sure you bring them to the house in the morning, as early as possible. I'll be there by seven. Be sure to spread the word to all of the other chapter members."

"Good." Penny checked something off on her clipboard. "We're almost done." As the group finished discussing the final preparations, Rory's phone vibrated. She looked at the display to see a text: *Answer your phone when it rings.* Moments later, it vibrated again and an unfamiliar number popped up on the display.

Rory slipped into the back room of the store to answer the phone. "Hello?" she said in a quiet voice so she wouldn't disturb the meeting still going on in the adjoining classroom.

"Rory, it's me," a voice Rory recognized as Zelena's said. "I wanted to tell you—What are you doing?"

The sound of a struggle followed by a crash and a yell of pain came over the line. Then the phone went dead.

Chapter 6

"Zelena! Are you all right?" Rory said into her cell. She repeated her friend's name several times, but all she heard was dead air. When she tried calling back the number, the phone rang and rang and no one answered.

The buzz of conversation in the next room died down. Liz popped her head around the door followed moments later by Jeanne and Penny.

"Everything okay back here?" Liz said.

"We heard you call Zelena's name. Was that her on the phone?" Penny added.

Rory headed back into the classroom and sat down in her chair. She took a deep breath and told them about the phone call.

"She just hung up?" Teresa said.

"Did she say where she was?" Penny asked, a worried tone in her voice.

"The phone went dead in the middle of the conversation." Rory looked down at her hands. "I'm not sure the hang up was voluntary."

"She's been kidnapped, hasn't she?" Liz said.

"Kidnapped?!" everyone said at the same time.

"We shouldn't jump to conclusions, but it sounded like someone else was with her. And I think there might have been a struggle." Rory closed her eyes and tried to remember any background noises that would confirm her belief, opening them moments later with little else to report. "That last bit might be my imagination. I'm pretty sure someone else was there, though."

"I knew as soon as I saw the article in the paper that something was terribly wrong." Teresa took off her glasses and rubbed the bridge of her nose before replacing them. "There's no way she'd leave town before the Halloween Holiday Boutique opened. It's her baby. It was her idea in the first place. She's been in charge of it for years."

"But she's not in charge *this* year," Jeanne said.

"Whose idea was that?" Teresa replied.

"You all agreed I had better ideas. That we needed to update the event," Jeanne grumbled. "I can't help it if she went off in a huff."

Penny held up her hands in a quieting gesture. "Ladies, ladies. Squabbling isn't getting us anywhere. At least we know she's alive." She turned to Rory. "How can we help?"

"I already filed a missing persons report and you heard from the newspaper article that the police have set up a tip line. I'm going to call them right now and give them an update. Maybe they can trace the call. Why don't all of you see if you can think of something that might help find her. Some place she might have gone or someone who might know her whereabouts."

Everyone nodded their head in agreement.

Rory went into the back room for some privacy and dialed Martin Green's number, leaving a message on his voicemail briefly describing the call and what she heard in the background.

When Rory returned to the classroom, Penny clapped her hands to get everyone's attention. "Why don't we go around the room and see what everyone's come up with. I'll start." She placed her palms on the table and took a deep breath. "She asked me not to tell anyone, but under the circumstances...Zelena has a stalker. Or at least she thinks she does. She told me about it at the meeting on Saturday. It started a few months ago with little presents left on her doorstep. She thought they were from parents of one of her kindergarten students. Then it turned into emails that were a little too...personal. I guess that's the right word. After she ignored them, they became insistent. She wasn't worried about them until she thought she was being followed."

That confirmed what Zelena wrote in her Beyond The Grave email, Rory thought. "Did she have any idea who it was?"

Penny shook her head.

"What did the police say when she told them?" Liz asked.

"She didn't report it. She didn't want to tell me about it either. I had to drag it out of her."

"Why didn't she tell the police?"

"She didn't really have any proof. She didn't think they'd believe her without it."

"But the emails," Rory said.

"She deleted all of them and they stopped coming. That's all I have. I wish I knew more."

The others only had vague impressions that something was wrong, no details. They had just finished going around the table when Rory received a text from Martin, informing her the police would look into the phone call.

Moments later, the group adjourned the meeting, everyone going their separate ways until only Rory and Liz were left alone in the classroom.

"I wish there was some way we could trace her." Liz cocked her head at Rory. "You know, we should probably install location apps on our own phones. With your track record, it seems like a good idea. That way, the next time you get into trouble, I can come to the rescue. I don't know what I'd do if something happened to you."

Rory gave her friend a quick hug. "That's a good idea. Hopefully there is no next time."

A short time later they had installed the apps, vowing not to use them unless it was absolutely necessary.

"Let's check *Vista Beach Confidential*." Rory brought the blog up on her phone and scrolled through the comment section of the post on Zelena's disappearance. "A few people supposedly spotted her in the last few days. Lots of different places. On the beach, in someone's car."

"Let me see." Liz pored over the entries. "This one says they saw her in Las Vegas. I doubt that one's real. She hates that town."

The two were talking about the purported sightings when Liz's phone rang. She walked to the opposite end of the room to answer it. The conversation started in English then switched to Japanese after a "But, Mom!"

"You heard?" Rory said to her own mother when she appeared in the doorway.

"Most of it," Arika said.

Rory sank down into a nearby chair. "Martin's looking into Zelena's disappearance, but I'm still worried."

Arika sat down next to her daughter. "He's good at his job. If anyone can find her, he will. You've done everything you can. Who knows? Maybe she'll contact you again. While you're here, why don't I get you that cat food I was telling you about the other day." She disappeared into the back room and returned moments later with a paper bag.

Rory looked inside the bag filled with canned cat food. "I thought Buster liked this brand," she said, referring to her mother's aging orange tabby.

"The older he gets, the pickier he is. Hopefully Sekhmet will approve."

"If not, I'll give the cans to the local animal shelter. I'm sure they can find a use for them."

Liz ended her call and, shaking her head in frustration, walked toward them. "Sorry about that. Family drama."

"Is your mom still giving you grief about her cousins?" Rory asked.

"I don't know what she expects me to do. I've showed them every property I can think of that meets their specifications. Guess I'll have to get creative." Liz slung her purse over her shoulder. "I've got to go. Let me know if you hear anything."

On her way home, Rory thought about Zelena and crossed her fingers that everything would turn out all right. When she walked through the back door into the kitchen, she found Sekhmet perched on top of the refrigerator.

"What are you doing up there? Come on down, I've got something for you."

The cat gracefully jumped onto the floor via a nearby counter, then brushed up against Rory's leg and meowed.

She took a can of cat food out of the bag and held it out. "Brought you some new food."

The cat sniffed the can, then walked over to sit beside her dish.

Rory placed the cans in the cupboard. "You're going to have to wait until dinnertime for this." She gestured toward the dispenser filled with dry cat food. "You've got your cat chow to tide you over."

Sekhmet stared at Rory as if hoping she'd change her mind. When that didn't appear to be a possibility, the cat headed toward the front of the house. A few minutes later, Rory followed, sat down on the couch beside the cat and stroked her fine fur. "What do you think I should do next? I feel like I should be doing something to help find Zelena."

Sekhmet opened one eye and stared at Rory for a moment before closing it again.

"I know, you're right. Leave it to the police. I have work to do, anyway."

After an hour of answering emails and writing code, she stared at the message from Beyond The Grave in hopes it would somehow tell her something new about her friend's disappearance. She cast her mind back to what Penny had said earlier that day about the disturbing messages Zelena received. She'd supposedly deleted them, but maybe they weren't really gone.

Rory logged into her friend's account, this time checking the trash and spam folders. In the latter, she spotted a suspicious message from a week before the chapter meeting. The photos attached to it, all casual shots of Zelena at various places around town including inside a public rest room, sent chills up her spine. Nothing about the cryptic name of the sender told her anything. She forwarded the email to Martin and her own account, hoping the police could get something from it she couldn't.

Rory looked through the rest of the messages to see if there was anything she missed, scrolling past payment receipts, documents Zelena sent herself for safekeeping, several of them marked latest draft, and messages from the local library regarding volunteer activities. The rest were similar to the ads and newsletters Rory herself received on a daily basis.

She'd moved onto Zelena's social media accounts when Martin Green knocked on her front door.

"What's up?" Rory smiled and stepped aside so he could enter.

"I got that message you forwarded. I put one of our tech guys on it to see if he could find anything."

"That was fast." Rory led the way into her work area where they settled down on chairs beside her desk. "Is something wrong?" Her face crinkled in worry. "You could have called me with the info. You didn't have to stop by."

Martin gently brushed a stray tendril of hair away from her face, sending tingles down her spine. "I wanted to see you," he said softly. He was leaning over to kiss her when his cell phone rang. "Dang it," he muttered under his breath. After a brief conversation, he stood up. "Sorry, I have to go."

"Is it about Zelena?" Rory held her breath.

"No, something else."

"Wait a sec." Rory headed into the kitchen and came back with a plastic container. "I baked some cookies for you. I was going to drop them off at the station later, but since you're here..."

He took a cookie out of the container and bit into it. "Mm. Chocolate chip. My favorite. I didn't have a chance to eat lunch. This will tide me over nicely. Do you want to try that new Italian restaurant downtown tonight?"

"I can't. I have a Neighborhood Watch block meeting. Mrs. Griswold insists everyone be there."

"Tomorrow, then. We can go there before the silent movie. What are we seeing again?"

"*Phantom of the Opera*. It's a Halloween tradition here in

town."

"I'm looking forward to it." He paused in the doorway. "You know, we can always cancel if you're not feeling up to it."

"I'm okay. Really."

He nodded and headed out the door.

After he left, Rory continued going through Zelena's social media accounts. She smiled at the pictures posted on Facebook of the teacher reading to a group of kids at the Vista Beach library. The caption on the most recent one said that Zelena was looking forward to reading at the children's storytime hour in two weeks. Rory consulted a calendar. The event was today at four p.m. She glanced at the time on her cell phone. She still had time to get there. Maybe someone at the library would know something that would help. Or maybe Zelena herself would show up. Rory crossed her fingers and headed out the door.

Rory made her way through the stacks toward the children's section of the Vista Beach library where a dozen kids wearing costumes were already sitting cross-legged in a semi-circle on the carpet facing an empty chair. She leaned against a post near the back, joining the cluster of parents and nannies standing behind the grade-school age children. Moments later, a young woman in a blonde bouffant wig and light blue ball gown sat down in the empty seat, carrying a picture book with a cartoon haunted house on the cover.

The children seemed fascinated by the young woman, especially when she introduced herself as Cinderella. After a few questions about Prince Charming (from the girls) and the mice (from the boys), she started to read from the book in an animated voice, displaying the pictures for each page. As soon as she mentioned the word "ghost," a little boy dressed as a pirate in the front row began to cry.

"What's wrong, Billy?" Cinderella leaned forward, a concerned look on her face.

"Sca-ared. Ghost." Billy hiccupped and wiped his nose on the sleeve of his white shirt.

"Ghosts aren't real, silly," a witch behind him said.

"Are too. I saw one," a boy wearing a vampire cape declared.

"Did not," the witch behind Billy countered.

Billy started to cry harder. The girl in a princess costume next to him put her arm around him and after a few moments, he quieted down.

The boy who'd declared he'd seen a ghost jutted his chin out. "Did too. Last night by the pier. It came out of the water and—"

"That's just a story," Cinderella said in a soft yet commanding voice. "Settle down everyone. There's no reason to be afraid."

Rory leaned over to the woman standing next to her and whispered, "Do you know what they're talking about?"

"You haven't heard the story?" the young mother whispered back.

Rory shook her head. "I've only lived here a few years."

The woman looked over at the kids who were once again quiet as they listened with rapt attention to Cinderella. "Let's go out here." She led the way into the corridor, far enough away their conversation wouldn't disturb the reading, but close enough she could keep an eye on the area. "I don't want to set the kids off again."

"I understand. What's this about a ghost near the pier?"

"There's a local legend. Supposedly, in the early 1900s a family was in a boat that wrecked off the coast near here. Happened around this time of year. Most of them survived, but one of the children, a boy, drowned. It's said the boy haunts the area near the Vista Beach pier. After dark, every October, he crawls out of the surf, bleeding from his eyes and mouth. One minute he's there, the next minute—poof!—he's gone." The young mother snapped her fingers.

"I take it you don't believe it?"

"I believe there was a boat wreck, all right, just not the part about the ghost."

"What about that little kid in there? The one who said he saw one yesterday."

The woman rolled her eyes. "Kids have vivid imaginations. They're constantly making up stories, especially ones this age. If you were around them all the time like I am, you'd know."

Moments later, the sound of hands clapping came from the reading area followed by a stream of parents and their costumed children exiting the room.

"Gotta go."

"Thanks," Rory said.

The woman made her way back inside and returned a short while later, leading the princess by the hand. Rory waited until the stream of parents and children slowed down to a trickle before heading back into the room and introducing herself to the young woman dressed as Cinderella.

"Zelena told me about you," the woman said. "You're part of her painting group, right?" She held out her hand. "I'm Megan. I work with Zelena."

"You're a teacher too?"

She nodded her head. "At VB Elementary. We both teach kindergarten."

"You know about Zelena, right?"

Megan sat down and sighed. "How she's missing? I saw the article in the *View*."

"It's nice of you to fill in for her on such short notice."

"But it wasn't."

"What do you mean?"

"Zelena called me over a week ago and asked me to be her backup in case she couldn't make it, so I wasn't surprised when I got the call." Megan looked off into space. "I can't help thinking she knew, you know. That she wouldn't be here today."

Rory sucked in her breath. "Did she say why?"

"Not really. It's like she had a premonition or something."

"She has a stalker."

Megan's eyes widened in surprise. "That explains a lot."

"What do you mean?"

"She's been so different lately. Really worried about something. I thought it had to do with one of her kindergarteners, but now...a stalker would explain it."

"Was there something going on in her classroom?"

"One of her students was acting out. The behavior problems had become bad enough she brought the parents in for a talk, but they didn't seem to take it seriously."

"Do you remember their names?"

"Uri and Tabitha Halliwell. Their daughter was at the reading dressed as a witch. Let's see if they're still here." She led the way into the main part of the library and pointed to a couple near the checkout desk. "That's them."

Rory's gaze locked onto the couple and the kindergartener next to them. As they started to leave, their blonde haired daughter sat down on the ground and refused to follow. The parents tried reasoning with her. When that didn't help, the father picked up the crying child and carried her out the door.

"Is she always like that?" Rory asked.

"She didn't used to be. She was the sweetest thing. No behavior problems whatsoever. Then, a couple weeks ago, she started having tantrums."

"Any idea what's causing them?" Rory said.

Megan shook her head. "It could be a lot of things. Maybe something's off at home. Children pick up on what's going on around them, even if they don't completely understand what's happening." She looked at Rory. "I hope Zelena's found soon. She's a great teacher and a good friend."

Rory nodded her head in agreement. She hoped so too.

That evening, Rory and the rest of her neighbors gathered at Mrs. Maldonado's house at the end of the block for the Neighborhood Watch meeting. Everyone sat in the living room, talking among themselves, while they waited for the meeting to begin. Mrs.

Maldonado kept on glancing at the clock. Finally, five minutes before the scheduled start time, she touched Rory on the arm. "Can I speak with you?"

"Sure." Rory followed her hostess into the neighboring kitchen.

"Have you seen Winifred today? I tried calling her, but she didn't pick up."

"Mrs. Griswold? Not today. It's not like her to miss a meeting, especially one she runs."

"I know. That's what worries me. I'll give her a little more time, then I'm starting without her."

When the Neighborhood Watch block captain still hadn't shown up fifteen minutes later, Mrs. Maldonado called the meeting to order. They were halfway through the agenda when Mrs. Griswold hurried in the door, looking tired and disheveled, with bags under her eyes. "So sorry, so sorry," she said. "I took a nap and lost track of the time."

Everyone quickly caught the block captain up on what they had discussed so far, then Mrs. Griswold took over until the meeting adjourned. When the group disbanded, Rory walked out the front door with her neighbor. "Are you okay?"

"I'm just a little tired. My age, you know. Thank you for asking."

"Did you know your outside lights don't seem to be working?"

"Don't worry. I'll get them fixed soon." Mrs. Griswold gave Rory a tiny smile. "There's something I've been meaning to talk to you about. Would you be interested in taking over my duties as Neighborhood Watch block captain?"

Rory's eyes opened wide. "Is anything wrong? You're not moving, are you?"

"No, just considering a change."

Rory sensed there was more to it than that. "Is there anything I can do to help?"

"That's very nice of you, but I'm fine. Let me know soon about being block captain." Mrs. Griswold quickened her pace, leaving

Rory trailing behind, wondering if the woman's late appearance at the meeting had something to do with her recent midnight run.

Chapter 7

Friday morning, Rory walked through the open doorway of a two-story Mediterranean-style house into a bustle of activity. Volunteers moved in and out, carrying decorations as well as completed projects in preparation for the next day's grand opening of the Halloween Holiday Boutique.

She carried a box filled with the items she'd painted into a living room decked out as if Christmas were just around the corner. A ten-foot tall pine tree dominated the room. Two volunteers hung ornaments on it, all of them painted by chapter members and available for sale once the doors officially opened.

"No, not there. I told you over *there*." Jeanne pointed to a table on the opposite side of the room. "Aren't you listening?"

The woman she was talking to looked confused. "But you said earlier—"

"You obviously misunderstood."

One look at the scowl on Jeanne's face and the volunteer scurried to do her bidding.

"Jeanne?" Rory said. "Where do you want me to put these?"

Jeanne turned to look at Rory, a big smile on her face. "Let me look at what you brought." She examined the pieces. "These are lovely, just lovely. They'll sell easily. You really are a wonderful painter, unlike some I could tell you about." She darted a glance toward one of the women hanging ornaments on the tree. "I know exactly where to put them. Follow me." She pointed toward the fireplace across the room. "The clock can go over there."

Rory set the clock decorated with a holly and berry pattern in the center of the mantelpiece.

Jeanne shifted it slightly. Once she was satisfied with its placement, she led the way into a room filled with ghosts, witches and spiders. "Each of the rooms has a theme so if someone is looking for a particular kind of decoration, they can look at all of the choices at once. All of the Halloween items are in here." Her gaze swept the room. She pointed toward a nearby table and the empty display stand that sat on it. "Your sign can go over there. That's the perfect place for it."

Rory set the domed sign painted with a design featuring a black cat and pumpkins where the woman had indicated.

"And last, but not least, your lazy Susan. Such a wonderful rosemaling design. Rogaland, if I'm not mistaken. Follow me." She led the way into the dining room where Rory placed the wood piece in the center of the polished mahogany table.

"Wonderful. Let me just check you off." Jeanne consulted a clipboard and verified the selling prices for the pieces. "I'll put up the signs in a minute."

When they were back in the other room, Rory said, "Where'd you get the Christmas tree?"

"Looks wonderful, doesn't it? It's artificial. I'd rather have a real one, of course, but it couldn't be helped."

"Have you seen Penny? She wanted me to check in with her when I arrived."

Jeanne waved her hand vaguely. "I'm sure she's around somewhere."

"What about Zelena?"

She looked down at her clipboard, a sober expression on her face. "I'm afraid not."

Rory took a tour of the rest of the downstairs, greeting volunteers and admiring items, making a mental note of which pieces she wanted to purchase for herself. In the backyard, she found the chapter president setting up a life-sized wooden Nativity set.

"Rory. Just who I was looking for." Penny straightened up and rubbed her lower back. "Liz is waiting for you upstairs to try out the escape room. She's already been briefed on the story line and clues. And could you thank your mother for me for being so understanding and for providing the sales personnel? I'll get that list of items we're selling to her as soon as possible so she'll know what to charge. And she shouldn't have any more problems with Jeanne. I had a long talk with her."

"I'll let her know. What was the issue with Jeanne, anyway?"

Penny sighed. "Just a misunderstanding. I'm afraid that was partially my fault. I didn't know about the deal Zelena had made with your mother last time."

"I don't understand."

"Your mother is getting a small percentage of the sales, enough to compensate her for the processing fees the credit card company charges her. Jeanne wanted her to do everything for free. Don't worry, it's all settled now."

"I see. Is there anything else?"

"I hate to ask you this, but could you do me a favor?"

"Sure, what is it?"

"After you're done trying out the escape room, could you swing by Escape Key and pick up a box of props Toby's loaning us to decorate the rest of the house? He forgot to bring them yesterday. I'd do it myself, but I really need to be here while we're setting up. You can tell him what you thought of the room at the same time."

"I'll take care of it. No problem."

"Thank you. That's a big help. I won't keep you any longer. The escape room is upstairs. Just follow the signs. You can't miss it. Oh, and don't forget that everything about it is hush hush. We don't want the solution getting out and ruining people's enjoyment."

As soon as she stepped inside the escape room, Rory felt as if she'd entered a cave. In the subdued lighting, she struggled to make out its contents. A cabinet, a roll top desk, a slightly battered trunk and a bookcase filled with leather-bound volumes and framed photos lined the edges of the room while a small round table sat in its center. A dark blue velvet tablecloth with gold tassels along the edge covered its surface. The cloth, embroidered with stars and other mystical symbols, didn't quite reach the ground, leaving the wood legs of the table exposed. A crystal ball sat in its center surrounded by flickering candles. Two straight-back chairs sat across the table from each other as if waiting for the mystic and client to appear.

When Rory stepped closer, she realized the candles were fake, battery-operated ones that only gave the illusion of flickering flames.

Dressed in a brightly colored skirt and top with astrological symbols embroidered all over them, a figure separated herself from the far wall and stepped forward. Gold and silver bracelets jingled as she raised her hand toward Rory.

"Welcome, Seeker of Truth," the figure intoned. "I am Madame Elizabeth. You have been called by the spirits to help us find the psychic to the stars, Madame Endora, who has been kidnapped. You have one hour to save—" Her hoop earrings swayed as Liz cocked her head and studied her friend. In her normal voice, she said, "What's going on?" She moved her hand in a circle in front of Rory's face. "Your aura's all messed up."

"It's a little dark in here. Can we have more light? People need to see the clues."

"Sure." Liz moved around the room, turning up lamps. "How's that?"

"Better." Rory walked over to the bookcase and picked up a framed picture of a large man dressed all in leather. The rotund biker sported a full beard and a tattoo of a red phoenix on his arm. Beside him stood a petite older woman. "Toby really went into detail, didn't he? Relatives of Madame Endora? Is this a clue?"

"You'll have to find out for yourself." Liz took the photo and returned it to its place on the bookcase. "You didn't answer my question. What's the matter? Is it Zelena? Has something new happened?"

"I didn't realize it showed."

"A friend can always tell when there's something wrong. Come tell Madame Elizabeth your troubles." Liz sat down at the table and gestured toward the chair across from her.

Rory sank down onto the seat. "I'm worried about Mrs. Griswold."

"Granny G? What's going on with her?" Liz pushed back the scarf that covered her head so her face was fully exposed.

"I'm not sure. She's been very secretive lately. More than usual. Every time I try to talk with her, she clams up."

Liz frowned. "That's not like her. She usually talks your ear off. Anything else?"

"She's been shirking her Neighborhood Watch duties. She showed up late for a block meeting last night. Said she took a nap and overslept. She's even talking about giving up being block captain."

"Whoa. Something's definitely wrong. She practically lives for that job."

"I know. Her outside lights aren't working properly, either. They flicker in and out and she hasn't gotten them fixed yet. That's so unlike her. She's always bugging everyone about keeping our yards lit up to deter burglars. Then there's the mysterious drive she took. I saw her leave after midnight the other day."

"The witching hour. I didn't think she liked driving at night."

"She doesn't."

Liz tapped her fingers on the table. "Maybe she's having a torrid affair and doesn't want her kids to know."

"She's in her 70s. I don't think they have any say in what she does."

"Doesn't stop some people from interfering."

"They live miles away from here and I haven't seen them around lately. Unless they have someone keeping tabs on her, they wouldn't know anything about any affair."

"Hasn't her son been bugging her about moving into a retirement home?"

"That's been going on for years. I have this feeling it's more than that though. I almost followed her the other night."

"What stopped you?"

"I felt bad about it. And I didn't know what to say if she spotted me."

"What about a tracking app on her phone?"

"She still uses an old flip-top. It wouldn't be right to do it, anyway." Rory sighed. "Some way to track her would be nice, though, wouldn't it? Then we'd know whether to worry about her or not."

Liz's eyes lit up. "We'll just have to tail her, then. I know how. I've been watching videos about it. She'll never know we're following her."

"You and your YouTube videos. Still..." Rory was mulling over the possibility when Teresa Mut poked her head in the doorway.

"Have you started yet? Should I lock the door?"

Rory stood up. "Sorry, we got to talking. Go ahead. Start timing me now." She turned to Liz. "We'll finish our conversation later. Start your spiel."

While Teresa closed and locked the door, Liz stood up and began again. "Welcome, Seeker of Truth..."

After she finished at the boutique house, Rory drove to a more industrialized part of town where Escape Key was located and pulled into the parking lot beside the repurposed warehouse that held the escape room business. In the reception area, one group sat in chairs waiting for their time to start while another checked in at the counter. While she waited in line, a tall, slim man with blond hair pulled back in a ponytail walked down the hallway toward her.

Toby Worthington smiled when he spotted her. "Hi, Rory. Penny told me you'd be stopping by."

"Liz and I tried out the escape room at the house today. It was great, but we had a few areas of concern." She handed him a piece of paper with their comments written on it.

He pushed his Harry Potter glasses up the bridge of his nose and studied the paper. "Good points, all of them. I'll send someone over to make the adjustments. This is why I like to have someone try out a new room before it goes live. Having someone new look at it points out problems we wouldn't notice otherwise." He stuffed the paper in the pocket of his jeans. "The box is in the garage. We'll go this way so you can see a bit of the place. We're all quite proud of it."

He led the way down a hallway that bisected the building, pointing out the four escape room doors, each featuring a different themed experience, and stopped at a bank of monitors. "This is where we keep an eye on the rooms in case there's an emergency. The person working here also gives clues when needed. Unlike the boutique house, we don't have an employee stationed inside each room."

"Do you allow cell phones in the rooms?"

"We don't prohibit them. Truth be told, they won't be much help, anyway. Cell service isn't great in this part of town, especially inside buildings. Everything they need to solve the puzzles is in the room, anyway."

They watched the activity within each room for a moment before moving on. As he led the way to the back door, Toby said, "Just an ordinary day here. Seems odd, doesn't it? Everything so normal while Zelena's missing. Has there been any news yet? Penny was pretty upset after the meeting yesterday. She told me about the phone call."

"Nothing yet, unfortunately. I was hoping the police would be able to trace the call, but they didn't have any luck. Did you know about Zelena's stalker?"

"Only heard about that yesterday. Penny knew earlier, but she never told me about it. I wish I'd known. Maybe I could have helped." He held the back door open for her. "Some things make more sense now."

"What do you mean?"

"Zelena seemed...anxious the last time I saw her. I don't know what about. I didn't really spend that much time with her. That's more Penny's department. She's the more social one in this marriage."

Everyone else seemed to have realized there was something going on with Zelena recently, even those who didn't know her that well. Rory wondered why she hadn't seen it herself.

They exited the building and crossed the driveway toward the side door of a garage that turned out to be large enough to house two or three moving trucks parked side by side.

"This is where we store the extra props."

Rory's gaze swept the room from the roll-up door that covered the front of the garage to the shelves near where they'd entered that held smaller items like vases, clocks and other bric-a-brac. Larger pieces of furniture of all types and styles lined the walls.

"Where do you get it all?"

"Depends. Buy some of it. Sometimes I rent from a prop house for a short-term project. That's what I did for the boutique house. The smaller stuff, I pick up here and there at thrift shops, garage sales... You name it, I've probably been there. I've even found some items discarded on the street. We change the escape rooms periodically so items move in and out of here on a regular basis."

She pointed toward a pile of wood stacked against a wall. "Do you build your own props too?"

"Sometimes, if I can't find exactly what I want." He picked up a box off a nearby shelf. "Here we go. Why don't I carry it to your car for you."

After placing the box in the trunk of her car, Toby rested his hand on the open lid. "There is something. I'm not sure how important it is." A worried look on his face, he looked off into the distance as if trying to decide whether to tell her or not.

Rory waited for him to continue.

Finally, he seemed to come to a decision. "Never mind. Probably nothing to do with her being missing, anyway." He smiled at her and closed the lid. "Thanks for taking this stuff to the house. Don't give up hope. I bet they'll find Zelena alive and well soon."

Rory watched him walk away, tempted to call after him and ask him what he was holding back. Certain she wouldn't have any luck, she got in her car and drove away.

Chapter 8

The audience filed into the Vista Beach State Theater Friday evening. Originally built in the 1920s to show silent movies, the lovingly restored theater, complete with its original Mighty Wurlitzer pipe organ, now periodically screened silents as well as classic films from the '30s and '40s.

Rory and Martin settled back in their seats in the darkened theater and laughed along with the rest of the audience at Laurel and Hardy's antics as the short film, *The Live Ghost,* played on the screen.

"It's nice to hear you laugh," Martin said to Rory when the lights went up for the intermission. "It's been a tough week for you."

"I've been looking forward to this movie all year. You're going to love this version of *Phantom of the Opera.* Lon Chaney is memorable in it."

"I've never seen a silent film with live organ music before." He brushed a wisp of hair away from her eyes and looked at her with concern. "I can take you home, if you like. You must be tired. I imagine you haven't gotten much sleep lately."

"Thanks, but I'm okay. It's nice to get out and focus on something else besides Zelena."

He squeezed her hand. "We're doing everything we can to find her. We'll just have to hope we'll catch a break soon."

"I know. I just wish there was more I could do to help." A chill ran up her spine. As surreptitiously as possible, Rory looked around the theater, but spotted nothing unusual.

"What is it?" Martin said.

"I'm not sure. For a second, I felt like someone was watching us."

His gaze swept the area. "I don't see anything suspicious."

"Just my imagination, I guess." She nodded toward the organist who was walking down the aisle toward his seat in front of the keyboard. "I think it's about to start."

Moments later, the lights dimmed and the organ music swelled as the title card for the *Phantom of the Opera* appeared on the screen. Martin took hold of her hand and they settled in for the silent film classic. Rory's attention was riveted on the screen when the row of seats rocked slightly and someone settled into the seat next to hers. She looked over at the newcomer. In the dim light, she could just make out a woman with a scarf over her head. After a brief glance, Rory turned her attention back to the movie.

She clutched Martin's hand tightly and gasped with the rest of the audience when Christine tore off Lon Chaney's mask. The Phantom's skull-like face reminded her of the skeleton found lounging underneath the Vista Beach pier. Moments later, the music swept her once again into the story and she became oblivious to the real world until *Finis* appeared on the screen and the last strains of music faded away. When the lights went up, the audience of silent film enthusiasts broke into applause.

"Amazing how the organist can play along with the film without sheet music," Martin said as they prepared to leave. "Thanks for suggesting this. It was fun."

"Excuse me," the woman in the seat next to Rory said. "Could I speak with you two a moment?"

The couple exchanged glances. Martin shrugged slightly and Rory nodded her head in agreement.

The woman removed her scarf, revealing long silver hair with a tinge of blue in it, and handed each of them a business card. "My name's Raven Leek. I have some information about the missing woman, Zelena Alvarez."

Hope filled Rory's heart. Maybe this was the break they had been looking for. She glanced down at the card and was instantly disappointed. Underneath the woman's name were the words "Psychic Advisor."

Martin handed the card back as soon as he looked at it and stood up. "I think we're done here."

Raven placed her hand on Rory's arm as she started to follow. "Please. Just hear me out. I won't take much of your time. What can it hurt?"

Rory shook off the woman's arm and glanced at Martin who shrugged as if to say it's up to you.

"I'll meet you outside." He headed toward the exit, a frown on his face.

Rory sat down in the seat Martin had occupied, leaving an empty one between her and Raven.

"It's better that the unbeliever is gone."

"What makes you think I'm a believer?" Rory said.

"You're at least willing to hear me out. Something the police don't seem inclined to do."

"Why do you think I'd be interested in what you have to say?"

"You are Aurora Anderson, right? I saw your name in the article about Zelena when she went missing. You do want to find her, don't you?"

"How do you know who I am? Did you follow me?" Rory looked around, relieved to see they weren't the only ones left in the theater.

"The universe wanted us to find each other." Raven glanced at the exit where the detective now stood, watching them. "I'll cut to the chase. I had a vision recently of your friend. She was surrounded by water. I got the feeling she's in danger."

Rory's pulse quickened, carried away for a moment by the purported psychic's words and tone of voice. She mentally shook herself and tried to think rationally. "That doesn't tell me much. We do live near the ocean."

The woman closed her eyes and swayed slightly in her seat as if going into a trance. "I see sand and shadows. Concrete." Her eyes flew open. "That's where you'll find her."

"Where? That doesn't tell me enough. You could be talking about dozens of places."

"That's all I saw. All I get are impressions." Raven stood up. "I'll let you know if I see anything else. I might be able to help more if the police would let me."

The woman walked toward the exit, Rory following closely behind. When she reached Martin, he took her hand and they headed toward his car. "What did she say?"

"Nothing very helpful. She had a vision of Zelena, but everything was very vague."

"You don't believe in that stuff, do you? Astrology, ESP, psychics?" He opened the passenger side door for Rory, then walked around to the driver's side.

As they settled into their seats, Rory mulled over his question. "Not really. But at this time of year it's easier to imagine. She mentioned something about the police not wanting her to help."

"She offered her...services to us after the article appeared in the newspaper. For a price, of course. We declined her offer."

"Have you ever used a psychic before on a case?" Rory asked curiously.

"Not me, personally, but I've known some officers who have. Caused more harm than good."

Rory thought about what the woman had said about concrete and shadows. A vision of her own popped into her head. "Can we take a walk on the beach?"

He cast a curious glance in her direction before starting the car and heading out of the parking lot. "Something tells me this isn't just a walk."

"Just a short one, down by the pier. It'll be romantic."

"This doesn't have something to do with that woman's vision, does it?"

"Just humor me."

Martin turned a corner and headed toward the ocean. He parked in a spot near the pier. They rolled up the legs on their pants and took off their shoes, then headed hand-in-hand across the sand. Enjoying the peaceful interlude, Rory forgot for a moment why she'd wanted to come there in the first place.

A late-night jogger ran along the edge of the water toward the pier. He'd almost reached them when an image in white rose out of the ocean. The jogger stopped and trained his headlamp on the figure that glowed from head to foot.

Rory gasped as the child turned its head, liquid streaming out of its eyes and mouth, just like the story she'd heard at the library. When it turned its head back toward the ocean, Martin mumbled something and ran forward.

The ghost child continued walking in the shallows as if none of them were there. Suddenly, it screamed and pointed, then broke out into a run on the packed sand, heading back toward the pier.

Instead of chasing the figure, Martin ran toward the jogger who was dragging a bundle out of the ocean. Rory walked as fast as she could across the sand. Her eyes widened when she saw the body that had washed up on the beach. Zelena's body, surrounded by water with concrete posts nearby, under the shadow of the pier. Just like in Raven Leek's vision.

Chapter 9

Rory stepped forward until she could see the body more clearly. Light from the lamps lining the pier above combined with moonlight to illuminate the area enough for her to confirm it was Zelena who had washed up on the beach.

For a moment, hope filled her heart when she saw her friend's chest move up and down only to be dashed when she realized it was merely the waves rocking the body.

Martin touched her arm. "Is that...?"

Rory nodded and a tear trickled down her face. "Is she...?"

"I think so. There's nothing you can do for her. Why don't we go over here?" After instructing the jogger to stay put, he gently guided her toward the pier until Zelena's body was an indefinable object being rocked by the waves. He hugged her and stroked her hair for a minute before going into detective mode.

Rory leaned against one of the concrete posts that supported the pier and slid down until she was sitting on the sand. After the detective talked to the jogger, he made some phone calls. Before long, the beach was swarming with activity. Martin spoke to everyone as they arrived, periodically walking over to check on her. When floodlights were brought in to illuminate the area so the police could better process the scene, Rory turned to face the opposite direction so she wouldn't have to see what was going on. She leaned against the post and cried a little inside for her friend.

Rory didn't know how long she'd been sitting there when a

familiar voice called her name. She turned her head to see Liz hurrying across the sand, her arms crossed in front of her, hugging her sweater to her chest.

Rory scrambled to her feet and the two wordlessly hugged. When they broke apart, Rory said, "What are you doing here?"

"Dashing D called me to take you home." Liz looked over at all of the activity. "So it's true, then? You found Zelena?"

"I'm afraid so."

"I'll never think of the beach in the same way again." Liz shuddered. "Come on, let's get out of here."

"Let me just tell Martin I'm going." Rory waved her hand until she got his attention, then pointed at Liz and mimed leaving.

He nodded and held his left hand up to his ear in the standard "I'll call you" gesture before returning to his work.

Rory and Liz silently trudged across the sand toward the parking lot. Only when they were in the car, heading toward Rory's house, did Liz speak. "That's tough finding her like that." She shivered. "It's lucky you came along when you did. If you hadn't she might have washed back into the ocean and we might never have known what happened to her."

"Something someone said led me there." Rory described the encounter with Raven Leek at the silent movie theater and how she had gotten the idea to walk by the pier from what the woman said.

"A real psychic? Here in town?"

"I'm not sure how 'real' she is. The things she said could be interpreted in a lot of ways. It was pure...I hesitate to call it luck...that we were there when the 'ghost child' found Zelena."

Liz glanced over at her friend, a puzzled expression on her face. "Ghost child?"

"Didn't I tell you about that?" Rory described what they had seen when they first arrived, how the jogger had pulled the body out of the water after the child screamed. "If it hadn't been for that mysterious figure, I don't think the jogger would have noticed Zelena's body."

Liz sucked in her breath. "You saw a ghost too? I'd forgotten all about that story."

"You know it?"

"My brother used to frighten me with it when I was growing up, but I never actually saw the ghost. Or know anyone who did, come to think of it. Up until now, that is."

"I don't think we saw it, either. That must have been another prank. It was pretty good though. Whoever it was must have painted his face and clothes with something that glows in the dark. And I could have sworn blood was coming out of the eyes and mouth."

"Do you think the ghost was a coincidence? Maybe it was involved in her death somehow."

"I'm leaning toward coincidence, but who knows." Rory leaned back in her seat. "I can't help wondering if we couldn't have prevented this somehow. If we'd known what was going on earlier, we could have hired a bodyguard for Zelena or...something."

"I know what you mean, but it doesn't help if we think like that," Liz said as she pulled into Rory's driveway.

"We need comfort food, but I'm not sure what I have in the house."

"I've got it covered." Liz reached into the back seat and produced a paper bag. "I got ice cream for us and kitty milk so Sekhmet wouldn't feel left out."

"Mint chocolate chip?"

"And chocolate moose tracks."

When they walked inside, they found the Abyssinian cat sitting by the front door as if she'd been waiting for hours, not the ten seconds Rory suspected she'd actually been there.

"That was nice of you, getting milk for my cat," Rory said.

"Sekhmet and me, we're like this." Liz crossed the index and middle fingers on her right hand and held them up so Rory could see. She bent down and scratched the cat underneath her chin. "Isn't that right, Sekhmet?"

After pouring some of the kitty milk in a bowl in the kitchen, they left the cat enjoying her treat and settled down in the living room, side by side on the couch. Rory took the pint of mint chocolate chip while Liz took the moose tracks. They ate in silence for a while, occasionally exchanging ice cream containers, until Liz finally said, "Do you think she drowned?" She spread a napkin on the coffee table and placed her container on top of it.

Rory stuck her spoon in her own pint and put it next to the other one. "Martin didn't really say what his first impression was, and I didn't think to ask. A part of me doesn't want to know." She cast her mind back to the scene on the beach. "It was pretty dark, hard to see much. Until they brought in the floodlights, of course. I couldn't face up to watching them work after that, so I turned around. All I can really remember is an impression of seaweed tangled up in her hair and the waves moving her body up and down."

Liz shuddered. "I'm glad I was too far away to see anything." She picked up her ice cream again. The spoon was halfway to her mouth when her eyes widened. "The boutique house opens tomorrow. We need to let everyone know."

"I hadn't thought of that. We should call the other board members." Rory glanced at the time on her cell phone. "It's after eleven. My mom taught me not to call anyone this late unless it was an emergency. I think this qualifies as one."

"Do you think it's possible someone in our painting chapter could be involved?"

"Why do you say that?"

"There's been a lot of tension since Jeanne joined the group eight months ago."

"Definitely not winning friends, that's for sure."

"But she is influencing people. She took control of the boutique away from Zelena. At least she's not president. Thank goodness Penny agreed to take the job when no one other than the Annoying One wanted it."

"Jeanne doesn't seem the stalker type. I don't know what she'd gain from sending those messages."

"Maybe that was the point." Liz tapped her temple. "Mind

games! Zelena would be so preoccupied with finding out who was stalking her, Jeanne could do whatever she wanted."

"I suppose it's possible," Rory said slowly. "But I'm not convinced."

They split up the list of board members and were about to start calling when Rory received a text from Martin. She replied to his *Are u still up?* and, less than a minute later, heard a soft knock on the front door.

He entered, a somber look on his face. Since Rory last saw him, he'd changed into a suit, indicating to her this was an official visit. "How are you two doing?"

"Hanging in there. What's the latest?" Rory said.

Martin sat down on the chair and leaned forward with his elbows on his knees. "We're still processing the scene. We'll know more after it gets light but, first indication is that your friend drowned. We won't know for sure until the autopsy is complete."

Rory sensed a "but" coming.

"There are...things that are suspicious. We're treating it as a potential homicide for now." He brought up a photo on his phone and showed it to Rory. "Is this what Zelena was wearing when you saw her at your meeting?"

Rory steadied herself to view the photo, breathing a sigh of relief when it turned out to be a close-up of clothes and not her friend's face. She peered at the screen, then handed the phone over to Liz. "Is that top the one she was wearing on Saturday? Didn't you say it was forest green?"

Liz squinted at the photo. "I can't really tell the color, but that's not what she was wearing. Different style entirely."

Martin took out a notepad and pen. "Do either of you know how to get in touch with Zelena's family? Parents? Brothers or sisters?"

"No brothers or sisters as far as I know. She grew up in East L.A. Her parents might still be there, but she hasn't talked to them in a long time," Rory said. "At least that's what a friend of hers told me."

"I found some old tabloid articles on her from years ago," Liz said. "She was legally emancipated from them when she was sixteen."

He looked up from his notes. "Did the articles say why?"

Liz twisted her lips in concentration. "Her father had lost all of the money she made on that sitcom she was on, *Mommy's Little Helper*, in a bad investment."

"Interesting." He jotted the information down in his notebook. "Was she dating anyone?"

"Not that I know of. Someone else in the chapter might know more. We were just about to call them. Or you might find something at her place. Hold on." Rory walked over to her work area and returned with a key. "Take this. It's to Zelena's apartment."

"The woman next door might be able to tell you something," Liz added. "She's very involved in the neighborhood."

"So I heard." Martin's lips twitched.

Rory drew Raven Leek's business card out of the pocket of her jeans. "You may as well take this too. Raven's vision did help us find Zelena."

He made no move to take the card. "Probably coincidence."

Rory wasn't so sure it was coincidence, but she wasn't yet ready to declare her belief in psychic visions. "Still, she might know something."

"Don't worry, we'll talk to her. We have her contact information at the station." He stood up. "I'll check in with you tomorrow. Walk me to the door?"

At the front door, he kissed Rory and said, "Be careful. Let me know if anyone in your painting group knows how to contact Zelena's family. Other than that, no investigating, okay?"

Rory nodded her head. When she returned to the living room, Liz was bringing out her phone. "It's time to make those calls."

With a heavy heart, Rory took her own phone off the coffee table and dialed the first number.

Chapter 10

When Rory entered the boutique house the next morning, everyone crowded around her and bombarded her with questions about Zelena's untimely death. She told them what she could, but the number of unanswered questions left the group unsatisfied.

As soon as she arrived, Penny gathered everyone in the living room for a short talk before they opened the doors. After making a few general comments, she said, "I know this is going to be hard. Some of you have suggested we close down the house, but Zelena would have wanted us to continue. This was her baby. We can't let down the cause she believed in. Before we open, let's take a moment to remember the caring person she was. Join hands, everyone."

They all solemnly gathered in a circle and held hands. Some bowed their heads, others closed their eyes. An occasional sniffle broke the quiet. After the moment of silence was over, the volunteers drifted away, taking up their stations as the house opened to paying customers.

Rory headed to her assigned post at the table outside the escape room where she was in charge of checking in customers as well as locking the escape room door. A couple hours later, Toby Worthington walked up to the table.

"Hi, Rory, how's the escape room going? Any problems?" He pushed his glasses up the bridge of his nose and peered earnestly at her.

"Everyone seems to be enjoying it. Most people finish by the end of the hour, though some have solved it earlier."

He scratched his chin where a beard was beginning to form. "Good. That means it's about the right level of difficulty. I want people to have fun but at the same time not get too frustrated. Any idea how many need clues?"

"No. You'll have to ask Liz—sorry, Madame Elizabeth. She's working the room right now." Rory glanced at the time on her cell phone. "The current guests should be exiting soon. You can ask her then."

Toby was opening his mouth to say something else when a woman and a young boy walked up to the table. He stepped to one side while Rory checked them in and pointed out chairs farther down the hallway where they could wait.

As soon as the two moved away, Toby approached the table once again and lowered his voice. "I was so sorry to hear about Zelena. I was really hoping they would find her alive and well. Thank you for calling and letting us know last night."

"How is Penny doing, really?" Rory's brow wrinkled in worry lines. "We didn't get a chance to talk much last night and I barely saw her this morning."

"You wouldn't know it, but she's devastated. She holds everything in, you know. Not healthy, not healthy at all." He kept his voice low, occasionally glancing at the people who were waiting, but they seemed oblivious to the topic of the conversation. "They were really close. Almost like sisters."

"I didn't realize that."

"They became almost instant friends when we moved here a year ago. Just one of those things, you know."

Rory nodded her head in understanding.

"I heard you were the one who found her. That must have been awful."

"I was there." Rory shuddered as a picture of the scene on the beach popped into her mind.

"Sorry, I didn't mean to upset you."

"It's okay. Has Penny remembered anything that might help the police with their investigation? I got the impression last night there was something she was reluctant to talk about."

Toby stared at the hardwood floor, avoiding Rory's gaze. Finally, he looked up. "I don't know if this counts, but Zelena was coming into a lot of money soon."

"Is that what you weren't sure you should tell me about yesterday?"

He nodded.

"When did Zelena talk to you about it?"

Looking uncomfortable, he absentmindedly scratched a scar on his forearm. "Not me, personally. She told Penny. She's not really sure if she should break Zelena's confidence since she was sworn to secrecy."

"But it might have something to do with her death. Penny needs to go to the police. I know the detective on the case. I could tell him, but he'd still have to talk to her."

Toby shook his head. "I'm not sure Penny will like that."

"Did I hear my name? Is there a problem with the escape room?" Penny said as she approached the table.

Toby jumped slightly when he heard his wife's voice. He plastered a smile on his face and turned toward her. "No, no problem. Everything seems to be going well."

Penny looked from one to the other. Her eyes narrowed. "What's going on?"

"We were just talking about Zelena." Rory cleared her throat. "Toby was telling me she was coming into some money."

"You told her? How could you do that? I told you about that in confidence," Penny said in a sharp tone of voice to her husband.

"Sorry, I thought it might have something to do with Zelena's death."

"It could help the police in their investigation," Rory said.

"Do they think it's murder then?" Penny sank down on the chair next to Rory's.

"It's a possibility. The police are treating it as one for now. You really should tell them what you know. I can get you in touch with them. I'll text you the detective's phone number." Rory picked up her cell from the table in front of her and sent the text.

"Do you really think it could be important?" Penny said in a whisper.

"Maybe. Did she say where the money was coming from?"

"I assumed it had something to do with acting. She was talking about getting back into the business."

"Really?" Rory made a mental note to ask Samantha if Zelena had broached the subject with her. "I thought she was happy teaching."

"Oh, she loved it. I got the impression it was more of a part-time thing. She does get summers off." Penny stood up. "I just stopped by to see how the escape room was going. If everything's fine here, I'll move along." She darted a meaningful glance at her husband. "I'll talk to *you* later."

"Something tells me I'm not going to like that," Toby said in a quiet voice, more to himself than anyone else.

Before he could say another word, they heard the click of a lock and the door to the escape room opened. A young couple emerged, triumphant looks on their faces. Rory congratulated them on their successful solution to the puzzles and handed them a printed certificate of completion with their names and the time it took them to solve the mystery written on it.

While Toby questioned the couple on how they liked the escape room, Madame Elizabeth poked her head around the door. "How much time?"

Rory glanced at her cell phone. "Ten minutes."

Liz nodded and disappeared back inside the room with Toby following closely behind.

"Thanks for coming along." Martin Green steered his car through the streets of Vista Beach. While Rory was working at the house earlier that day, he'd texted her asking her to accompany him on a call.

"Glad to help." Rory briefly laid a sympathetic hand on his arm. "Notifying relatives of a death must be very hard."

"It's not my favorite part of the job."

Rory stared at the businesses and houses as they passed by. "Are we heading to East L.A.? Isn't that where Zelena's parents live?"

"Turns out her father's here, staying at a nearby motel."

Rory turned her head to look at the detective. "He's here? Any idea why?"

Martin shrugged. "I assume he came to visit his daughter."

"But why stay at a motel? East L.A. is a pretty short drive."

"Maybe he doesn't have a car."

"And why isn't he staying at her place?"

"Perhaps he wanted his privacy. We'll have to ask." He turned on a blinker and pulled into the parking lot of a beige two-story building with a slightly crooked sign that read Vista View Motel. "We're here."

The motel landscaping was neat and tidy, but the stucco building was showing its age. Paint flaked off here and there and a gutter hung at an odd angle. Off to one side, Rory spotted a young couple and their two children splashing around in a small swimming pool surrounded by an iron fence.

Martin was pulling into a spot near the motel office when a lanky man wearing a name badge stormed out and marched toward a much shorter man dressed in jeans and a T-shirt who was putting a suitcase in the trunk of an old beater.

"You're not planning on leaving without paying, are you?" the motel employee said.

"What are you talking about? I paid through tomorrow," the shorter one said in accented English.

"Your check bounced."

"My daughter was supposed to put some money in my account. She probably forgot. Zelena Alvarez. You must have heard of her. *Mommy's Little Helper?*"

"I don't care who your daughter is or who she helped. I want my money." The employee moved closer and raised a fist.

The two started arguing in Spanish and appeared to be ready to come to blows.

Martin Green approached them and flashed his badge while Rory watched from the safety of the car. "Police. What seems to be the problem here?"

"This one was trying to skip out without paying."

Martin turned toward the man who stood beside the car. "Are you Tito Alvarez?"

Zelena's father nodded and turned pale. "How do you know my name? I've done nothing wrong. You can't deport me. I'm a citizen now."

"Don't worry, I'm not with immigration." Martin turned toward the motel employee. "Why don't you return to the office. You can straighten out the money issue later. Right now I need to speak with Mr. Alvarez." When the employee crossed his arms in front of his chest and refused to budge, Martin added, "It's important."

The employee studied the detective for a moment, then uncrossed his arms and nodded. Before leaving he turned to Tito and said, "I want money. Cash. Got it?" Without waiting for a response, he walked back toward the office, muttering to himself.

Once he was gone, Tito said, "I wasn't trying to skip out. Honest."

"That's not why I'm here. It's about your daughter. Could we speak inside?" Martin gestured toward the open door of the room the beater was parked in front of.

Tito closed the trunk of his car and nervously led the way inside. Martin gestured toward Rory who got out of the car and followed the two men into the motel room.

Rory's gaze swept the area. The place appeared clean but, at the moment, it was far from neat with its unmade bed and takeout containers that littered the desk and bedside tables. Empty tequila and vodka bottles filled the trash can. She leaned against the open doorway while Martin introduced the two of them.

"You know my daughter?" Tito said to Rory.

"We've been friends for a while now."

"Why don't we sit down?" Martin offered the only chair to Rory. When she indicated she preferred to stay where she was, he sat down on it while Tito perched on the edge of the bed.

Tito's gaze went from the detective to Rory and back again. "Why are you here? Has something happened to Zelena?"

Martin cleared his throat. "I'm afraid I have some bad news. We found your daughter's body."

"She's dead?"

"That's right."

"My beautiful *mija*." Tito crossed himself. His shoulders slumped and he looked down at his hands. "How did she die?" he said without looking up.

"At the moment, it looks like she drowned."

Tito studied the detective's face. "Did someone kill her?"

"Why do you say that?" Martin said.

"She couldn't swim. She was afraid of the ocean."

"I never said she drowned in the ocean."

Tito shrugged his shoulders. "This is a beach city. Where else would she drown?" He looked over at Rory. "Why are you here?"

"I've known your daughter for a couple years. You haven't seen her in a while so I figured I could answer any questions you might have..." Rory's voice trailed off when she realized how lame it sounded.

"What makes you think I haven't seen her?"

"Someone told me...I heard you two were...estranged."

Tito waved his hand in the air. "Tabloid nonsense. I was here visiting like I often do."

"Why are you staying in a motel? Your home's not that far," Rory said.

"Now and then I like to spend a few days at the beach."

"How long have you been here in town?" Martin asked.

"A week or so."

"And your wife? Is she here too?"

"No. She's visiting relatives in Mexico." He buried his head in his hands. "How am I going to tell her?"

Martin jotted something down in his notebook. "When was the last time you saw your daughter?"

"Sunday. We took a walk on the beach."

The detective looked up from his notes. "Are you sure it was Sunday?"

Tito looked at him in confusion. "Sunday? Did I say Sunday? I meant Saturday."

"Do you know if she was seeing anyone?"

"A boyfriend? She never talked about one."

"What about someone following her? Did she mention anything like that?"

"Like a stalker?" Tito shook his head. "She seemed...troubled though."

"Do you have any idea why?"

"She never said."

"Did she say anything about coming into some money? Maybe a relative passed away and left her something?"

"Money?" Zelena's father shook his head, but for a second Rory detected a gleam in his eyes. "Not an inheritance. Nobody in our family is rich."

Detective Green jotted something down in his notebook. "Do you know what her plans were for Saturday night?"

"She said something about painting." Tito glanced over at Rory.

She nodded. "We had a painting chapter meeting that night."

"Other than that, no. You know how daughters are. They don't tell their fathers everything."

Detective Green put his notebook in his jacket pocket and stood up. "I'm very sorry for your loss. We'll do everything we can to find out what happened. It would be helpful if you could stay in town for a few more days. If you do have to leave or if you remember anything else that might help, give me a call." He placed his business card on the nearby dresser.

Tito nodded and saw them to the door. When Rory didn't immediately follow Martin, he turned around, a question in his eyes. She inclined her head toward Tito and mouthed "one minute". The detective nodded and headed toward the car.

"Mr. Alvarez, are you going to be okay?" Rory asked the man, concern in her voice.

"I'll be fine, thank you."

She handed him her own business card. "If you ever need anything, give me a call. Even if you just want to talk. Or I can help you with...arrangements." She hesitated. "Do you need money? A loan, of course," she hastily added. "Just to tide you over."

For a fraction of a second, an eager look came over his face, then he shook his head. "No, thank you."

But he didn't object when she took a twenty out of her wallet and handed it to him.

"*Gracias.*"

"What was that about?" Martin asked when she got in the car.

"Just gave him my card in case he needed anything."

"You're entirely too generous, you know." He put the car into gear and headed out of the parking lot.

"What did you think?" she said.

"About Zelena's father? I think he's holding something back. It might be important, might not."

"He's lying about how often he saw her, you know. Samantha Granger told me they haven't seen each other in years."

"Zelena's former manager? Do you believe her?"

"If anyone knows the details of Zelena's relationship with her parents, it would be Samantha."

They spent the rest of the drive in silence. When he dropped Rory off at her place, Martin drew a key out of his jacket pocket and handed it to her. "Almost forgot. You can have this back."

"You're done with Zelena's apartment?"

"Not quite, but we got another key from the landlord. I thought you might want it back in case you need to get something for a memorial service."

"Thanks." Rory gave him a quick kiss good-bye and headed inside.

Chapter 11

The next day after the mid-morning church service, Rory was fishing her car keys out of the pocket of her khakis when a car screeched to a halt in front of her in the parking lot. The passenger side window rolled down and someone called out her name. She bent down and looked into the silver Honda to see who was driving.

Veronica Justice leaned over and said, "Get in."

"Why?"

"I need your help. It's about Zelena's case."

Rory's gaze traveled to her own sedan.

"This won't take long. Leave your car here. It'll be fine. It's a church parking lot. What can happen to it?"

After making sure her car was locked, Rory opened the Honda's door and sat down on the passenger side. Her legs bent at an uncomfortable angle, she pushed the seat back until she no longer felt as if her knees were in her chest. She'd barely fastened her seat belt when Veronica gunned the engine and peeled out of the parking lot, narrowly missing a Mercedes that was backing out of a spot.

"Where are we going?" Rory said through gritted teeth. She gripped the armrest as Veronica navigated the streets of downtown Vista Beach.

"To see Edgar Geller."

"The CEO of Beyond The Grave? Didn't you already interview him for a story?"

Veronica took her eyes off the road to glance at an incoming text on her cell phone. "I want to do a follow up, but he's not doing any interviews right now. That's where you come in."

Rory said a silent prayer for their safe arrival wherever they were going. "What can I do? I don't know him. I've never even met him."

"But you knew Zelena. Just bat those pretty eyes of yours at him and let me do most of the talking."

Rory peered at the buildings they passed as they careened around a corner. She spotted the ocean dead ahead. "Where are we going? Didn't we just pass his office?"

"He's not there today, but I know where to find him."

Veronica parked in a space a block from the ocean and headed toward a portion of the beach where a series of volleyball nets were set up. Her gaze swept over the khakis and blouse Rory had worn to church. "You're not exactly wearing appropriate clothes for the beach, but you'll be fine. You can always take off your shoes and roll up your pants if you have to. Come on."

Rory followed the reporter down the incline toward one of the groups playing volleyball, trying not to think about what she'd seen the last time she was in the area.

The slap of palm against ball greeted them as they crossed the bike path and stopped at the edge of the sand. Her gaze swept the group of six middle-aged men and women, four of them playing two-on-two while the others sat on the sand nearby watching and waiting to sub in when needed.

"Which one is he?"

"Don't you recognize him? His photo was in the paper. I guess he looks different in casual clothes. The one in the blue swim trunks and white T-shirt." Veronica pointed to the court where a muscular man was serving the ball. Even in casual clothes, Edgar Geller exuded the air of a businessman.

Moments later, the volleyball came hurtling toward them, landing steps away from Veronica's feet. When she grabbed it, the players motioned for her to throw it back, but she held onto it, shouting that she wanted to talk with Edgar.

Veronica nudged Rory. "Go on. Bat those baby blues at him."

Rory gave a slight shake of her head.

Edgar walked toward the two women and frowned when he spotted the reporter. "I said I wasn't giving interviews. You can wait for the press conference like everyone else. The ball, please."

Veronica threw it to him, then gave Rory a meaningful look. He was heading back to the group when Rory called after him, "I'm the one who received Zelena Alvarez's email."

He threw the ball to a woman sitting on the sidelines, indicating with a wave of his hand she should sub in for him. When he once again stood in front of Rory and Veronica, he said, "I'm sorry for your loss. What can I do for you?" His gaze rested on the recorder in the reporter's hands. "Everything I say is off the record, understood?"

Veronica put her recorder back in her purse, tightened her lips and nodded.

He turned his attention back to Rory, a strained look on his face. "How can I help you?"

Rory studied the CEO of Beyond The Grave, trying to decide how to start. "How well did you know Zelena?"

"About as well as I know any of my customers."

"So...?" Veronica prompted.

"Not very well. Why the questions?"

"We're trying to find out what happened to her."

A puzzled look came over his face. "I thought she drowned in an accident. I assumed that's why the event was triggered and the email sent. She drowned days before but her body only washed ashore recently. At least that's the impression I got from everything I read online."

"The police are investigating it as a possible homicide," Rory said. "She was alive the day before her body was found. She called me."

"Oh." Edgar stared off into space. Rory could almost hear the wheels turning in his brain as he digested the implications of this new information. Finally, he turned his attention back to them. "What do you want to know?"

"Did you see the message she sent me? Do you know if there were others?"

"No on both counts. All messages are completely private. No one at my company has access to the contents of any emails a client sets up."

"When did she sign up for your services? Did she say why?"

"Must be two, three weeks back now, maybe more."

"Do you know anything about a stalker?" Veronica added before he could continue.

"Stalker? Is that what she said in her message?" A troubled look came over his face.

Rory nodded.

"I only met her once. I try to talk with all of my high-profile clients to assure them my company is discreet. I know what you're thinking, she taught school. But she was once a very well-known child actress. From what I gathered, she generally led a quiet life, but she still got the occasional fan letter."

Rory's ears perked up. "Anything that would fall in the stalker category?"

"She mentioned some disturbing emails but didn't know who they were from. And she thought she was being followed."

"You didn't think to tell the police?" Veronica said.

He held up his hands, palms forward. "Wait a minute. You can't blame what happened, whatever that was, on me or my company. We're not in the habit of revealing secrets."

"But—" Rory said.

He started back over the sand toward the volleyball game still in progress, calling over his shoulder, "Wasn't my story to tell."

Rory studied him as he returned to his group. She sensed he hadn't told them everything he knew. She turned to Veronica and said, "Sorry you didn't get an interview on the record."

Veronica waved away the concern. "You don't win every game." She checked something on her smart phone. "I've got somewhere to be. I'll drop you off at your car."

While the two drove back to the church, Rory mulled over everything the CEO had told them, trying to figure out if any of it could help them figure out what happened to her friend.

Chapter 12

Rory was putting the finishing touches on a painting project that afternoon when Tito Alvarez called and asked her if she'd accompany him to his daughter's apartment.

"The police are done processing it?" Rory said.

"For now. They said I could go in. I understand you have a key."

"That's right."

He cleared his throat. "I was also wondering if you could help me pick out clothes for...you know."

"Of course."

Half an hour later, Rory met Zelena's father on the sidewalk in front of the apartment. They were starting up the walkway toward the front door when Rory noticed the same woman she'd met before peering at them from around the hedge.

Rory touched Tito's arm and directed his attention to the woman. "We should introduce ourselves."

When they were steps away from the neighbor, Rory waved and smiled. "You're Doreen, right? I'm Rory. This is Zelena's father, Tito Alvarez." She put a slight emphasis on the word father, figuring that would prevent the woman from calling the police again.

Doreen's face softened. She clasped one of his hands between both of hers and held it for a moment. "So sorry for your loss. Your daughter was a lovely woman." She called over her shoulder. "Don!

Zelena's father is here." Moments later, the woman's husband appeared in the doorway of the house. They waited in silence as he slowly made his way across the lawn toward them. As soon as he reached them, Doreen said, "I was just telling Mr. Alvarez how sorry we are about his daughter."

Don scratched the bald spot on the top of his head. "I don't understand what's going on in the world today. To have that happen to such a nice girl."

"You knew her well?" Tito said.

"We talked now and then. She was always bringing us the best chocolate chip cookies. We'll miss them. And her too of course." Doreen nudged her husband who nodded his head in agreement.

"Did you notice anything unusual with her lately?" Rory said.

The couple exchanged glances. Some message seemed to pass between them.

"She seemed excited about something the last week or so," Doreen finally said.

"Excited, pleased, or excited, worried?"

"Oh, pleased, definitely pleased," Don said.

"Something about coming into some money that would make her dreams come true," Doreen added.

That confirmed what Toby said the previous day. "When did she tell you this?"

"Not so much tell us. More like overheard," Don said.

"Not that we were eavesdropping, mind you," Doreen added. "You know how people are, especially the younger ones, always talking on their cell phones, carrying on all kinds of conversations in public. Seems like no one understands privacy anymore. Even politicians—all their business is talked about in the press and on that bird thing."

"Twitter?"

"That's it. I remember when FDR was president. I was an itty bitty thing, then, of course, but I still remember it well," she continued. "Everyone knew he used a wheelchair, but the press never splashed it across the pages of the paper. They had respect.

Not like today."

"Did either of you see anyone you didn't recognize hanging around lately? Someone in a car or following Zelena?" Rory said.

"The police asked us the same thing. I'll tell you what we told them. There was a car with a man in it. And someone in her front yard once or twice. Not sure it was the same person. Could have been." Doreen poked her husband in the ribs. "Right, Don?"

He nodded.

"Did you get a good look at him?"

"Only saw part of his face. There was something familiar about him, but I can't put my finger on it." She seemed about to say more when they heard a man shout "Stop!" from the far side of the triplex followed seconds later by sounds of running.

The woman's helpful demeanor changed to one of suspicion. "Are you really Zelena's father? Or were you two just keeping us busy so we wouldn't notice a break-in?"

Don placed a hand on his wife's arm. "Doreen, I'm sure that's not what happened."

Rory assured her they had no idea what was going on. The woman calmed down, but Rory sensed they wouldn't get anything else out of either one of them for the rest of the day.

While Rory talked to the couple, Tito headed toward the far side of the triplex to see what all the shouting was about.

"Don, call the police," Doreen said.

Sure nothing she could say would convince the woman to hold off notifying the authorities, Rory said, "Go ahead. I'll see what's happening."

Don headed into the house to make the call while Rory followed the sound of voices to the far side of the triplex where she found Tito talking with a man who was leaning out of one of the windows on the second floor of the middle unit.

"What happened?" She looked up at the window.

"Someone was trying to get in the side door of Zelena's place." The man pointed toward the partially open door that led into the front unit. "He ran down the walkway and into the alley at the back."

"Going in or coming out?"

The man scratched his head. "Hadn't thought of that. Could've been either, I suppose."

"Did you get a good look at him?" Tito asked.

"Just a general impression."

"I'd better go in and see if the place is all right," Tito said.

"We should probably wait for the police," Rory said. "Just in case there's someone else inside."

"You called them?"

Rory nodded toward the house next door. "Neighbors did."

They didn't have long to wait before a police cruiser drove up and parked in the driveway. A uniformed officer Rory knew as Officer Yamada stepped out and nodded at her. If he was surprised to see her, he didn't show it. "Ms. Anderson. What seems to be the problem?"

Between the three of them, they explained what had happened and what they had each seen. Once the officer made sure no one was lurking inside, she and Tito checked it out to see if anything had been disturbed. Other than the side door, nothing seemed out of place.

"Detective Green is going to want to hear about this," Officer Yamada said. "Could one of you stay?"

Rory glanced at the time on her cell phone. "I don't know how long I can wait. I'm supposed to be working at the house soon. I suppose I could call and tell them I'll be late."

"I'll stay," Tito said. "You go do what you have to do."

"But the outfit..."

"It's all right. We can do that some other time."

Reluctantly, Rory walked back to her car and headed to work at the boutique house.

At home that evening, she was reading emails when her phone chirped, alerting her to new content on *Vista Beach Confidential*. Her eyes widened when she scrolled through the new post. After she reread it to make sure she understood it correctly, she called a familiar number.

"What's up?" Liz said.

"Have you seen the article Veronica just posted on *VBC*?"

"Hold on."

Rory leaned back in her desk chair and waited patiently while her friend read the short interview with the psychic who'd interrupted the date at the silent movie theater. Liz uttered a few "whoas" and sucked in her breath several times, then came back on the line.

"What do you think?" Rory asked. "You believe in ESP and all that stuff. Do you think Raven's vision is real?"

"I don't know. She's very specific about seeing Zelena at a trailer park and hearing sounds of the ocean nearby and planes overhead."

"I wish she'd given the name of the park."

"That's not the way it works. Unless the vision included the image of a sign, she would have no way of knowing where it took place."

"There's only one I can think of around here that fits that description: Ocean View Rest Stop."

"Right. One of my clients parked their trailer there while she was house hunting. Said it was nice, but really hated the planes taking off overhead."

"It's worth checking out."

"Are you going to call Dashing D?"

"I'm not sure he'll be that interested. He already rejected Raven's offer of her services when Zelena went missing. Interrupting our date didn't help. Plus he doesn't think much of psychics." Rory sat up straighter. "I'll tell him about it, but I think we should still check it out ourselves."

"First thing tomorrow?"

"First thing tomorrow."

After Liz hung up, Rory dialed Martin's number. Relief washed over her when the call went straight to voicemail. She left a brief message describing the article, omitting the part about their intent to investigate on their own.

She was heading to bed around midnight when she saw Mrs. Griswold driving away in her car. Rory sensed a pattern developing.

Chapter 13

The next morning, Rory pulled her sedan into a spot in the beach parking lot adjacent to their destination. Before heading to the ocean side RV park next door, she and Liz split up the investigation tasks.

"You see if anyone in the office has seen her. I'll ask some of the people in the park if they know anything," Rory said.

"Check."

While Liz headed toward the park's office, Rory took off her tennis shoes and socks and walked onto the sand. The roar of a jet taking off from LAX momentarily drowned out the hum of traffic on the road above. She shaded her eyes from the sun and looked at the plane flying west over the ocean. Before heading toward the RV park, she glanced up at the hill above her where cars traveled back and forth along the coast.

Ocean View Rest Stop, really just a parking lot with a little over one hundred marked spaces large enough to accommodate various sizes of motor homes and trailers, was three-quarters full on this October day.

Rory was walking along the sand in front of it when a teenager dressed in a wetsuit, carrying a surfboard under one arm, climbed over the knee-high fence that separated the RV park from the sand and headed toward the ocean. Rory followed him as fast as she could and called after him.

A question in his eyes, he turned around and stopped so she

could catch up.

"Excuse me," Rory said. "You're staying at the RV park, right?"

He nodded his head in acknowledgement and waited for her to continue.

Rory brought up Zelena's photo on her phone and showed it to him. "Have you seen this woman around the park?"

He leaned forward slightly and studied the photo. "Sorry. Haven't seen her. Maybe my parents can help. They're in the motor home. Slot 110."

"Thanks." Rory walked back to the park while the teen continued on his way. She walked through a gap in the fence surrounding the RV park and headed toward the space the teen had indicated. There she found a forty-something couple sitting around a picnic table next to their motor home, sipping coffee. She showed them the photo, but neither one of them had seen Zelena around.

Rory was heading toward the next occupied space when Liz jogged across the pavement toward her.

"Any luck?" Rory said.

Liz shook her head. "The man in the office hasn't seen her."

"That doesn't mean she wasn't here. Whoever kidnapped her could have had her tied up inside the RV when he drove it into the lot. I suppose he wouldn't give you a list of who's here?"

"That would be too much to hope for. He doesn't have any problem with us asking around, though."

The two of them went from RV to RV asking anyone who was there if they had seen Zelena in the last week. They didn't have any luck until they met an older man wheeling his bicycle across the lot toward the bike path. He studied the photo and nodded his head. "Sure, I've seen her." He pointed to a motor home a few spaces down from where they stood. "I think she's in that one."

Hopeful that they had finally discovered where Zelena had been held, they marched with determined steps across the pavement toward the RV the man had indicated.

They were steps away when Liz touched Rory's arm and held her back. "What if the killer's in there?" she whispered.

Rory considered the question. "We'll tell them a relative is thinking of staying here and we're going around asking how people like it. You can secretly take a photo of them while I ask the questions."

"Sounds like a plan." Liz drew her cell phone out of her purse and held it in her hand.

While Rory knocked on the RV's door, Liz looked down at her phone and pretended to be texting, waiting for the right moment to snap a picture. Rory called out "Anyone home?" and knocked several more times, but the door remained firmly shut. She pressed her ear against it, listening for telltale sounds of occupation. "I don't hear anything. I think it's empty." Rory looked over at Liz. "Do you have any Kleenex?"

Liz rummaged around in her purse and produced a small package of tissues.

A tissue in her hand, Rory looked around to see if anyone was watching, then tried the door. To her surprise, it opened right away. The two looked down at the floor, making sure they weren't inadvertently destroying any possible evidence, before they cautiously stepped inside and closed the door behind them.

A slightly musty smell pervaded the interior. The coverings on every window were duct taped around the edges so no one could see inside. A curtain separated the cab and living areas. Rory drew it aside, giving them more light in which to examine the RV. Her gaze swept the interior from the sofa, table and kitchen appliances to the carpeted floor that looked like it had seen better days. She moved further inside, her gaze zeroing in on a bed at the far end. In the hallway, bits of rope were scattered across the floor. "Those ropes must have been used to tie her up."

Liz motioned toward a used piece of gray duct tape less than a foot away. "I bet the kidnapper put that across her mouth."

Tears pricked at Rory's eyes while she thought about her friend gagged and tied up on the bed, unable to cry out for help. She wiped away the tears and straightened her shoulders. "We're going to get them, whoever they are."

"What's this?" Liz bent down and reached toward a piece of irregularly shaped black plastic on the carpet.

"Don't touch it," Rory said. "It could have a fingerprint on it." She bent down beside her friend and stared at the piece of plastic. "It could have come from a cell phone. Maybe the one she used to call me."

"The kidnapper must have found her making the call and smashed it to bits." Liz stood up and looked around. "I don't see any other pieces, do you?"

They searched the rest of the RV but didn't spot anything else that could have come from a cell phone. Bundled up in a closet were the clothes Zelena had been wearing at the meeting on Saturday.

"I wonder why the kidnapper had her change clothes," Liz said.

"That is odd." Rory sniffed the blouse and pants. "These smell like she threw up on them. Maybe that's why. Do you see her purse anywhere? The police haven't found it yet."

"No. The killer must have tossed it."

"Let's look around and see if there's anything that indicates who else was here."

Touching as little as possible, they searched the RV for something that would tell them about its occupants, but found no mail or other personal items anywhere.

"Is that...blood?" Liz pointed to a red-brown speck on the edge of the table.

Rory stared at the spot. "It might be. I think it's time to call Martin. The police will be able to get more information out of this place than we can."

Liz nodded in agreement. Moments later, Rory pushed open the door to discover a woman about her mother's age brandishing a cast-iron frying pan in a threatening manner.

"What are you doing here?" the woman said.

Rory and Liz held up their hands.

"We're just looking for a friend of ours. We were supposed to meet her here. Maybe you've seen her." Rory put her hand in the pocket of her jeans to retrieve her phone.

The woman eyed her narrowly and waved the pan at her. "Be careful what you do. This frying pan hurts, you know."

"I'm just getting her picture." Rory showed Zelena's photo to the woman.

"I can't see it. Come on out, slowly, so I can get a better look." She glowered at the two of them. "And no funny business. I may be older than you are, but I'm fast."

The woman stepped back to allow Rory and Liz to exit the motor home. As soon as they closed the door behind them, Rory held out her phone again. "Her name's Zelena."

The woman lowered her arm and laid the frying pan down on the nearby picnic table, careful to keep it within arm's reach. She sat down on the bench and studied the phone. "She was here in this RV all right." She handed it back to Rory.

"Did you see anyone with her?"

The woman's eyes narrowed. "I thought you said you were meeting her here."

Rory looked at Liz who gave an almost imperceptible nod of agreement.

"We think she was being held here," Rory finally said.

"Like a prisoner?" The woman's face grew thoughtful. "That would explain it."

Rory's heart skipped a beat. "Explain what?"

"I only saw her once. Late at night. She was with someone. A man. They went walking on the beach. He had his arm around her like he was her boyfriend, but it could have been something else."

Like making sure she didn't escape, Rory thought. "When was this?"

"Monday night, I think. Don't know the exact time, but after the sun went down."

"What about the man?"

"I saw him more often. He came twice a day. All bundled up so I couldn't see his face. Every day at lunch time and in the evening, too, carrying bags of food. Takeout by the looks of it."

"Do you remember the name of the restaurant?"

The woman shook her head. "The bags are probably in the trash. Doesn't come until Friday." She pointed toward the far edge of the property where a pair of dumpsters stood.

"Could it have been a woman you saw?" Liz asked.

She considered the question. "If it was, it was a broad-shouldered one."

"Jeanne," Liz said in a quiet voice.

"What?"

"Never mind," Rory said. "Is there anything else you can tell us?"

The woman hesitated for a fraction of a second, then shook her head.

"Thank you, you've been very helpful." Rory handed her a business card. "If you think of anything else, call me."

The woman took the card and nodded.

As the woman picked up her frying pan and got up to go, Rory said, "I'm curious why you didn't call the police. Our friend's photo was in the local paper."

"Don't read the paper. Don't look at the internet. Too much negativity out there."

"You'd better call Dashing D," Liz said.

"Who's that?" the woman asked.

"He's a detective with the Vista Beach police department. He's the one looking into our friend's murder."

The woman's eyes widened. "Murder? You didn't say anything about murder." Before Rory could respond, the woman clutched her frying pan and headed across the lot, looking around her nervously.

"What do you think that was about?" Liz asked.

"Probably doesn't like the idea of the place where she's staying being involved in a murder."

"We don't know if Zelena was killed here or not."

"True. Martin will find out." Rory called him, briefly telling him what they'd found. While they waited for the police to arrive, they looked inside the half-full dumpsters at the far end of the lot, but didn't see any takeout containers or a purse on the top of either one.

"We'd better leave the dumpster search to the police. I've had enough of that to last a lifetime," Rory said.

While they sat at the picnic table by the RV and waited, Rory looked over at Liz. "What was that about Jeanne?"

"I told you. She's involved somehow. I just know it."

"Why do you say that?"

"She's broad-shouldered and tall. Put her in the right clothes and she'd look like a man from a distance."

"Why are you so fixated on her, anyway?"

"She's mean. Just the sort to kill someone."

"Anything else?"

Liz mumbled something Rory couldn't quite make out.

"What did you say?"

Liz spoke louder. "Fine. She said my Madame Elizabeth costume needed more pizzazz. I have plenty of pizzazz. Plenty."

"I know you do."

Less than ten minutes later a police car entered the park followed closely by an unmarked car driven by Martin Green. Shortly after that the woman they had talked to earlier drove out of the lot, apparently feeling the need to leave as soon as the police arrived.

Chapter 14

"You should have called me as soon as you found the RV. Someone could have been inside and hurt you. Not to mention you've contaminated the scene." An angry look on his face, Martin Green stood, arms crossed in front of him, and stared down at Rory and Liz where they were sitting at the picnic table next to the suspicious motor home.

"Sorry, but we were very careful. We disturbed as little as possible. Even used Kleenex when we touched things. See." Rory held up a tissue. "We didn't want to bother you unless it was important. I did leave you a message last night about the park."

"I didn't expect you to come here on your own. I should have known better." The detective took a package of Tums out of his pocket and popped one into his mouth. He paced the length of the RV, mumbling to himself. Finally, he took a deep breath and walked over to the two of them. "You can go now. No. More. Investigating. Understand?"

Rory and Liz nodded their agreement. A bit subdued, they headed back into town. They were driving through downtown when they spotted a crowd forming in front of the glass and metal building that housed the headquarters of Beyond The Grave. A podium and microphone had been set up in the courtyard in front of the building.

"What's going on there?" Liz pointed to the crowd. "Is that Veronica?"

"That must be Edgar Geller's press conference. I completely forgot about it."

"Press conference?"

Rory quickly brought Liz up to date on yesterday's visit to the beach with Veronica. "I think we should go see what he says. Do you have time?"

"I'll make time."

Rory found a parking space on the street a few blocks away. By the time the two of them had walked back to BTG headquarters, the press conference appeared ready to start. Edgar Geller stood behind the podium flanked by two men in suits with blank expressions on their faces.

Rory and Liz slipped into the crowd beside Veronica who was uncharacteristically standing near the back.

"You're just in time," the *Vista Beach View* reporter said to them. "I wish I could get closer, but this press conference has attracted way more people than I expected."

"Why do you think that is?" Rory asked. "Zelena's previous fame?"

"That would be my guess." Veronica's gaze swept the crowd. "I see several reporters who usually deal with Hollywood news. Something tells me this story is going to blow up in a big way." She nodded toward a half dozen people holding bouquets of flowers. "Any idea what's going on there?"

Rory and Liz shook their heads. "No clue."

Before Veronica could say anything else, Edgar asked for everyone's attention. As soon as the voices died down and the crowd was focused on him, the press conference started.

"Thank you all for coming," he began. "As most of you know, I'm Edgar Geller, the founder and CEO of Beyond The Grave. Here at BTG, we pride ourselves on providing an important service to our clients. One of those clients was Zelena Alvarez, a former child actor but, more importantly, a teacher here in Vista Beach and a great contributor to our community. We did what she asked us to do when the unthinkable happened." He paused and gazed solemnly at the audience. "Here at BTG clients are family. We want to do more. My company is announcing a reward of $10,000 to whoever provides information that leads to the identification and arrest of the person or persons who stalked, kidnapped and killed Zelena Alvarez."

A collective gasp went through the crowd at the mention of a stalker, a detail that had been kept from the press so far.

"That's all I have. I'll take a few questions now."

"Are you working with the police?" Veronica shouted from the back of the crowd.

"I've informed them of the reward. Next?"

While Edgar continued answering questions, Veronica looked at Rory who plastered a noncommittal expression on her face and shrugged.

When the reporter turned her attention back toward the podium, Rory leaned over to Liz and whispered, "I don't think Martin knows anything about the reward."

Liz mouthed a "wow."

After a few more questions, one of Edgar's minions whispered in his ear. The CEO immediately thanked everyone for coming and walked back into the building, flanked by his two bodyguards. While the crowd dispersed, a crew moved in and quickly dismantled the podium and sound system.

Rory glanced down at the scribbles on Veronica's notepad. She caught a glimpse of "Security footage" with a check mark beside it before the pad disappeared into the woman's tote bag. "You've seen the footage from the drugstore?"

Veronica frowned. "It's not nice to read over someone's shoulder."

"Sorry."

Veronica moved off to the side, motioning with her head for Rory and Liz to join her. She lowered her voice and said, "My sources at the police station say it's a dead end. Apparently, half the city seems to have visited the place."

"So there's nothing on it that will help us figure out who

dropped Zelena's phone in the bin?"

"Could have been anyone." Veronica adjusted her tote bag on her shoulder. "I'd better be off."

"Thanks for the information," Rory said.

"Too bad the video couldn't help," Liz said as the two headed back to their car.

The men and women who'd been in the crowd carrying flowers walked past them, all headed in the same direction.

Rory nodded toward them. "Let's find out what that's about."

The two attached themselves to the tail end of the group. It wasn't long before they realized they were headed toward the pier.

Halfway down the pier, a makeshift memorial had spontaneously sprung up on one side, overlooking the spot where Zelena's body had washed up. A piece of plywood leaned against the railing, preventing anything from falling onto the sand below. In the center of the memorial was a current photo of the elementary school teacher. Zelena smiled out at them, brown eyes sparkling and long hair pulled back in a ponytail. The group they had been following placed their bouquets among the stuffed animals, flowers and pictures drawn by grade school kids that had already piled up.

"Why so many brown bears?" Rory gestured toward the stuffed animals that were propped up everywhere.

"Don't you remember?" Liz said. "On *Mommy's Little Helper*, Zelena's character had a stuffed bear named 'Bear'. She carried him everywhere. He had a stuffed animal friend named 'Tiger'. If the show were on today, Bear would probably have his own Facebook page."

They were studying the memorial when a couple and two kids walked up. Rory recognized the younger child as the kindergartener who'd had the tantrum in the library. The blonde-haired girl clutched a piece of paper, while her brother who looked to be about high school age, stood nearby engrossed in his phone.

Tabitha Halliwell gently pushed the little girl forward. "Go ahead, Dana."

She looked at her parents for reassurance. They nodded

encouragement and Dana placed a crayon drawing next to one of the bears.

Rory smiled and knelt down so she was at eye level with the girl. "Did you draw that?"

Dana nodded shyly.

"It's very good. Miss Alvarez would have loved it."

Dana smiled and hid behind her parents. Rory straightened up and introduced herself to the Halliwells. "She was in Zelena's class?"

Tabitha nodded. "She was really wonderful to our little girl. Really looked out for her."

For a split second, annoyance washed over Uri's face. "Maybe too much."

"What do you mean?" Rory said.

He seemed about to say more, but one touch on his sleeve from his wife and he clamped his mouth shut.

"Did you know Zelena well?" Tabitha said.

Rory and Liz explained about their painting chapter. While the adults talked, Dana headed toward another kindergarten-aged girl who was standing nearby.

Uri nudged his son's arm. "Look after her."

His gaze fixated on his smart phone, the high schooler nodded and placed himself so he could watch his sister if he ever bothered to look up from the screen.

"Oh, I just realized," Tabitha said to Rory. "You were the one who found her. That must have been awful."

"I wasn't the first one who spotted her, though." Rory explained about the ghost child emerging from the water underneath the pier.

"Just like that old story," Liz said.

"I'm sure it wasn't a ghost. Must be another one of those pranks," Tabitha said.

"Whoever it was, the police are looking for them. Just in case they noticed something we didn't."

"I doubt they'll find them," Tabitha said. Uri nodded his

agreement.

The older boy chuckled, drawing everyone's attention in his direction. The teen stared at his phone, still chuckling to himself, while Dana and the other little girl looked through the railing, pointing down at the beach twenty feet below.

The next time Rory looked over at the two girls, they had climbed the railing and were leaning over, staring down at something.

Everyone shouted at once. Uri and another man sprang toward the two girls, plucking them off the railing before they went over. The man, who must have been the other girl's father, tightly held his child's hand and dragged her away while Uri scolded his own daughter. As soon as Dana was safely by her mother's side, Uri snatched the phone out of his son's hands. "We asked you to do one thing, Keith, one thing. Look after your sister. She could have gotten seriously hurt."

"She was fine. She climbs on all kinds of things all the time."

"She's five. You're eighteen now. You need to grow up and be more responsible."

"I'm thirsty." Keith scowled and walked away toward the cafe at the end of the pier.

Dana tugged at her mother's sleeve. "Mommy."

Tabitha leaned down. "What is it, honey?"

The five-year-old was pointing at the railing when a tennis ball sailed through the air and landed with a thud next to the memorial. Plop, plop, plop. One by one, balls rained down onto the pier. Uri and Tabitha shielded their daughter from the onslaught while everyone else on the pier ran for cover, hiding behind trash cans and benches until the bombardment stopped.

Rory and Liz cautiously looked over the railing to the beach below them where the balls seemed to have come from, but didn't see anyone acting suspiciously.

"What are those?" Liz pointed to a line of cylindrical objects sticking out of the sand. A man picked one up and examined it.

Rory shouted down to him. "What is it?"

He dumped the contents onto the sand. "Looks like a firecracker stunt," he shouted back, holding up a tennis ball so she could see it. "This one's a dud. Come down and I'll show you."

Rory and Liz quickly made their way down the stairs. When they were beside him, he showed them what he found. "I used to make these when I was a kid. Just stick a lit firecracker in a tennis ball can and put your projectile on top. It'll launch it in the air. For some reason, this one didn't go off."

Rory looked around, spotting at least half a dozen cans buried in the sand parallel to the pier. She suspected she'd find a similar row on the other side of the pier. "How long would someone have to get away before it went off?"

"Thirty seconds or so."

Long enough to blend into the crowd, Rory thought.

"At least no one was hurt," Liz said.

"I didn't notice if any of the balls hit the memorial. Let's go and make sure it's okay." Rory led the way up the stairs and onto the pier to see what damage had been done by the latest prank.

Chapter 15

That evening, Rory was working at the sales table set up in the entryway of the boutique house when Samantha walked inside, carrying a sheet of paper. She looked uncertainly around her until she spotted Rory. With a faint smile, she approached the table where Rory was processing a sale for a customer.

As soon as she was done with the sale, Rory turned to the woman and smiled. "Hi, Samantha. Is this your first time at our boutique? I see you have a map of the rooms in the house." She nodded at the paper in the woman's hand. "Can I answer any questions?"

Samantha glanced around, her gaze not really settling on anything. "It's lovely, I'm sure. Can you take a break? I'd like to talk to you about something. It's important."

Rory glanced at the time on her cell phone. "I'm off in ten minutes. Can you wait until then?"

Samantha nodded.

"While you're waiting, why don't you take a look around? We have a lot of nice items for sale. The proceeds go to a good cause."

While Samantha wandered into the next room, Rory dealt with several sales in a row. As soon as Arika arrived to relieve her, Rory went from room to room in the house in search of Zelena's former manager. She found her in the room set aside for the Halloween decorations, staring at a wooden board painted with a complicated pattern of fall leaves and pumpkins. A card propped up in front of the piece indicated it had been painted by Zelena Alvarez.

"Such a waste of talent," Samantha said without taking her eyes off the board.

"She was a good painter. I know we'll miss her. She always had a lot of energy and contributed a lot to our painting chapter. Not to mention all of the hours she spent teaching kindergarten and the volunteer work she did around town."

"Most people couldn't keep up with her. Loads of energy. She was like that as a child too." Samantha looked over at Rory. "I'd like to buy this. Can you set it aside for me while we talk?"

"Sure. I'll just take it to the sales table and put your name on it. It'll be there when you're ready to pay for it. Wait here." Rory put Samantha's name on the identifying card, picked up the piece and brought it to the entryway where she handed it into her mother's care.

When she returned to Samantha's side, an older couple and a young woman were milling around the room, examining the pieces for sale.

"Why don't we find somewhere more private to talk? The backyard has a bench we can sit on and the area's pretty well lit," Rory said.

After Samantha nodded in agreement, Rory led the way through the house to the backyard. Lights near the back door illuminated the ten-foot-deep yard. Camellias with red blooms surrounded the small lawn while trees sheltered the yard from neighbors' prying eyes.

They crossed the grass, passing a man hauling away a piece of the life-sized Nativity set, and headed toward the other side of the yard where a wooden bench stood.

Once they settled down side by side on the bench, Rory turned to the other woman and said, "What did you want to talk to me about?"

"Are you investigating Zelena's death? I hear you've solved several murders since you moved to town."

"I may have run across information that helped the police

solve a few crimes," Rory said cautiously.

"That's not what I've heard, but no matter." Samantha waved her hand in the air as if to say let's move on. "I'd like you to investigate this one. I'm not sure I trust the police to solve it."

"Why not? They're very capable."

Samantha gave Rory a shrewd look. "That's right. You're dating that Detective...Green, is it? Do you trust him?"

"With my life," Rory said softly.

Samantha studied her face and nodded. "Still, I'd like you to keep track of the investigation. I'll help any way I can. She was like a daughter to me."

"I'll do what I can, but I'm not a professional. And I won't do anything that interferes with the official investigation." While she thought about what to say next, Rory settled back in her seat and studied the man dismantling the Nativity set. He slung the final piece, a shepherd, over his shoulder and headed down the side of the house toward the street. "There's something I've been meaning to ask you."

"What is it?"

"Was Zelena going back into acting?"

Samantha stared at Rory, a puzzled expression on her face. "Not that I'm aware of. Not that she couldn't have. She was always getting offers for small parts here and there. She turned down a number of jobs over the years. There was even talk about an *MLH* reunion, but nothing much came of it."

"Someone told me they'd heard she was thinking of getting back into the business."

Samantha stared into space for a moment, then her face cleared. "You must mean the movie script. She was trying to get it produced."

"Movie?"

"She wrote a script for a film. Couldn't get anyone to bankroll it so she started a KickStarter campaign." Samantha brought up the website on her smart phone and showed it to Rory. "Unfortunately, she couldn't raise enough money."

Rory studied the page. "There's not much information here. Do you know what the movie's about?"

"All I know is that it's a caper film, part of it loosely based on events in her own life."

"Can you send me the link?" Rory said.

Samantha tapped her phone and, moments later, Rory heard an alert on her own cell.

"Do you know if anyone else was going to invest?"

"Not as far as I know. She thought she had a lead once, but it didn't pan out. She was still trying, though. She didn't give up on her dreams easily. She had tenacity, that one."

Rory thought back to last year's boutique, which Zelena had run before Penny and Jeanne joined the group. Even though the venue for the boutique had fallen through at the last minute, Zelena had spent hours calling around until she'd found another one that could accommodate them on such short notice.

Samantha stood up. "I have to go. You'll let me know if you learn anything useful?"

"I promise. Don't forget to pick up that piece Zelena painted."

A thoughtful expression on her face, Rory followed Samantha across the lawn into the house.

Chapter 16

The next day, Rory was three doorways away from the front entrance of Arika's Scrap 'n Paint when she spotted Mrs. Griswold exiting the store and walking down the sidewalk away from her. As soon as Rory entered the painting and scrapbooking supply store, she headed toward the cash register where her mother was studying a piece of paper. "Was that Mrs. Griswold I saw leaving just now? Is she going to start painting?"

Arika looked up from her paper. "Winifred is going to be working here part-time starting next week."

Rory's mouth gaped open. "Really? I thought she was retired."

"Even retired people need jobs sometimes." Arika placed the piece of paper underneath the counter. "You're here for those flowers, aren't you? Let me get them for you." She went into the back room and returned moments later with a bouquet of yellow roses.

"They're beautiful," Rory said as she took them from her mother. "Zelena's favorite flowers."

"Thank you for dropping them off at the memorial. I'd go with you, but I have a big delivery coming and I want to be here for it."

"No problem. I was going there anyway. This is what I'm putting on it." She held up a framed photo of Zelena with the rest of the painting chapter, taken at one of their meetings.

Arika studied the photo and nodded her head in approval. "That's a great picture of all of you. One of my customers told me about a fireworks prank. Was there any damage to the memorial?"

"Just a few crushed flowers. Most of the tennis balls landed in the middle of the pier."

"That's good." The store owner's gaze drifted to the front window where a brown truck had pulled up. "Looks like my delivery's here."

"I'll see you later." Rory tucked the photo and flowers under her arm and smiled at the delivery man as she headed out the door.

While she walked toward the pier with the items to place on Zelena's memorial, she dialed Liz's number. "Guess what I just learned about Mrs. Griswold," she said as soon as Liz came on the line.

"What's up with Granny G now?"

"She's going to be working part-time at my mom's store starting next week."

"Really? She never struck me as someone who likes crafts."

"I know. She knows I paint, but she's never really asked me about it." Rory stopped at an intersection and waited for the light to change. "Needs the money, I guess."

"I wonder why she needs money all of a sudden. Her retirement earnings seemed to be enough before."

"I don't know. Something changed." Rory crossed the street and headed down the hill toward the pier.

"Maybe it has something to do with her midnight runs. Next time we should follow her."

"If we can figure out when that is in advance. She's been out Wednesday and Sunday so far. At least that's when I noticed her leaving. Maybe she'll go again this coming Wednesday."

"If she does, we'll be ready!"

"Listen, I've got to go. I'll call you later and we can figure out the details."

When Rory reached the memorial, she placed her mother's bouquet and the framed photo on the mound of items that had doubled in size since she was there last. She was looking at some of the latest additions when she heard someone come up beside her.

She glanced over to find Zelena's father, Tito Alvarez, staring at the memorial, a bouquet of mixed flowers in his hand. He stared down at the photo at its center. "My beautiful *mija*," he said softly.

He nodded a greeting and placed the flowers next to the picture of the painting group. They stared silently down at the display of teddy bears, stuffed tigers, flowers and *MLH* memorabilia stacked against the edge of the pier.

Tito took a photo of a young Zelena out of his wallet and added it to the display. "How long do you think the city will let this stay?"

"I don't know." Rory made a mental note to ask Martin about it. The flowers would probably be thrown out, but she could see the stuffed animals being cleaned and donated to a local children's charity.

"It's nice to know so many people loved her." Tito sighed and looked out at the ocean and the seagulls flying overhead. "When she was little I used to call her my little bird because she was always running around. She ran so fast it almost looked like she was flying." He looked up at the sky. "I like to think she's up there flying now."

Rory wiped a tear from the corner of her eye. "The press haven't found this place yet."

"*Gracias a Dios* for that."

"It might be a good thing to have press coverage. Someone might see the story and provide information that'll lead to finding out who killed her."

"I need to go and finish making the arrangements. I wonder...would you be willing to go to Zelena's place with me again? I still need to pick out some clothes."

"Of course. I have the time right now. I'll meet you there."

When Rory arrived at Zelena's apartment, she found a media circus. Television transmission trucks took up all available parking spaces in front of the apartment. She drove past, looking for a place to park, but a slew of other vehicles occupied the rest of the spaces on both sides of the street, up and down the block. She finally squeezed into a spot three blocks away.

When she approached the triplex, she found Tito standing at the edge of the crowd, looking overwhelmed and nervous. Relief washed over his face as soon as he saw her.

"Thank God you're here. I'm not sure what to do."

Rory surveyed the crowd of reporters. Zelena's neighbor, Doreen, chastised a man dressed in a polo shirt and casual pants for trampling her flowers while her husband stood nearby and shouted something about calling the police. Veronica Justice walked around the edge of the crowd, taking photos.

Rory pointed to the reporter. "Maybe she can help." She caught Veronica's eye and motioned for her to join them. They moved far enough away from everyone they wouldn't be overheard by the other reporters. The three stood to one side as if they were merely neighbors observing the unusual activity.

"We need to get in there." Rory nodded toward the triplex. "Any idea how we can get to the door without anyone noticing?"

Veronica studied them and cocked her head. "What's in it for me?"

Rory drew Tito aside and they quietly talked. When they returned to Veronica's side, Rory said, "This is Zelena's father. He'll give you an exclusive interview after you get us in and out of there. After."

Veronica's eyes lit up for a second, but she didn't immediately reply as if she didn't want to advertise her eagerness. "Done."

"What's your plan?" Rory said.

"We need a distraction, something to focus their attention on." Her gaze swept the crowd. "It's mostly reporters from out of the area. That's good news. They don't know either one of you. You could be anyone. I could pretend to live in the back unit. They'd pounce on me and you two could slip by."

"Won't they recognize you?" Rory said.

"They don't know me, either," Veronica said in a bitter voice.

"I'm not sure that's good enough," Tito said.

Veronica's face lit up. "But I know what is. Wait here." She whipped her cell out of her tote bag and stepped to one side. After a brief conversation, she joined them again, a big smile on her face. "Shouldn't be long now."

"Who did you call?" Rory said.

"You'll see."

Less than ten minutes later, Edgar Geller, dressed in a casual shirt and pants, walked up to the crowd of reporters and waved.

"How did you get him here?" Rory said. "You didn't tell him it was a ruse to get us inside, did you?"

Veronica smirked. "Of course not. I just said the press were at Zelena's place and eager to follow-up on the reward he's offering. What CEO can resist an opportunity to talk about their business?"

Edgar stood in the street and, almost immediately, the group turned its back to the front door and crowded around the CEO of Beyond The Grave. Everyone trained their cameras on him and a woman dressed in a suit thrust a microphone in front of his face.

"Now's your chance," Veronica whispered. "Use the side door."

Rory and Tito turned their faces away from the group and slid behind the crowd. When they passed Doreen and Don, Rory thought for a moment the couple would give them away, but their attention remained riveted on Edgar's impromptu press conference. Rory and Tito made their way across the lawn and down the walkway on the far side of the triplex, moving as quietly and as swiftly as possible. Before long, they had made it to the side door and safely inside.

"Whew!" Rory said as Tito locked the door behind them.

When they stepped into Zelena's bedroom, Rory spotted a brown bear on the bed, dressed in a silver astronaut uniform with a U.S. flag sewn on one sleeve. A fishbowl helmet completed the costume. "Is that Bear? From *Mommy's Little Helper?*"

Tito nodded and wiped a tear from the corner of his eye. "The production company sold a lot of them when the sitcom was airing. That's the original, the one she used in every episode. Every October she dresses him in a costume made by the show's wardrobe department. This one is—was—her favorite."

"Where's Tiger? Aren't they a team?"

"Here he is." Tito bent down and picked up a stuffed tiger off the carpet and placed it beside the bear on the bed.

While the two went through the possible outfits to bury Zelena in, Rory caught bits and pieces of the impromptu press conference that drifted through a partially open window. At one point, she parted the curtains and dared to peek outside at Edgar who was still expounding on his company. The reporters appeared bewitched by his words, jotting down everything he said.

She quietly closed the curtain and returned to her work. They had settled on an outfit and were wondering how to get past the still milling reporters when they heard the whoop of a siren. Rory peeked outside once again. Two police cruisers were parked in the middle of the street and two officers were talking to Edgar and the reporters. "The police are here."

A short time later, the crowd began to disperse.

"Looks like everyone's leaving," she said to Tito. She stared out the window, occasionally ducking down when someone looked her way. "The coast is clear. We can go now."

Once they were outside, Tito shook Rory's hand and said, "Thank you for your help."

"Of course. Let me know when the service is or if you need anything else."

They both headed to their respective cars. She was walking by the house next door when a stout figure popped out from behind a bush.

Rory involuntarily jumped. "Hi, Doreen. You startled me."

Doreen looked around carefully. Satisfied no one was watching, she said in a low voice, "He was the one."

Rory stared at the woman, a puzzled expression on her face. "He?"

"The man talking to the press."

"Edgar Geller?"

"If that's his name." The woman looked at Rory expectantly.

"I'm sorry. I'm not sure what you're trying to tell me."

Don poked his head out the front door of the house. "Leave it alone, Doreen."

She waved her hand behind her back at her husband, urging him back inside, keeping her focus on Rory. "Ignore him. This Edgar was the one I saw in Zelena's front yard. The one I told you about."

Rory's pulse quickened. "Are you sure?"

The woman nodded. "I recognized him from his photo in the newspaper. That's what I was trying to remember when you were here last time."

"What about the car? Was he in that as well or was that someone else?"

"Now that I've had time to think about it, I'm pretty sure he was the one in the car too."

Don walked across the lawn, calling his wife's name. "Come inside."

"All right, all right!" Doreen yelled back. She turned to Rory. "Just thought you should know."

Before Rory could say anything else, Doreen headed up the steps to her house.

On the short walk to her car, Rory wondered if Edgar had a legitimate reason for being at the apartment before that day or if he could be Zelena's mysterious stalker.

Chapter 17

"Do you really think Edgar could be the stalker?" Liz asked as Rory drove them from the boutique house to downtown Vista Beach at eleven that evening.

"He doesn't really seem the type, but I think we should look into it. He might have a perfectly reasonable explanation for being at Zelena's apartment. Or Doreen could be mistaken. I'll go down to his office tomorrow and talk to him."

"Is that wise? What about what Dashing D said?"

For a split second, Rory wondered if talking to the CEO would be too risky, but quickly brushed the concern aside. "I'll be in his office. I promise not to go anywhere alone with him. Don't worry, I won't take any unnecessary chances."

"What excuse are you going to use to see him?"

"I'll think of something." Rory eased into a parking spot in the alley behind Arika's Scrap 'n Paint. "You haven't talked about your cousins in a few days. Did you find them a house?"

"Not yet, but I'm hopeful. I sent out letters to some people who own places similar to the ones they like, to see if they're interested in selling. Fingers crossed I come up with something."

As soon as they walked through the back door of the store, they deposited the cash box and receipts from the boutique house in the safe in the back room. They were heading back outside when Liz stopped and cocked her head. "Did you hear something?" she whispered.

They stood stock still and listened. The faint sound of breaking glass followed by muffled giggling reached their ears.

"I think it's coming from the front," Rory whispered back.

They tiptoed through the classroom and peeked around the doorway onto the sales floor. A nearby street lamp that usually shed light on the front door was out, leaving the area in shadow. Twin beams of light shone onto the front window display.

Once Rory's eyes adjusted to the dim lighting, she could make out three figures on the sidewalk outside. Two held flashlights while a third sprayed something on the front window of the store. Rory and Liz retreated to the back room.

"Looks like those pranksters are at it again," Rory whispered. "They must have knocked out the street light with a rock."

"Let's go after them," Liz whispered back. "There must be something in the store we can use for protection."

"If we go through the front room, they'll see us and get away before we can unlock the door."

"Not if we shimmy across the floor like army troops do." Liz moved her shoulders back and forth to simulate a crawling motion.

"How about this? You call the police, then cross the front room and get a picture of them through the window. You can shimmy all you want." Rory handed her friend the keys to the store. "Unlock the door, if you can. I'll sneak around the side and see if I can identify them. One of us is bound to get a good look at them."

Liz put her thumb and forefinger together in an okay sign and picked up the receiver of the store's landline.

Rory slipped out the back door and ran as quietly as she could down the alley and into a narrow passageway between buildings that led to the sidewalk and the street beyond. She stopped once she got to the front of the building and peeked around the corner. Three figures dressed all in black and wearing green masks huddled around the front window, taking turns spraying paint on the glass. Resembling a carved pumpkin, the masks covered most of their faces with holes for eyes, nose and mouth. The three of them were so engrossed in their artwork, they didn't hear her approach until

Rory was almost upon them.

A flash of light momentarily stunned the pranksters. Another flash and they all raised their hands to cover their eyes at the same time, dropping their cans of spray paint on the sidewalk. Rory grabbed for the mask of the one closest to her. The Velcro holding it in place ripped apart and it dropped to the ground. As soon as the prankster realized she could see his face, he pushed her aside and ran down the sidewalk.

Liz flung open the front door of the store, hitting the shortest one in the calf. The injured prankster hopped around on one leg and cried out in pain while the other one took off down the street.

The one who was left behind scooped one of the cans off the ground and pointed it at Rory's face. Rory flung her arm in front of her eyes and felt the paint splatter on the sleeve of her hoodie. When she heard the sound of running feet, Rory took off after the figure down the street and into a nearby park. With a burst of energy, she closed the distance between them, her long legs giving her an advantage over the much shorter teen. Reaching forward, she grabbed the straggler's shirt and wrestled the teen to the ground. A knit cap fell off, revealing long brown hair which cascaded around the girl's shoulder. Rory tore off the green mask and stared into a teenage girl's angry eyes.

She twisted around, trying to escape, but Rory held on firmly and the girl ended up face up on the grass.

"Let me go," the wriggling girl said.

Carrying a can of spray paint in one hand and a phone in the other, Liz caught up to them moments later. "Hold her still." She raised her phone and snapped a photo.

Rory sat on the girl's legs to keep her down. "What are the names of your friends?" she said after the picture was taken.

"I'm not going to tell you. We weren't doing anything that bad, anyway. The window's washable."

"Doesn't matter," Liz said. "I recognize one of them from the business club at the high school."

Rory twisted her head around to look at her friend. "The club you help out with?"

Liz nodded. "The police should be at the store any minute now."

At the mention of the police, the girl went limp as if all the fight had gone out of her. "My parents are going to kill me. Do you have to turn me in? Us girls have to stick together, right?" She appealed to them with her eyes.

"You should have thought of that before you started all those pranks." Liz's gaze darted from one to the other. "If you're okay here, I'll run back and tell them where you are."

"I'm fine. You have her photo. If she runs, we can easily find her."

Liz dropped the paint can on the ground next to Rory's leg and headed back toward the store.

"We've got some time. Let's have a little chat. You're one of the ones responsible for all those pranks around town, aren't you? Egging the houses and changing the names on those street signs? That was you and your friends, right?"

For a split second, the girl looked as if she was going to deny it then, sighing in resignation, she nodded her head.

"Were you responsible for the tennis ball stunt? It's lucky no one was hurt."

The girl shook her head. "That wasn't me. I have no idea how to do something like that."

"What about the skeleton? Was that yours?"

The girl giggled.

"What are you laughing at?" Rory asked.

"That one was our best so far. The visor and the board shorts were an inspired touch. Mrs. Breyer had a fit when Sid went missing."

"What about the necklace? Where'd you get that? Did you steal it?"

"No way, we wouldn't do that."

"You stole the skeleton."

"We *borrowed* it for a little while."

"I painted that necklace," Rory said.

The girl's mouth formed into an "O".

"And gave it to a friend of mine," Rory continued. "A friend who was murdered."

The girl's face went pale. She sat up on her elbows. "A murder? We didn't have anything to do with that."

"Where'd you get it then?"

"I'm not supposed to tell."

"This is serious," Rory said. "Someone was killed."

The girl gulped. "Okay. Someone gave it to us. Told us to put it on the skeleton."

"Who was it?"

"Some old lady."

As far as the teenager was concerned that could mean anyone from thirty to ninety, Rory thought. "Do you know her name?"

The girl shook her head. "Never saw her before. She caught us carrying the skeleton to the beach Tuesday evening. We thought she was going to turn us in, but instead she gave us the necklace."

"And you didn't find that suspicious?"

"She said she was playing a prank of her own on someone."

"You can get up now," a deep voice said. "I'll take it from here."

Rory glanced behind her to find Martin Green standing a few feet away. She stood up and brushed off her jeans. "She's all yours, Mart—Detective. She has a lot to tell you."

Chapter 18

The next day, Rory stood in the reception area of Beyond The Grave and studied the artwork on the walls.

"Mr. Geller's assistant will be right out," the receptionist said.

Rory nodded and resumed her perusal of the paintings. When she heard the click click of high heels on hardwood she turned to discover Tabitha Halliwell walking toward her, a welcoming smile on her face.

"Tabitha," Rory said. "I didn't realize you worked here."

"I thought I recognized your name, but I wasn't sure. I'm Mr. Geller's assistant. Shall we go back?" She gestured toward the hallway that led into the more private areas of the company.

Rory followed Edgar's assistant down the hallway, past offices filled with employees talking on the phone and typing on the computer. "How's your daughter doing?"

"She misses her teacher, of course, but the young ones bounce back pretty quickly."

"And Keith? Is that his name?"

Tabitha looked worried for a moment, then her face brightened. "Busy with college applications. He's a straight A student. We're hoping for Harvard or Princeton. Here we are." She knocked on a partially closed door before opening it. "Ms. Anderson to see you, Mr. Geller."

The first thing Rory noticed when she stepped inside the office was the view. From the second story window, she could see the pier and the waves washing onto the beach below. She stepped forward and gazed through the glass in awe.

Edgar came out from behind his cherry wood desk and stood beside her. "Spectacular, isn't it?"

"I'll say."

They drank in the view for a minute before the CEO gestured toward one of the leather chairs in front of his desk. "Please, have a seat. Coffee? Water? Soda?"

"Water, please."

Edgar nodded to Tabitha who slipped out the door and reappeared moments later with a bottle of water that she placed on the desk.

After one last glance at the view, Rory made her way across the office and sat down.

Instead of taking the chair behind his desk, Edgar sat in the one next to hers. "What can I do for you? You mentioned that Zelena had left something for me?"

Rory took a sip of water. "I may have misspoken."

"Oh?" He settled back in his chair and steepled his fingers.

Rory recapped the water bottle and placed it on the desk in front of her. "When we talked before, you said you didn't know Zelena well. That you'd only met her once."

His brow wrinkled. "That's right."

"Someone told me you were at her apartment several times."

"Who?"

"Doesn't matter. You were seen in a car watching the apartment and in the front yard."

"What? Like a stalker?" Edgar roared with laughter.

When she didn't respond, his smile faded. "You're serious?" He sat forward in his chair, put his elbows on his thighs and looked at her earnestly. "I'm not a stalker. Okay, I admit I may have known Zelena slightly better than I indicated. She told me she thought she was being followed. I was worried and felt a bit protective of her. I remembered her from when she was on that sitcom. Still thought of her as that vulnerable young thing, I suppose. So I may have stopped by her house a time or two, just watching to see if there was anything out of order."

"I see. And was there? Anything out of order?"

He shook his head. "Not that I noticed. I wish I *had* seen her stalker. Then maybe she'd still be alive."

A knock followed by a discreet cough sounded from the doorway. "Your ten thirty is here, Mr. Geller."

"Right. Thank you, Tabitha. I'm almost done here." He stood up, effectively ending the conversation. "I hope I've explained everything to your satisfaction."

"Thank you for your time."

"Whatever I can do to help. Tabitha will show you out."

As they walked toward the reception area, Rory thought about her conversation with the CEO. He seemed genuine enough. Until new evidence came to light that implicated him, she'd give him the benefit of the doubt and assume he was telling the truth.

At the elevator, Tabitha turned to Rory and said in a hushed voice, "Are you investigating the murder, then?"

"Zelena was a friend. I want to know what happened."

"I hope you find out." Tabitha waited for Rory to board the elevator then, with a thoughtful expression on her face, headed back to the CEO's office.

Ten minutes before midnight, Rory peeked through the blinds of her front window at Mrs. Griswold's house where the outside lights had winked out moments before. Seeing no activity next door, she covered her hair with a black knit cap, slipped out the front door and closed it softly behind her.

Seagull Lane appeared tucked in for the night. No cars or pedestrians made their way down the narrow street. A single street light, newly installed, and a scattering of porch lights lit her path as she carefully picked her way down the sidewalk.

Wearing black from head to toe, Rory peered into the parked cars as she passed them. Two doors down from Mrs. Griswold's place, she spotted the one she was looking for. As she climbed into the passenger seat of the dark colored Prius, she said to the figure dressed in a black turtleneck behind the wheel, "Where'd you get the car? I don't recognize it."

"Borrowed it from my dad. It's a lot quieter than my Lexus," Liz whispered back.

"I don't think we have to whisper. No one can hear us."

"Can't be too careful." Liz thrust a pair of binoculars in Rory's direction. "You're in charge of these."

Rory turned them over in her hands. "I don't know how much help they'll be. It's pretty dark."

"They're night vision. You'll be able to see no matter what."

"Where'd you get them? Candy?" she said, referring to the private investigator they had met several months ago.

"That's right. She showed me how to use them. Here..." Liz gave her friend a quick lesson on the binoculars.

Rory trained them on a lawn across the street and spotted a neighborhood cat prowling among the bushes. Satisfied she knew how to use them, she placed the binoculars on her lap and waited.

Less than five minutes later, a silver Camry backed out of Mrs. Griswold's driveway onto the street. Rory nudged Liz's arm and nodded toward the car. "There she is."

"It's go time." Liz started the Prius, waiting until Mrs. Griswold was almost at the end of the block before following. She hunched over the steering wheel, gripping it tightly, while Rory kept her eyes on the car.

"Don't get too close or she'll see us," Rory said.

"Don't worry, I know what I'm doing."

Liz hung back, keeping what she determined to be a safe distance while Rory periodically looked through the binoculars at the Camry, advising Liz on the various turns the car made.

At a four-way stop, another sedan got between them and Mrs. Griswold's car.

Liz loosened her grip on the wheel. "At least now I don't have to worry as much about her noticing me. Where's Granny G going, anyway?"

"This is the route to the freeway. Maybe that's where she's headed."

"Let's hope she doesn't get on. I'll lose her for sure then."

At the edge of Vista Beach city limits, Mrs. Griswold turned onto a side street and pulled into a parking lot next to a non-descript two-story office building. Liz slowed down as they drove past.

Rory trained the binoculars on Mrs. Griswold's car. The woman parked it in a dark corner of the lot. When she got out, she looked around before heading inside the building.

"She went inside. Pull into the next driveway," Rory said.

Liz slowly pulled into the lot, backing into a parking space so the front of her car was directly opposite the building's entrance. "We'll use the mirrors. That way it's less conspicuous."

Rory nodded in understanding. Liz kept her gaze glued to the rearview mirror while Rory looked into the side one, waiting in silence for something to happen.

"Who do you think she's visiting this late at night?" Rory finally said.

"Who knows."

"You keep watch while I check my phone and see who has offices here." Rory was typing the address into her phone's browser when Liz grabbed her arm.

"She's coming out," Liz said.

"Already?" Rory checked the time on her cell phone. "It's only been ten minutes." She twisted around in her seat and pointed the binoculars at the front of the building.

Mrs. Griswold stepped into a circle of light given off by a fixture beside the front door and stared straight at their car.

Rory ducked down and held her breath. She counted to ten, then carefully peeked over the seat and looked at the entrance. "I don't see her. She must have gone back inside. You don't think she spotted us, do you?"

"I don't want to chance it. Let's get out of here." Liz started the engine and headed out of the parking lot back the way they came.

They were turning a corner after a stop sign when red and blue lights flashed behind them followed by the whoop whoop of a siren.

Rory glanced over her shoulder. "It's the police. You'd better pull over."

"I don't know what I did. I made a full stop."

While Liz eased the car to the side of the road, Rory slid the binoculars as far underneath the seat as possible.

Liz turned off the car, rolled down her window and placed her hands on the steering wheel so they were clearly visible. The officer approached the car and shined his flashlight on their faces.

Rory squinted in the bright light. Before either of them could say a word, the officer let out a sigh and said, "I should have known it would be you two."

Chapter 19

A short while later, Rory and Liz found themselves sitting side by side in an interrogation room in the Vista Beach police station. An awkward silence filled the room as Martin Green leaned against the table opposite them and stared at them, an exasperated look on his face.

Hands clasped on her lap, Rory avoided his gaze. When the silence became unbearable, she peeked out from under her lashes.

Martin folded his arms in front of him. "You two do know following someone is against the law, don't you?"

"We weren't—," Rory said.

"How did you—?" Liz asked.

The detective held up his hand to stop them, then glanced over at the half-open door where Mrs. Griswold peeked around the corner. He walked across the room, said a few words, then gently closed the door and returned to lean against the table once again. "You were saying?"

"How do you know we were following anyone? We were just on our way home," Liz said.

"From where?"

"Nightclub. We went dancing," she said at the same time Rory declared they had been at a friend's house.

"We went dancing at a club, then went to a friend's house afterwards," Liz quickly said.

His gaze swept over their black pants and turtlenecks, finally landing on the knit caps that rested in their laps. "Uh-huh."

"Black is all the rage these days." Liz nodded her head emphatically.

Martin picked up the night vision binoculars sitting on the table next to him. "And these?"

Liz held out her hand. "Just holding them for a friend. They're not illegal. Can I have them back, please?" After he gave them to her, she said, "I don't know what the fuss is all about. PIs follow people all the time."

He cocked an eyebrow. "Does one of you have a PI license I don't know about?"

They both shook their heads.

"We were just worried about her," Rory said.

"It doesn't matter. She called us as soon as she realized someone was following her." Martin ran a hand through his hair. "Look, it's late. You two need to take this seriously. She decided not to file a complaint so I'll let you off with a warning this time, but only if you apologize to her and promise never ever to follow her again. Can you two do that?"

"We promise." Rory crossed her heart and Liz murmured her agreement.

"You understand me, right? No following on foot or in a car, no stakeouts, ok?"

"We get it," Rory said.

He stared at the two of them for a moment, then seemed satisfied. "I think you two owe Gran—Mrs. Griswold that apology now." He opened the door and motioned Rory's neighbor inside. "I'll leave you to it. Remember what I said."

Mrs. Griswold sat down in a chair facing them and the detective stepped outside, closing the door behind him. "Well?"

"We're sorry we followed you," Rory said first.

"We won't do it again," Liz added.

"We were just worried about you," Rory said. "You haven't...been yourself lately. You left so late, we wanted to make sure you were okay."

Mrs. Griswold's expression softened. "Thank you for your concern, but I'm fine." Her eyes hardened once again and she stood up. "But where and when I go is my business, not yours. Understand?"

After they both nodded, she headed out the door, closing it behind her without saying another word.

Rory and Liz sat quietly, thinking about everything that happened.

"I guess that's that," Liz finally said.

"I guess so. I'm still worried about her."

"I know." Liz lowered her voice. "In the car you were looking to see who had offices in the building she went to. We never had the chance to talk about what you found out."

Rory stared at her friend in disbelief.

"What? We're not following her, just looking at some public information. Come on, what did you find out?"

Rory kept an eye on the closed door while she brought up the building's website on her phone and scrolled through the list of tenants. "Nothing obvious here. No doctor's offices or lawyers. Just architects, construction companies and the like. She must have ducked in there when she realized we were following her."

"To get us off the scent. Smart."

When they exited the room moments later, they found Martin leaning against the wall, waiting for them. "What took you two so long?"

"Just talking about...stuff. Girl stuff." Liz looked from the detective to Rory and back again. "I'll wait down the hall for you."

"We were worried about her," Rory said when they were alone.

"I know it came from a good place, but whatever's going on with her, you need to let her come to you. You could have ended up in a situation I can't get you out of." Martin rubbed his forehead as if he felt a headache coming on.

She studied his face. "You look tired."

"I don't enjoy being awakened in the middle of the night." He looked at her, a sadness in his eyes she hadn't seen there since they started dating. "I don't know if this is going to work out."

"What? You can't mean…?"

He kissed her on the cheek and motioned towards the exit. "Ignore me. I'm just tired. Go home and get some sleep. I'll see you at the costume shop this afternoon."

A stunned look on her face, Rory headed down the hall toward the exit where Liz stood waiting.

"What's going on?" Liz said as soon as she saw her friend. "You look like you got some bad news."

"I'll tell you about it in the car."

Once they'd settled down in their seats, Liz said, "Okay, spill. What did Dashing D say that's got you so upset?"

"I think he's going to break up with me," Rory said softly.

"What?! That can't be. He adores you. What did he really say?"

"He said he didn't know if our relationship was going to work out."

Liz stared at Rory with her mouth open. "Is it because we followed Granny G? You told him that was my idea, right?"

"Doesn't matter. He gets worried about me. You know what happened to his wife. How she died taking a bullet for him. I think he's afraid something similar is going to happen to me."

Liz leaned over and gave Rory a hug. "I'm sure he's just tired. He's still going to the costume store with you, right? That's a good sign. Let's go home. Everything will look better in the morning."

As Liz maneuvered her car down the empty streets, Rory sat back in her seat, praying that would be true.

When the couple met that afternoon at Trick or Treat at the Beach, a temporary Halloween store set up in an unused space downtown, neither of them brought up their earlier conversation. Rory hoped it was just one of those bumps in the road that occurred in any relationship.

She held up a doublet and its accompanying white shirt. "How about Romeo and Juliet?"

Martin looked up from his perusal of a rack of costumes in the next aisle and shook his head. "I don't do tights."

Rory held the Juliet dress up in front of her and squinted into a nearby mirror, trying to visualize it on her body. She sighed and returned the dress to the rack. "Maybe not."

"There's not a lot of choice here." He surveyed the store. Half a dozen people milled around, hunting through the largely depleted racks of costumes for something that appealed to them.

"That's what we get for waiting until the last minute, I guess." She stepped over to the next rack and started going through it. She opened her mouth to ask about the case, almost immediately closing it. Suppressing her itch to know the latest, she continued her search, occasionally glancing over at Martin.

After several minutes of silence, he looked over at her. "Did you want to ask me something?"

"Just wondering how everything's going."

"It's fine." Martin picked up a pirate outfit complete with eye patch and stuffed parrot and examined it closely before returning it to the rack.

Rory stared at a mermaid costume and immediately dismissed it. She couldn't imagine wearing it for any length of time. "I've been keeping an eye out for Zelena's purse. No luck so far. Maybe the woman at the RV park I told you about saw it. I forgot to ask her about it. I'm not sure she'll answer your questions though. She seemed rather jittery when I mentioned the police. I gave her my card. Maybe she'll call."

When he didn't immediately respond, Rory looked over at him to see if he'd heard her.

A hand on the rack of costumes, he stared at her, exasperation written all over his face. "You're not planning on going back there, are you? You need to leave the investigating to us. This is murder, not a game." He faced the rack and continued his search. "If you really want to help, why don't you volunteer on the tip line."

"That's still up? I thought you closed it down as soon as Zelena was found."

"We're using it to field calls about her murder now. Even the smallest bit of information can be useful."

"That makes sense. How do I sign up?"

"Contact this guy. He's scheduling the volunteers." Martin pulled out his phone.

Moments later, Rory heard a quack coming from the pocket of her jeans, indicating a text had arrived. She glanced at it and nodded, then picked up a black cape with red satin lining. "I've got an idea." She held it up so he could see. "You can be Count Dracula and I'll be one of your victims. Black jeans and a black T-shirt and you're all set."

"I like the sound of that. I saw some fake fangs near the checkout stand. I can put the cape over my suit tomorrow when I help out with the trick or treaters at the station."

One afternoon each October, downtown businesses participated in a Safe Halloween event, handing out candy and treats to costumed children, providing a secure environment for trick or treaters.

"The police station's participating?"

"We do it every year. This is my first time, though." Martin put his elbows on the rack. "I still haven't had a chance to try that escape room of yours. Didn't want to sign up and not be able to go."

"You can do it at the party on Sunday."

"Sounds like a plan." His gaze swept the store. "What are you going to wear?"

Rory studied the displays, searching for something that would go with the vampire costume. "Not sure yet. I could go in a lot of directions."

Martin's phone beeped. He glanced down at the screen. "Sorry, I have to leave. Chief Marshall needs me," he said, referring to Vista Beach police chief Redmond Marshall.

Rory looked up, concern on her face. "How's he doing?"

"Cancer's in remission. He lost some weight, which he probably needed to do, anyway. He's back to his usual self, I think."

"That's good. I can't imagine the city without him."

He leaned over the rack and kissed her good-bye. "Can't wait to see what you're going to wear." With the cape draped over his arm, Martin walked toward the checkout stand near the exit.

As soon as she was done at the costume shop, Rory headed to the boutique house. When she walked in the front door, she found half a dozen customers clustered around the sales table, waiting to be rung up. She rushed to help her mother process sales and, before long, the back log was taken care of.

Rory walked around the house to see if anyone had any questions or needed help. In the dining room, she came across the teenage girl they had caught vandalizing the store. Beside her stood a woman who resembled the girl enough she was probably her mother. The two examined the lazy Susan Rory had painted and the piece next to it.

When she spotted Rory, the mother nudged her daughter.

The girl looked down at the floor. "Sorry about, you know."

"That's between you and my mother."

"We cleaned the window."

"That's good."

The mother pointed at the lazy Susan. "You painted this?"

They were discussing the different painting techniques used in the project when the girl's eyes opened wide. Rory looked over her shoulder to see what had startled her so, catching a glimpse of Jeanne scurrying out of the room.

When the mother picked up the lazy Susan and headed toward the sales table to pay for it, the girl hung back. She looked uncertainly at Rory.

"What is it?" Rory said.

"That woman..."

"Broad shoulders? Tall?"

"That's her. She...she was the one who gave us the necklace to put on the skeleton."

"Are you sure?"

"Positive."

"Thanks for letting me know."

The girl nodded and headed toward the doorway where her mother stood holding a shopping bag, waiting for her.

"Was that one of the pranksters?" Liz said as she walked up to Rory.

"Yeah. She said the oddest thing." Rory related what the girl had said about Jeanne and the necklace.

"I knew it! Jeanne was involved in Zelena's disappearance! And probably her murder too."

"We don't know that yet. We don't even know if what the girl said is true."

"We need to ask her. Right now." Liz marched toward the doorway.

Rory went after her and touched Liz's sleeve, stopping her. "Let's wait until it's quieter so we can get her alone. Jeanne's more likely to answer our questions then."

Liz looked disappointed, but nodded her agreement. For the next hour, they tried to get Jeanne's attention, but every time they walked into a room where the woman was, she came up with an excuse to leave.

Finally, they found her sitting by herself at the table in the kitchen, sipping a bottle of water while she studied some paperwork.

Rory stood in front of the table while Liz sat down on a nearby chair.

"Jeanne, we need to talk to you," Rory said.

The woman looked up from her work and frowned. "Can't you see I'm busy?"

"It's important."

She leaned back in her chair, an exasperated look on her face, and flicked her hand, indicating Rory should continue.

"Did you give a necklace to one of those pranksters to put on the skeleton?"

Jeanne stared at the two of them, then howled with laughter. "Why would I do that? That's the stupidest thing I ever heard. Who told you that?"

"The person you gave it to. She said you saw them with the skeleton. Instead of turning them in, you gave them the necklace to put on it."

"Why ever would I do that? And what would I be doing with a bunch of painted tombstones and witches? Not my style."

"We never said what the necklace looked like," Rory said.

"Didn't you say you were talking about one Zelena had?"

"We never mentioned her name," Liz said. "Admit it, you were involved with her abduction. You were seen at the RV park and you gave her necklace to the kids. The one Zelena was wearing when she went missing."

Jeanne took a sip of water. "I don't know what you're talking about. What's this about an RV?"

Rory studied her. She seemed genuinely confused about the RV park, but that didn't mean she didn't know about the necklace. Rory walked over to a nearby counter and picked up a paper bag. When she returned to the table, she grabbed the water bottle Jeanne had been drinking from. Careful to only handle it by its cap, she placed it in the bag.

Jeanne stood up and leaned over the table until her face was inches away from Rory's. "What are you doing? That's my water bottle!"

"I'm giving it to the police. They can compare the prints on it to the ones they found on the necklace."

Jeanne sat down abruptly. "All right, all right. I gave the necklace to the kids to put on the skeleton. I found it on the street. It was just a prank. I had nothing—" she slammed her hand on the table, sending a pen flying onto the ground. "—nothing to do with Zelena's death or abduction."

"Where'd you find it?"

"In some bushes a few blocks away from the beach. I recognized it as hers. She was being such a pain about the boutique house, I thought I'd have some fun with it. I had no idea at the time that she was missing."

"Didn't you find it odd it was in the bushes in the first place?"

Liz said.

Jeanne shrugged. "I figured she lost it on one of her walks. That was her thing, you know. Did two or three miles a day from what I hear. I figured the clasp came undone and fell off. It's happened to me enough times."

"What were you doing out so late at night, anyway?" Rory asked.

"I couldn't sleep so I went for a walk myself."

"What about the matching earrings? Did you see those too?"

"I only saw the necklace." Jeanne motioned toward the paper bag still in Rory's hands. "There's no reason to give that to the police now."

Rory studied her, then set the bag on the table. "Fine, I won't give the bottle to them. But you should really tell them where you found the necklace."

Jeanne grabbed the bag and bobbed her head up and down in agreement. "Absolutely."

Through the open window behind Jeanne, Rory saw a hand waving at them. Teresa Mut mouthed words Rory couldn't understand and motioned toward the side of the house.

"Is there anything else?" Jeanne said sharply.

"No, nothing at all," Rory said.

While Rory and Liz headed toward the front door, Rory whispered, "Did you see Teresa in the backyard? She wants to see us."

"Maybe she has some new information for us," Liz whispered back. "Speaking of information, you've been holding out on me. You didn't tell me they found prints on the necklace."

"As far as I know they didn't."

"But you told Jeanne—"

"It got her to talk, didn't it?"

"Sneaky, very sneaky." Liz dug her car keys out of her purse. "Do you think she'll tell the police about the necklace?"

"I doubt it, but I'll make sure they know."

Liz opened her mouth to say something, but Rory beat her to

it. "I never said I wouldn't *say* anything to them about it, just that I wouldn't give them the bottle."

They exited the front door and went around the side of the house where Teresa stood next to a row of garbage cans, waiting for them.

"I heard you talking to Jeanne about Zelena. Window was open so I couldn't help overhearing. Did you know they had a big dust up about the boutique house?" Teresa said.

Rory and Liz exchanged glances.

"I knew Zelena wasn't entirely happy about the changes," Liz finally said, "but I didn't realize they had a fight about it."

"How do you know about this fight?" Rory said.

"I heard them talking by their cars before one of our board meetings. You weren't there yet. There was a big argument. Jeanne threw her water bottle at Zelena and Zelena yelled something about how she knew things about Jeanne that she wouldn't want told."

"Do you know what those things were?"

"No idea, but I wouldn't be surprised if Jeanne had something to do with Zelena's death." Teresa looked nervously over her shoulder. "I've got to go. I'm supposed to be working. Don't tell anyone where you got the information from, okay?" She headed down the side of the house toward the backyard.

"Told you Jeanne's involved," Liz said.

"Sure looks like she has something to hide, anyway."

While she drove home, Rory wondered what Zelena could have found out about Jeanne that might lead to kidnapping and murder.

Later that evening, Rory opened her front door to discover Tabitha Halliwell on her doorstep.

"You left this in the office the other day." Tabitha smiled and held out a cell phone. "Sorry I didn't return it sooner, but I just found it. I hope you don't mind me coming to your house."

Rory stared down at the unfamiliar phone. "It's not mine."

"Really? I was sure it was yours." Tabitha pressed it into Rory's hands. "Maybe you can help me figure out who it belongs to. Go on, take a look at it. Maybe you'll recognize a phone number or something."

Rory cast a puzzled glance at the woman before examining the phone. Only a half dozen calls had been made on it, all to a number that seemed familiar. "Come on in. Let me check something."

Rory led the way into her work area and picked up her own cell phone. She scrolled through her contact list until she found the same number that was on the mystery phone. She sank down onto a chair. "This was used to call Zelena." When Tabitha didn't respond, Rory looked at her more closely. The woman avoided Rory's gaze.

"But you know that, don't you?" Rory said softly.

Tabitha sat down on the other chair. "I don't know what you're talking about."

Rory laid a reassuring hand on the woman's arm. "Where did you *really* find this phone?"

Tabitha looked up. "In Mr. Geller's office. That's the truth."

"But you knew it wasn't mine."

She slowly nodded her head. "I didn't recognize it so I looked at it to see if I could figure out who it belonged to. When I saw what was on it, it scared me."

"Did you recognize the phone number?"

"No. It's the emails. Look at them."

Rory flipped through the messages. One of them matched the email from the stalker Rory had found in Zelena's spam folder. When she checked the photo gallery on the phone, she found even more pictures taken of Zelena shopping, entering and exiting her apartment as well as walking around town. "I see what you mean."

"I wasn't sure what to do with it. I was afraid, well, that Mr. Geller might be involved with Ms. Alvarez's death somehow. I didn't want to bring it up with him. My job, you know. Then I thought of you, how you have experience investigating these kinds of things."

"You did the right thing, bringing it to me. I'll see the police get it." Rory carefully placed the phone on her desk. "I'd better not handle it anymore. There might be prints on it. Why do you think Edgar's involved?"

"He's been acting a little weird lately. Especially when Zelena's name comes up."

"Have you ever seen him with this phone?"

"Maybe. I'm not really sure."

"Exactly where in the office did you find it?"

"Under his desk."

"So anyone could have dropped it there." Rory wrinkled her brow in thought.

"I wouldn't say anyone. I'm there throughout the day. I'd have noticed if someone went into his office."

"What about lunchtime? Bathroom breaks?"

"I eat at my desk. I get our lunches delivered most days. I suppose someone could have slipped in while I was in the bathroom or on an errand, but they'd have to get by the receptionist and the other offices. Someone would have noticed someone who didn't belong there."

"Put together a list of everyone who's had appointments with Mr. Geller in the last couple weeks."

Tabitha nodded. "I'll get right on it."

As soon as the woman left, Rory called Martin and told him about the cell phone.

Chapter 20

Friday afternoon, Rory was in Arika's Scrap 'n Paint when Edgar Geller walked in the store with a little girl dressed in a child-size pants suit, carrying a tiny briefcase. The two joined the line of kids and parents patiently waiting for their share of candy.

Rory smiled at them and headed into the back room to call Martin Green. She whispered into the phone, "Have you talked with Edgar Geller yet?"

"Haven't been able to find him. He's been doing a good job of avoiding us."

"He's here, in my mom's store. He brought his daughter in for the business to business trick or treat event."

"Keep him there. I'll be right over."

When she returned to the sales floor, Edgar and his daughter were at the front of the line. After Arika dropped candy into the open briefcase, they stepped to the side so the little girl could check out what she'd gotten.

Rory greeted Edgar, then leaned down and extended her hand to his daughter. "Hi, what's your name? Mine's Rory."

The little girl shook Rory's hand. "I'm Grace."

"How old are you, Grace?"

She frowned. "Mommy says it's not nice to ask a lady how old she is."

Rory bit her lip to keep from laughing and straightened up. She eyed Grace's costume. "Are you a lawyer?"

Grace shook her head. "A business person, like Daddy." She looked up at her father with adoring eyes.

Rory smiled and turned to Edgar. "Have you been to many stores yet?"

"This is only the second one." He looked around at the painted decorations and Halloween scrapbooking pages displayed throughout the store. "I like what you've done here."

"My mom likes a festive atmosphere." She pointed to a wooden cookie jar lid in the shape of a pumpkin displayed on a nearby shelf. "That was one of my first projects. I painted it when I wasn't much older than you are now, Grace."

She stared at it, wide-eyed, and looked at her father who seemed to sense what she wanted. "Go ahead, look around, but no touching."

The little girl was examining the jar lid close up when Detective Green walked into the store. In a quiet voice, he said, "Mr. Geller, could we talk?"

"Okay, but I want to stay in sight of my daughter."

Rory pointed to the empty seating area near the back of the sales floor. "Why don't you sit over there. I'll make sure no one disturbs you."

Martin led the way and the two men settled down on the couch. Rory stood within earshot, straightening nearby shelves while she kept an eye on the conversation.

The detective pulled a bag containing a phone out of his jacket pocket and placed it on the coffee table in front of Edgar.

The man's eyes widened for a split second, then returned to normal. "Am I supposed to know what that is?"

"It's not yours? It was found in your office."

Edgar held up both hands in front of him. "Whoa. What are you saying? I had nothing to do with Zelena's death."

"I didn't mention her name."

A look of panic came over his face. "I may have seen Zelena with it," he said weakly.

Grace tugged on the sleeve of her father's shirt. She'd

approached so silently, none of them had realized she was there.

When he looked down, his face softened. "What is it, honey?"

"Can I paint a punkin?" She pointed toward the doorway into the classroom where Arika had spread out a project for kids to work on.

He looked a question at Rory who said, "My mom's teaching them how to paint faces on miniature pumpkins."

He smiled at his daughter and said in a gentle voice, "Go ahead. Have fun. I've got to talk to these nice people. Stay inside the store until I come to get you, okay?"

He watched her skip into the other room, then turned to the detective and said, "That should keep her occupied for a while. Let's go outside and talk."

Rory hung back, itching to follow but not sure if she should.

Edgar motioned with his hand. "You might as well come with. You received the email from Zelena. I want you to hear this too."

The three of them stood to one side of the front entrance to Arika's Scrap 'n Paint. Trick or treaters walked past, going from business to business, loading up on candy from each of the participating stores. The bell over the entrance to the craft store rang almost continuously as children and their parents moved in and out.

"This is a little busy, but I don't want to go too far." Edgar looked up and down the block. "Let's go over here." He led the way to a store that was currently unoccupied and they settled into the relative quiet of its doorway. "That phone isn't mine. I had nothing to do with those stalker emails."

The detective raised an eyebrow. "How did you know it was used to send the messages?"

A defeated look in his eyes, Edgar looked from Rory to Detective Green and back again. "I can explain..." He stared at the ground for a moment, then looked up at them, an earnest expression on his face. "I didn't send those. I don't know how that phone ended up in my office."

"If you didn't send them, who did?"

"Zelena."

Rory gasped and felt a surge of anger that the man would accuse her friend of such a thing, especially since she was no longer around to defend herself.

"To herself?" Skepticism was written all over the detective's face. "You expect us to believe that?"

"It's the truth."

"What about the photos? They don't look like selfies," Rory said.

"What photos?"

"The ones attached to the emails."

"Fine. I took those. It was all part of the plan."

"What plan?" Martin said.

Edgar leaned against the doorway and crossed his arms in front of him. "It's hard to explain. There's a bit of a gray area."

"Start at the beginning." Martin brought out his notepad and started taking notes.

"Zelena and I had a...mutually beneficial...agreement. I was going to bankroll her movie."

That explains the money she was going to come into, Rory thought. "What was she giving you in return?"

"That's the gray area." He took a deep breath. "She was going to pretend to have a stalker and be kidnapped. BTG's automatic email system would kick in and you'd be notified."

"I don't understand. How was that supposed to help you?" Rory cast a puzzled expression in the CEO's direction.

"Publicity," Martin said. "You got plenty of it when that article appeared in the paper. I hear you've signed up quite a few more customers since."

"She wasn't supposed to die." Edgar shook his head, a sad expression on his face.

Anger welled up inside Rory. She didn't know whether she was madder at Edgar or Zelena for concocting such a scheme. "What was supposed to happen?" She practically bit out the words.

"She was supposed to be found wandering by the pier. She was going to say she'd been drugged and couldn't remember much. That her stalker let her go after all the news reports about Beyond The Grave and her disappearance. We'd do a joint press conference and there'd be a lot of publicity for her and her movie as well as for my company."

Rory shook her head in disgust.

"What happened?" Martin asked.

"She got cold feet. She saw the article on that blog, *Vista Beach Confidential*, and got worried about you, Rory, how you were taking it." He directed his attention to her. "I caught her calling you and grabbed the phone out of her hand. We had a bit of a fight." He rubbed the side of his face. "She throws—threw—a mean punch."

"So you admit you kept her in the RV at the park?"

"I didn't keep her anywhere. She was there voluntarily."

"The rope and the duct tape?"

"Props in case someone found the RV. I didn't expect anyone to find it, but if they did, I made sure no one would know I was involved. I always wore gloves and bundled up so no one would recognize me. What gave me away?"

"We found your blood in the RV," Martin said.

"The nosebleed. I thought I'd cleaned up all that."

"We also found takeout containers in the dumpster that led us to a restaurant where they recognized you as a frequent customer."

"Guess I should have thrown those out at home. Probably should have driven the RV out of the lot right away, too, but I didn't want to attract undue attention. I figured I'd wait until after the period I had reserved ended."

"What were you going to do if the owner reported the RV stolen?"

"He wouldn't have. He's a friend of mine."

"That's not what he said to me," the detective said. "He told me it was stolen from the storage place where he kept it. Just didn't notice it was gone until we came to see him."

"That's what I told him to say."

"He didn't think that was odd?" Rory asked.

Edgar shrugged. "We've known each other a long time. He was just returning a favor. I assured him I wasn't doing anything illegal with it. That's all he needed to know."

"She died there and you dumped her body later, then?" Martin said.

Edgar straightened up and waved his hands in front of his body. "No, no, no! She said she didn't want any part of it anymore and stormed out. I have no idea what happened after that, but she was alive the last time I saw her."

His words had the ring of truth to them but, after everything the man had done, Rory wasn't sure if she could trust him. "We found the clothes she was wearing Saturday night in a closet in the RV. They didn't smell that great."

"She had a bad reaction to some food I got for her so she changed into the extra clothes she brought with her. She was supposed to put the old ones back on when she was found so it would look like she was taken when she was walking home from the meeting. I even tossed her necklace out the window of my car when I drove back into town. If anyone found it, they'd think she lost it in a struggle when she was abducted."

"Did she have her purse with her?" Rory said.

Edgar shrugged. "I suppose so. I didn't see it anywhere after she left."

"What about her phone? The one we found at the drugstore," the detective asked.

"I dropped her phone in the recycling bin so no one could track her. That was Zelena's idea." Edgar slumped against the wall and said in a quieter voice, "This was not supposed to happen."

"Did you try to break into her apartment?"

"I wanted to make sure there was nothing inside that would point back to me, but I didn't get very far. Someone saw me so I ran."

"And the reward? You knew she didn't have a stalker so why mention that at the press conference?"

"Anyone in the know thought she had a stalker so I couldn't

leave it out. And I really do want to help find her killer."

"I still don't understand about the BTG email. Why did Zelena choose to send it to me?" Rory said. "Did she really want me investigating? What if I found out the truth?"

"We planned on ending it before you discovered too much."

Rory was processing the new information when she heard her name called. She looked over and saw Arika gesturing to her from the store doorway. She excused herself and headed over to see what her mother wanted.

"Are you going to be long? Grace is looking for her father."

Rory glanced down the block to where Edgar and Detective Green were still talking. "Keep her occupied for a little while longer, okay?"

Arika nodded and headed back inside the store.

When Rory returned to the two men, she said, "Grace is looking for her dad."

Edgar straightened up and a worried expression came across his face. "Oh, Lord. I forgot about Grace. She's only five. I'm a terrible father."

"Can your wife pick her up?" the detective said. "I'd like to go over a few more things down at the station."

"You're not arresting me, are you?"

"We're just going to have a quiet chat."

Edgar nodded. With the detective's permission, he pulled out his cell phone and made the call. After he explained the situation to his wife, he hung up and said, "Can I talk to Grace for a minute?"

The three trooped back into the decorative painting supply store where Edgar pulled his daughter aside and explained that he had to go to work and that her mother would be there shortly to pick her up. He'd no sooner finished than a frazzled looking woman ran in the front door, sending the bell madly tinkling. She looked wide-eyed at her husband and the detective.

Edgar placed a reassuring hand on his wife's arm and said, "I'll explain when I get home."

The two men walked out the door followed moments later by

Edgar's wife and daughter, the two of them holding hands. Clutching a pint-sized pumpkin painted with a jolly face, Grace looked back at Rory and her mother and shyly waved goodbye.

Chapter 21

"Rory, you made it just in time! Veronica's ready to take our picture for the paper." The Wicked Witch of the East gestured for Rory to join the group gathered in the entryway of the boutique house. Twelve women stood in front of the sales table waiting for instructions, half of them wearing Halloween costumes.

Rory peered at the green-faced woman dressed all in black sporting a grape-sized wart on the tip of her pointed chin. "Penny, is that you? Were we supposed to wear costumes?"

"Not required," Penny said. "But some of us thought it would be fun."

Rory took her place beside Jeanne in the back row while the others arranged themselves so everyone could be seen in the photograph. Dressed in her fortune teller's outfit, Liz sat down in a chair up front, holding a painted sign with the chapter name written on it. Penny took the seat beside her, adjusted her pointy hat and placed a large photograph of Zelena on her lap.

Veronica snapped a few pictures, then wrote down on her notepad everyone's name along with their position in the rows.

At the end of the photo session, Penny said, "Too bad Zelena couldn't be here."

"At least we had a photo of her," Liz said.

"If only we knew who was stalking her, we'd be able to find out what happened and get some closure." Penny returned the two chairs to their positions behind the sales table.

"About that..." Rory quickly brought them up to date on everything that had happened at Arika's Scrap 'n Paint earlier that day, including Edgar's confession about his arrangement with Zelena.

Veronica jotted down the details while Rory talked. "So there was no stalker? Very interesting. Where's Edgar now?"

"As far as I know, he's still at the police station, answering questions."

"I'd better get down there." Veronica stuffed her camera and notepad back in her tote bag. "I'll send you copies of the photos and let you know when I post them on *VBC*. Penny, I'll let you pick the one that appears in the paper." She slung her bag over her shoulder and exited the house.

"If it wasn't a stalker, then who killed her?" Penny sank down onto one of the chairs.

"I'm sure the police will figure it out," Rory said.

"You would say that. Conflict of interest, if you ask me." Jeanne crossed her arms in front of her ample chest. "I'm glad I'm working here instead of going to the candlelight vigil. You all should consider staying away too."

Penny stared at Jeanne, her mouth open. "Why ever would you say that?"

"She was a fraud. She pretended to have a stalker and be kidnapped. For what? Monetary gain. That's not someone we should be celebrating."

"Like you've lived a perfect life! She was a good person who made a mistake. She didn't deserve to die," Penny said.

"Maybe Edgar killed her. He was the last one to see her, that we know of, anyway," Liz said. "Just because he confessed to the publicity stunt doesn't mean he's innocent."

"But, if he killed her, why would he admit to their agreement?" Rory said. "Wouldn't he want to keep his mouth shut? As far as I can tell, no one else knew about it."

Penny scratched the wart on her chin, a bit of the green makeup coming off on her fingers. "His back was up against the wall. It's better to confess to that harebrained scheme than murder."

"But he offered a reward for information that would lead to her killer. Would he do that if he was guilty?" Rory crossed her arms in front of her chest and leaned against the table.

"Probably covering his tracks," Jeanne said.

"I wish we knew where she went after she left the RV."

Liz's eyes lit up. "I've got an idea. I'll be right back."

Before anyone could ask what it was, she took her phone out of her purse and headed outside.

"Where's she going? The house is about to open and she's working!" Jeanne stared in disbelief at the front door.

"I'm sure she'll be right back." Rory glanced at the time on her cell phone. "We've got a few minutes left. We're only here for a couple hours, anyway, until we leave for the vigil."

"I still think you all should boycott it." Jeanne tapped her watch and clapped her hands. "It's time to open up. Places everyone."

No sooner had the words left her mouth than Liz came back in the front door, a satisfied look on her face. "They're lining up outside. Big crowd tonight."

"What did you find out?" Rory whispered as the two walked up the stairs toward the escape room.

"We've got an appointment tomorrow evening that should shed light on everything. I hope so, anyway."

"What are you talking about?"

"You'll see." Liz looked behind her. "We'd better get to it. Our first guests are coming up the stairs now." She slipped into her Madame Elizabeth persona and headed into the escape room while the first group of customers checked in with Rory.

Rory looked at the sea of faces surrounding her. Half the city seemed to have gathered on and around the Vista Beach pier right before sunset for a candlelight vigil honoring Zelena Alvarez's life.

She stood beside Liz on the beach below the pier with several other members of their painting chapter, waiting for the program to begin. Everyone had changed out of their Halloween costumes for the event. They each held a currently unlit white candle with an attached drip protector they'd picked up from a table when they arrived.

Liz stood on tiptoe and craned her neck. "Where's Dashing D? I don't see him."

"I'm sure he's around somewhere. He said he'd be working," Rory said. "There are so many people here, it's hard to spot anyone unless you're right next to them."

Liz dropped back down onto her heels. "I figured the vigil would be popular, but I didn't realize so many would show up."

"She was well-liked in the community. Even her recent lapse in judgment doesn't seem to have made much difference in how most people view her. Though I suppose maybe not everyone has found out about that yet." Penny pointed to several news vans parked in a lot on the hill above them. "Of course, the media coverage might also have something to do with the large turnout."

Rory looked up at the pier above them where a podium and microphone had been set up. Spotlights were trained on the area where a woman and two men stood. "I see Martin. He's up there with the mayor and a man I don't recognize."

"That's the principal of Vista Beach Elementary," Liz said.

"Edgar Geller's not here," Rory said. "At least I don't see him at the podium."

"Do you blame him?" Liz asked.

"I suppose not."

"I wonder if the $10,000 reward is still on," Liz said.

"He seems to want to find whoever killed Zelena so my guess is yes."

"Who's that talking to the mayor now?" Penny asked.

Rory stared at the podium where another man had joined the group. "Tito Alvarez, Zelena's father."

"That explains it. Family's never easy."

Rory stared at Penny. "What do you mean?"

"Did they get along? Zelena and her father?"

"I'm not sure. Zelena never talked about her parents with you?"

"Not really. I know she declared emancipation years ago."

"He was here visiting. Maybe they were mending fences," Rory said. "Is something wrong?"

"I don't know. I saw them together Saturday morning, here on the beach. Toby and I were taking a walk. Such a beautiful morning. We really love it there in the winter. I like the weather better and there aren't as many people around. Anyway, we saw them arguing. Zelena looked really angry. I only heard bits and pieces of the conversation. Something about him always asking for money." Penny wrinkled her brow in thought. "Then she said she wasn't going to give him any more handouts."

"Did she tell you anything about it at the chapter meeting?"

"No, she was more upset about her stalker. I'm sure it's nothing. Like I said, family's never easy."

Rory was mulling over this news when the sun slipped down into the ocean. The crowd quieted down and silently watched the colorful sunset. As soon as darkness fell, everyone directed their attention toward the podium where the mayor now stood. She cleared her throat and spoke into the microphone.

After welcoming them all and thanking them for coming, she said, "You've all seen the articles on social media and in the paper about Zelena Alvarez, how she was a child star, well known for *Mommy's Little Helper*. But she was so much more than that to this community. She loved this city, and she loved children. She was a teacher, beloved by her students and colleagues alike, as well as the driving force behind various charity projects, including the Halloween Holiday Boutique that she and her fellow painting chapter members put on each year. Proceeds go to a charity that was dear to her heart, one that provides art supplies and instruction to not only children here, but also in less affluent areas." The mayor stopped to catch her breath. "We will never forget her. Now, Principal Walters of Vista Beach Elementary will say a few words."

She turned the microphone over to a middle-aged man dressed in casual pants and a button-down shirt.

"Zelena was well loved," he began. "We will all miss her at Vista Beach Elementary." After a few anecdotes about the kindergarten teacher that made everyone smile, he said, "I speak for everyone at the school when I say how touched we are by the outpouring of support for us and her family. We'll be moving the memorial from the pier to VB Elementary at eight a.m. tomorrow morning. Anyone who can help, please stop by."

The principal eyed the man standing beside him. "Now, a few words from Zelena's father, Tito Alvarez. Mr. Alvarez?"

Tito stepped up to the podium and cleared his throat. He started to say something, but he'd only gotten half a dozen words out before he broke down and dissolved into tears. The mayor gently led him to the side and took his place at the podium. Her voice wavered as she continued, "The police department would like to say a few words. Detective Green?"

Martin stepped up to the microphone. "The same tip line that was set up when Ms. Alvarez went missing is now being used to field calls about her murder. If anyone knows anything that can assist us in the investigation, please call. You don't have to give us your name. You can remain anonymous. We could also use more volunteers to cover the phones. Just call or come by the station to sign up. Thank you."

"Did you know about the tip line?" Liz said to Rory.

"Martin told me about it the other day. I'm working it on Sunday. I'll text you the name of the person handling the volunteer schedule after we're done here."

As soon as the detective stepped away from the podium, the mayor instructed everyone to light their candles and raise them to Zelena.

The lights on the pier winked out and candlelight started popping up everywhere. The people at the end of each row lit the candle of the person next to them and so on down the line. Those who didn't have candles held up lighted cell phones in solidarity.

A soft voice began singing, "Stand By Me", Zelena's favorite karaoke song. Before long everyone joined in. After that, the crowd spontaneously broke into the theme song from *Mommy's Little Helper*. A scream split the night air during the final words of the song. The singing died down and everyone's attention became riveted on the area near the base of the pier.

"What is it?" Liz jumped up and down, trying to get a glimpse of what was at the center of the flurry of activity. When someone screamed again, she said, "Quick! Put me on your shoulders."

Rory extinguished both of their candles and bent down so Liz could climb onto her shoulders. As soon as Liz said she was ready, Rory stood up. "Can you see anything?"

"Hold on." Liz shifted her weight, momentarily losing her balance. She put her hands around Rory's head to steady herself.

"Eyes! Eyes!"

Liz removed her hands from in front of Rory's eyes. "Sorry."

"Hurry up. I don't know how long I can carry you."

From her vantage point above the crowd, Liz reported on what was going on. "Dashing D's there. There's something in the water." She sucked in her breath. "The ghost! It's back. It's pointing at something. Whatever it is, they're dragging it out of the water. It looks like—oh no!"

"What is it?" Rory said.

"I think it's another body."

Chapter 22

Rory momentarily forgot someone was on her shoulders and leaned forward to see what was going on, throwing herself off balance. Once the wobbling stopped and Liz was safely on the ground, Rory said, "What was that about a body?"

"Sure looked like one to me, but it's hard to see with all the people around."

"Did you say something about a ghost?"

"There was a figure in the water, pointing at something. I glanced away for a moment and it was gone." Liz looked wild-eyed at Rory. "Do you think it only appears when someone's dead?"

Cries of "it's another body" and "it's a kid" rippled through the crowd. Some people headed toward the commotion, phones held out to capture the moment, but the vast majority surged forward, moving in the opposite direction. In the panic that ensued, lit candles landed everywhere, their flames extinguished as soon as they hit the sand.

The lights on the pier came on and the mayor spoke into the microphone. "Calm down, everyone. There's nothing to worry about. There's no need to rush. Make sure you extinguish your candles safely and deposit them in the bins."

The panic lessened and people walked in a more orderly fashion toward the nearby street. Going against the tide, a woman shoved her way through the crowd, scanning the faces around her. Only when she was within a few feet did Rory recognize her.

"Tabitha, is everything okay?"

"Have you seen Keith? I can't find him anywhere." Desperation in her eyes, Tabitha craned her neck, looking around at each face. "Did I hear something about another body? You don't think...?"

"I'm sure it's not. Do you want help looking for him?"

"Would you recognize him?"

"I think so," Rory said. "Show us a photo just to be sure."

Tabitha brought up a current photo of her high school-aged son on her phone before the three of them split up to look for him.

Rory scanned the thinned-out crowd as she walked toward the pier. When she reached the area where the body washed up, she looked down at the object lying in the sand. A boy-sized mannequin dressed in shorts and a T-shirt lay on the ground. A sign encased in plastic with "Trick or Treat" written on it in block letters was pinned to its chest.

"This is getting ridiculous," a man said. "When are you going to do something about these pranks?" He stared at Martin Green who was kneeling down beside the mannequin, examining it.

A small crowd gathered around them.

Martin rose to his feet and calmly addressed the man. "We've already identified two of the culprits. It's only a matter of time before we get the rest."

The information seemed to satisfy the man who nodded and headed toward town. As soon as he left, the rest of the crowd dispersed and Rory walked over to where the detective stood.

She nodded her head at the mannequin. "Do you think the two kids you arrested were involved in this?"

"If they were, they're incredibly stupid. It's probably one of their friends, the ones we haven't caught yet."

"The girl's not talking? She had plenty to say the other night."

"She decided she'd said enough. Or her parents decided for her."

Liz walked over. "Any luck?"

Rory shook her head.

Martin eyed the two of them. "Is there a problem?"

"Just looking for someone. I'm sure he's around somewhere."

Liz glanced down at the mannequin. "I saw that in the window of the kid's clothing store downtown. The pranksters must have stolen it." She gave the details to Martin who wrote them down in his notebook.

The two left the detective to his work. They were looking for Tabitha when they heard her voice coming from their right. Two high school age boys emerged from under the pier, goofy grins on their faces. Tabitha walked beside her son, talking angrily to him. When the three of them walked past, Rory caught a whiff of alcohol.

"I guess we know what those two were doing," Liz said.

Rory peered more closely at the teenager accompanying Keith. "Isn't that one of the ones we caught vandalizing the store?"

"That's him all right. Maybe Keith knows something about the other pranksters."

"Maybe. Or he's one of them."

Rory and Liz followed the rest of the crowd toward the parking lot, depositing their candles in a bin as they passed by.

"I'm going to help move the memorial to the school tomorrow morning. Do you want to come along?"

Liz shook her head. "I wish I could. I have a lot of appointments. Saturday's always a busy day for me. Plus we're working at the boutique house in the afternoon."

"No problem. I'm sure there'll be more than enough people there." Rory picked her way across the sand. "This was a nice tribute to Zelena, but I'd rather have her back. I wish we knew what happened."

"I know what you mean," Liz said. "But aren't you a little angry at her? I am. She shouldn't have put you through all that worry just to get her movie financed."

"I was at first, but she did change her mind and try to call me. I can't stay mad at her now that she's gone. It doesn't accomplish anything."

"Can you imagine what it's like for her father? It's pretty sad his last memory of her was an argument."

"One he neglected to tell the police about. That's pretty suspicious."

"Everyone argues with family at some point or another."

Rory cast a sympathetic glance in Liz's direction. "This thing with your mother's cousins is really getting to you, isn't it?"

"I just wish I knew why they're being so insistent. They never struck me as inflexible before. They were all excited at first. Now it's almost like they don't want to find anything."

"I'm sure you'll work it out."

"Do you want to have dinner? Or do you and Dashing D have plans?"

"No plans. He's busy updating Chief Marshall on the pranks and Zelena's case."

"How about getting takeout from that new Hawaiian place? I hear their vegetable fried rice is awesome. We can take it back to your house and discuss the case in private."

"Spam fried rice would be great."

Liz wrinkled her petite nose. "Spam, ugh. Don't know how you can eat that. It's not even real meat."

"It's good in small doses. Sekhmet agrees with me."

When they stopped to put on their shoes at the edge of the sand, Rory sniffed the air. "Is that...beef I smell?"

They stepped over to the freestanding shower beachgoers used to wash the sand off their feet. A city employee stood beside it, examining a stream of water coming from it. He turned off the water and unscrewed the shower head.

"Is that smell coming from the shower?" Rory asked him.

"'Fraid so. Looks like someone put a bouillon cube in the shower head. Got complaints of a strange smell so I walked over to check it out."

"That's two pranks in one night," Rory said. "I guess it was a coordinated attack. At least two people must have been involved."

"They could have put the bouillon cube in the shower head anytime," Liz pointed out. "No one would know about it unless someone used it."

"That's true. Let's get out of here. I'm starving."

A short while later, they settled down on the couch in Rory's living room. Between bites of fried rice, they discussed Zelena's case.

"Looks like Edgar's out as a suspect," Rory said.

"Is he, though?" Liz waved her fork in the air. "I wonder. Like I said before, he was the last person we know for sure who saw Zelena alive. Plus there's motive with her refusal to continue with that publicity stunt."

"I'm not sure that's reason enough to kill her. She wouldn't have said anything. She wouldn't want anyone to know about what she'd planned on doing. She might have lost her job if the school board found out."

"It could have been an accident. They did have a fight. He could have killed her in the RV and disposed of her body off the pier in the dead of night."

"Someone sure wanted us to believe he's guilty, anyway. They planted the phone in his office."

"We need to know who was there, who visited him after Zelena went missing."

"Tabitha said she'd put together a list of people who had appointments recently." Rory made a mental note to get it from her.

"How do we know she's telling the truth, anyway? She could have said she found it in his office. You didn't actually see it there, did you?"

"What's her motive?"

"Maybe Tabitha was playing Overprotective Mama. If Keith is one of the pranksters, Zelena could have found out and threatened to expose him. Now Mama's covering her tracks."

"Having issues with the police wouldn't look good on his college applications, that's for sure. Ivy League schools probably wouldn't be eager to admit someone with a mark like that on their record. Still, I'm not totally convinced." Rory took a bite of her

Spam fried rice and munched on it thoughtfully. "Where'd the phone come from in the first place? I wonder if Zelena had it on her."

"If she did, wouldn't she have used it to call you instead of that other phone?"

"I don't think so. It was used to send the 'stalker' messages. She probably wouldn't want to use it for anything else."

"Maybe it was at her place. The police could have missed it when they searched her apartment or someone took it before that." Liz screwed up her face in concentration. "Who had access?"

"Edgar broke in or tried to, anyway. Her father. Not sure who else."

"Penny said Tito had an argument with Zelena on Saturday about money. Maybe he met her later on the pier and pushed her off when she refused again to give him anything." Liz made a shoving motion with her hands. "Jeanne's still in the running too. She did have Zelena's necklace."

"But Edgar said he threw it out the window of his car."

"I'm still not ruling her out. She could have gotten into Zelena's apartment the same way we did. As long as she replaced the key, no one would know."

"With Doreen watching the area like a hawk?" Rory said.

"She has to take a break sometime."

Sekhmet wandered into the room and sniffed the air. Rory gave her a piece of Spam, then set the half-eaten container of fried rice on the coffee table, closing the lid so the cat couldn't get at the food. "There are too many possibilities. We need more info. What was that appointment you were talking about earlier?"

"We're going to see Raven tomorrow night. With her psychic abilities, she might be able to tell us something."

"Raven Leek? *That* was your big idea? You've got to be kidding."

"Do you have a better one?"

"I suppose it couldn't hurt," Rory said grudgingly.

Liz stuck her fork in her food and closed the lid. "There's got to be something else we're not thinking of." She took out her phone and selected a play list of dance-worthy songs. "Come on, stand up. Let's dance it out. I heard somewhere that exercise helps you think." She started doing dance steps Rory had seen on *The Ellen DeGeneres Show*.

"I don't think I can move like that."

"Just jump up and down and raise your hands to heaven, then." Liz demonstrated, then pulled on Rory's hands, trying to get her to her feet. "Come on. No one's going to see you."

Rory glanced out the living room window. Satisfied the house was set back far enough from the street no one would notice what she was doing, she pranced around the room to the music, releasing all of the tension built up since Zelena's disappearance. Liz was showing her a new move when Rory glanced outside and spotted a man peering into the window, an amused expression on his face. She jumped back and collided with the sofa. As soon as she looked at him, Martin pointed to the door.

Rory nodded at the window and turned off the music. "Martin's here. Not a word about Raven, okay? He doesn't think much of her."

"I rang the bell and knocked. Guess you didn't hear me," Martin said when she answered the door.

"Sorry. The music was too loud." She led the way into the living room. "How did your meeting with the chief go?"

"Nothing new to report." He sank down onto a chair and hungrily eyed the containers of food on the coffee table.

"Do you want the rest of my Spam fried rice?" She pushed the carton toward him. "I'll get you a fork."

While he ate, Rory and Liz told him what they had heard about the argument Tito had with Zelena on Saturday.

"Interesting." He took a final bite and set the food down with a satisfied sigh. "That hit the spot. Thanks."

"Anything useful on the tip line?" Rory said.

"Lots of calls, but nothing worthwhile so far."

"Any news on the other pranksters, then?" Liz said.

"We have some leads, but we can't make anything stick. Not yet, anyway." He sat back in the chair. "Enough about my work. Tell me how the Halloween Holiday Boutique is doing."

While they shared stories of the house, thoughts of Zelena were in the back of Rory's mind. She hoped some new information would soon come to light that would help identify her killer.

Chapter 23

"Rory? Have you come to help?"

Rory looked in puzzlement at the twenty-something red-haired woman standing in front of Zelena's memorial on the pier. She looked vaguely familiar, but Rory couldn't remember where she'd seen her before.

The redhead's smile faded slightly. "It's me, Megan. From the library. You know, Cinderella."

"Megan! Sorry, I didn't recognize you out of costume." Rory looked around at the half dozen men and women who were carrying bouquets of flowers toward the van parked in the lot nearest the pier. "Is there someone in particular I need to talk to about helping?"

"Everyone checks in with me. Principal Walters left me in charge." Megan glanced around at the other volunteers. "How about you help me pick out all the stuffed animals? We're going to clean them and take them to the children's hospital."

They both picked up armfuls of tigers and bears and put them into empty boxes lined up nearby.

"Is it true that Zelena didn't have a stalker? That she made it up?" Megan said.

"I'm afraid so." Rory leaned against the pier railing. "She made a deal with Edgar Geller, the CEO of Beyond The Grave. He'd finance her movie if she went along with the publicity stunt."

"I would never have thought she'd do anything like that."

"Me either. But it looks like she decided not to go through with it, after all."

Megan picked up the final bear, stuffed it into a box and closed it up. "Do you think that's why Edgar killed her?"

"The police aren't sure he did. Neither am I."

"Then what happened?"

"I wish I knew. If we could find out where she went after she left him, we might be able to figure it out."

The two women carried the boxes of stuffed animals to the van, then helped the other volunteers put the rest of the pictures, flowers and miscellaneous bits and pieces in the cargo area alongside the boxes. Before long, the pier was empty with only a handful of stray flower petals to indicate the memorial had ever been there.

"Would you mind riding to VB Elementary with me and helping me unload? I'll drive you back here afterward," Megan said.

"Sure, but you don't have to bring me back. I walked here. I'll just walk home."

On the way to the grade school, Rory sat back in the van's passenger seat and stared out the window at the businesses they passed on the way to the school. Finally, she said, "How are Zelena's kindergarten students doing?"

"Not bad, considering. They're getting used to their new teacher. Kids are pretty resilient."

"What about the little girl you told me about before? The one we saw at the library."

"She's the same." Megan stopped at a light and glanced over at Rory. "Why do you ask?"

"Just wondering. What do you know about the girl's parents?"

"The Halliwells? They have money, that's for sure."

"And they still send their kids to public school?"

"We have great schools in this city, always ranked highly in all the standardized tests. A lot of them, including VB Elementary, have won awards for excellence. No reason to spend money on something they don't need. That's how the rich stay rich, you know."

"What do the Halliwells do?"

"He's a big-time lawyer. Takes high-profile cases, a lot of celebrities. She works at a company downtown, assistant to some bigwig. Not sure the name of it."

"Beyond The Grave."

"Edgar Geller's company? I didn't realize."

"Like you said, she's his assistant. Makes you wonder if she knew about his plan." Rory glanced over at Megan, but she didn't seem surprised to know that Rory knew who Tabitha worked for. "She told me Keith is going to some Ivy League school. Or at least, that's what they're aiming for. Even if he has good grades, I wonder if they'll accept him."

"What do you mean?"

"He was under the pier at the vigil, drinking with one of the kids I caught defacing my mother's store. I can't help wondering if he's involved in all the recent pranks."

Megan's face turned thoughtful. "Maybe that's why Dana's been acting out. Tension at home could cause her behavior problems."

"Do you think Zelena knew?"

"Possibly."

"Wouldn't she have told the parents?"

"If she did, I'm not sure they'd do anything about it."

Rory's ears perked up. "What do you mean?"

Megan bit her lip as if holding something back. "I'm not sure if I should say anything. It might be just a rumor, but...I'm pretty sure it's true. I think it's okay to talk about it."

"Is it about Keith?"

"A few months back he was caught shoplifting expensive sunglasses, and I mean really expensive, a month of my salary expensive, from a store downtown."

"Was he charged? If he was arrested, I can't see any Ivy League school accepting him."

"No. His father paid off the store owner so he wouldn't press charges. From what I hear lots of money changed hands."

"I guess a lot of parents would do that if they could."

"The Halliwells? They'd do anything for their kids to ensure their future." Megan pulled into a parking space labeled *Miss Megan.* "We're here." She hopped out and pointed toward a spot on the grass beside a sign that read *Vista Beach Elementary.* "We're going to put everything there."

Rory helped unload the van and place the memorial items around the sign.

After they finished, Megan said, "I boxed up Zelena's personal items in her classroom. Could you see that her father gets them? I don't know how to contact him."

"Sure. There's something I want to talk with him about, anyway."

"Wait here. I'll go get it." Megan jogged down the sidewalk toward one of the classrooms. She returned a short time later with a cardboard box. "I'd better drive you home. This is heavy enough you shouldn't have to carry it."

"Thanks, I'd appreciate that." While they drove to her place, Rory wondered how far the Halliwells would go to protect their son's future.

As she turned off the street, Rory scanned the parking lot of the Vista View Motel but didn't spot Tito's old beater. She walked toward his room on the off chance he'd parked somewhere else. She found the door open and a maid inside, cleaning the room. The woman indicated Tito had left.

Rory headed to the motel office to see what she could find out. "I'm looking for someone who was staying here, Tito Alvarez. I understand he checked out. Did he say where he was going?" she asked the man in the office.

"I make it a rule not to talk about guests. Bad for business." The motel clerk cocked his head and peered closely at her. "Say, aren't you the one who was here the other day with the policeman?"

"That's right. We told Mr. Alvarez the bad news about his daughter."

The clerk shook his head. "Shame about her. Feel a bit sorry for her dad even if he did try to leave without paying. She was great on that sitcom. *Mommy's Little Helper*, right? Too bad she turned to the dark side. Hollywood types. I'll never understand them."

Rory mentally objected to his characterization of her friend, but she kept her expression neutral, trying not to show her true feelings. "What do you mean, the dark side?"

"You know, that bit about her pulling that disappearing act as a publicity stunt."

"Where did you hear about that?"

"Saw it on *VBC*, the blog that hot reporter chick writes. Va-va-voom. Wouldn't mind having her stay here, if you know what I mean." He narrowed his eyes. "What do you want with this Tito, anyway?"

"I loaned him some money," Rory said.

"Ah, you want to get it back." The clerk leaned forward. "I shouldn't do this, but seeing as he owes you...He mentioned something about packing up his daughter's place. Left, uh—" He consulted the clock on the wall. "—about an hour ago. Rented one of those U-Haul trailers, the kind that attaches to a car."

"Thanks."

"He has money now, a wad of cash. Don't let him tell you otherwise." He winked at her. "Come back, anytime. Day...or night."

As soon as Rory stepped out of the office, she spotted Toby leaving a nearby room. She ducked into the shadow of an overhang, behind the ice machine, and waited until he drove out of the lot before heading to her car. She'd just sat down and closed the door when a broad-shouldered woman with salt and pepper hair emerged from the same room Toby had left minutes before.

Rory ducked down, rolled down her window and, as surreptitiously as possible, snapped a photo of Jeanne with her phone. She texted it to Liz, briefly explaining the situation. Less than five minutes later, Liz called.

"Is Toby having an affair with Jeanne?" Liz burst into speech as soon as Rory answered.

"Looks like it. I suppose there could be another explanation, but I'm not sure what it is."

"But Jeanne? I mean *Jeanne*? She's so...bossy."

"She has some redeeming qualities. She's very organized and she's done a great job with the house."

"She doesn't even like him."

Rory thought about all of the times she'd seen the two of them together. "True. She's never had a kind word to say about him since they met."

"Maybe that's been to throw us off the scent. They do that on TV shows all the time."

"Did you know Penny and Toby were having trouble?"

"Haven't heard a peep. They're always together—okay, obviously not all the time," Liz said. "Maybe Penny already knows."

"She doesn't strike me as the type to put up with it if she found out her husband was having an affair."

Liz's voice grew excited. "Didn't Teresa say Zelena knew something about Jeanne? Some secret. I bet this was it. Zelena could have threatened to tell Penny so Jeanne offed her."

Rory mulled over the possibility. "It's worth looking into, though I'm not sure the secret is worth killing someone over."

"Maybe they have one of those open marriages." Liz sounded almost disappointed as she raised the possibility.

"Maybe. But what am I supposed to do when I see Penny today?"

"That's right. You're going on that Halloween decoration tour this afternoon, aren't you? Teresa and some of the others will be there. Just hang out with one of them. It should be pretty easy to avoid Penny."

"Zelena sure had more disagreements with people than I expected. I'm headed over to talk to her father now."

"Raven will give us some insight tonight. I'm sure of it."

Rory made a noncommittal sound and hung up, promising to report on her conversation with Tito.

When she arrived at Zelena's apartment, she found the front door wide open. As she got out of her car, Tito emerged from the apartment carrying a small table and headed toward a U-Haul trailer parked in the driveway.

Rory walked over to him with the box Megan had entrusted to her. "Mr. Alvarez. Do you have a minute?"

He placed the table in the trailer and turned to her, a smile on his face. "Anything for such a good friend of my *mija*. Before I forget—" he pulled a twenty dollar bill out of a wallet that seemed to be jam-packed with money. "Thank you for the loan."

Rory tried to keep her face neutral as she eyed the bulging wallet. "You're welcome."

"What's that?" He nodded at the box in her hands.

"Zelena's personal belongings from her classroom at Vista Beach Elementary. They thought you might like them."

"Thank you for delivering it." He placed the box in the half full trailer. His gaze swept over the boxes and small pieces of furniture inside. "So much stuff. I'll have to come back for the larger pieces. My wife and I will sort it all out when I get it home. There's so much about her life we don't know about."

"Zelena's mother is back in the U.S. now? Tell her how sorry I am for her loss."

"She's still in Mexico, but she should be home soon." He faced Rory. "I need to get back to packing up her things. The landlord wants everything out in the next few days."

"Let me help you."

Between the two of them, they soon had everything in the bedroom packed up. While they worked, she tried to figure out a way to talk to him about his argument with his daughter.

They were boxing up the office when she finally found the courage to ask. "Mr. Alvarez, I need to talk to you about something."

"Oh?" He dumped the contents of a desk drawer in a box and

looked up. "What is it?"

"It's about the Saturday you walked on the beach with Zelena."

His face softened. "The last time I saw my *mija*."

"Someone saw you. They said you were arguing about money. You never said anything about it before."

He sat down on the desk chair and hung his head. "I didn't want you to think bad of me."

"Did you often argue?"

"Not always. It was nothing. Just a silly misunderstanding."

"But didn't you lose all of her money from her acting days in a bad investment?"

Tito pounded his fist on the desk. "That tabloid nonsense again!"

"But it's gone, right?"

"I lost nothing. That manager of hers hired a bad man who stole it."

"Samantha Granger? Are you sure?"

"Of course. Why would I lie?" He stood up. "Thank you for your help. I'll handle the rest myself. You can leave now."

"Will you let me know about the service? Several of us in our painting chapter would like to attend."

"No service. We thought it better that way. Her death is a private matter. There's been too much publicity already."

She stared at him in disbelief at the unexpected news, then headed to her car.

Rory was about to drive off when she received a text from Samantha inviting her to lunch. She texted back her agreement, hoping it would give her an opportunity to get to the truth about Zelena's money.

Chapter 24

Rory's gaze swept over the customers in Buddy's Rockin' Diner until it rested on Samantha Granger sitting in a corner booth. The woman waved and Rory lifted her hand in response.

She slipped into the seat across from Samantha. "I'm glad you called. There's something I want to talk to you about."

"Me first. Several of the cast members of *MLH* reached out to me. They want to attend Zelena's service. Maybe even participate, say a few words. Do you know anything about the arrangements?"

"There isn't going to be one."

Samantha's mouth gaped open. She sat back in the booth, a bewildered look on her face. "No service? Are you sure?"

Rory shrugged her shoulders. "I'm as surprised as you are. That's what Zelena's father told me when I saw him today. He seems worried about all of the recent publicity."

"That doesn't sound like him. He always courted it in the past. Of course, there has been some backlash about her faked disappearance, though it's fairly minor as those things go. It'll probably blow over soon. Maybe he'll change his mind after it does. If not, I'll put something together. She deserves to be remembered." Samantha leaned forward and placed her arms on the table. "Now, what did you want to talk to me about?"

The waitress arrived to take their orders, giving Rory time to figure out how to broach the subject of the lost money.

A shrewd look in her eyes, Samantha took a sip of her coffee.

"Okay, what's going on? Out with it."

"Zelena's father said something to me today that...puzzled me. I figure you'll tell me the truth."

Samantha cocked her head and waited for Rory to continue.

"I know Zelena lost all of the money she made on her sitcom. The tabloids said her father lost it in a bad investment."

Samantha stirred more sugar into her coffee. "That's right."

"But he told me *you* were the one responsible. That you hired someone who stole it."

She blinked several times, then became so still she could have been a statue. When Samantha finally opened her mouth, Rory could almost see the fumes coming off her. "What a load of...poppycock. Tito Alvarez..." She practically spit out his name. "...is a greedy so-and-so who never cared a whit about his daughter. She was his little cash cow. All he was interested in, from almost the moment she was born, was how much she could make for him."

"What about her mother? Was she just as interested in exploiting her daughter?"

Samantha shook her head. "Too scared to stand up to her husband. He's mad at me because I encouraged Zelena to find her own voice and get free of his influence."

"You helped her sue for emancipation?"

"She knew it was the right thing to do. She just needed a little emotional support."

"And the money?"

"That was all on him, not me." Samantha paused while the waitress delivered their food. She waited until they were alone once more before continuing. "Tito was always looking for the big payout. The commercials Zelena made over the years didn't cut it for him. He finally got it with *Mommy's Little Helper*. Then he lost it all."

"How?" Rory took a bite of her burger.

"Greed got the better of him. Plain and simple. He trusted the wrong person. I don't know if you know this about him, but he's not the best at handling money. It seems to slip through his fingers as fast as he gets it."

Rory thought back to the day she'd first met Tito and how he was trying to skip out on the motel without paying. "I'm not surprised to hear that."

"When the money started coming in, he hired someone to handle it. An investment 'professional'." Samantha air-quoted the last word. "Only he turned out to be a con artist. Tito should have known better when he promised to double his money in a short period of time. Instead, he took off with it."

"Aren't there laws protecting underage actors?"

"They don't always work."

"So Zelena sued for emancipation after that."

"She might have forgiven him if he hadn't tried to hide it from her. She wanted to know how much money she had for college. He kept putting her off until he couldn't anymore and the truth came out. She cut all ties with her parents and moved in with me for a while." Samantha toyed with her salad. "Any money she made after that she handled herself. She put herself through college, got out of the acting business and started teaching. It's only recently that she got the urge to go back."

"Her father was packing up her apartment when I saw him."

Samantha stabbed the air with her fork. "Mark my words. Half of Zelena's stuff is going to end up on some auction site. Probably soon, real soon."

Rory thoughtfully chewed her burger. She made a mental note to look out for auction items associated with Zelena's name or her sitcom.

The two finished their lunches in silence.

Samantha pushed her empty salad plate to one side. "Even with all the problems with her family, Zelena didn't let it get her down. She used it as inspiration for her script, the one she was trying to find financing for when she died. There's been a lot of interest in it recently. Several people have contacted me about it."

"Why did they come to you?" Rory said.

"Everyone knows I used to manage her and she kept in touch

with me. They figured I could find out about it."

That seemed understandable to Rory. "Does Tito have to sign off on anything?"

Samantha gave a self-satisfied smile. "It's out of his hands. Zelena gave me the go ahead to try and sell it before she died. The contract she signed gives me full rights and control if anything happens to her."

Rory stared at her in astonishment. "So you get to keep all the money it earns?"

"That's right."

"Is that usual?"

"Doesn't matter. It's a done deal."

"When you told me about the script earlier, you didn't say anything about signing a deal with Zelena."

"Didn't want you wasting your time on something that isn't important." Samantha stood up and placed money on the table. "Lunch is on me. I'll let you know about any service I put together."

Rory stared, open-mouthed, at the woman as she walked toward the exit.

"All right, ladies." Penny addressed the four painting chapter members gathered on the lawn in front of the boutique house. She distributed small notepads and pens to each one of them. "Remember, we're looking for ideas for the future. We hardly did anything about decorating the outside of the boutique house this time. Next year we need to do better."

"What do you want us to do with these?" Teresa held up her notepad and pen.

"I know paper is a little old-fashioned, but it'll be easier for me to put a report together if I gather everyone's notepads at the end of the tour. Jot down whatever comes to mind. Write, draw, whatever. Whenever you see a Halloween decoration you particularly like, take a picture of it and write down your thoughts. You can email or text the photos to me, whichever you prefer. Are we ready?"

Everyone nodded and the group started moving down the street. Penny stopped Rory and touched her arm. "Is everything all right? You seem a little out of sorts."

"I'm fine." Rory did her best to smile and appear normal, but all she could think about was Jeanne and Toby and their rendezvous at the Vista View Motel.

Penny looked doubtfully at her. "Whatever's bothering you, I'm here if you want to talk." She moved to the front of the group and led the way to their first stop a block away.

Teresa fell back so she was walking beside Rory at the rear of the group. She eyed her curiously. "What was that about?"

"Nothing. I think Penny's just hyper-sensitive about everybody after what happened to Zelena." Rory smiled her biggest smile. "This should be fun. I've driven by some great decorations recently."

Moments later, the group stopped in front of a modern house that looked more like an office than somebody's home. Everyone exclaimed over a line of child-size ghosts that paraded across the lawn. One of them wore black plastic-rimmed glasses and carried a backpack.

Rory dutifully took a photo with her phone and jotted down possibilities for transforming the ghosts into painting enthusiasts. "We could put paint stains on some of the sheets and replace that backpack with a painted piece of wood," she said to Teresa who nodded enthusiastically and made her own notes.

The group continued walking up and down the blocks, taking photos and notes of everything they saw. They passed houses infested with gigantic spiders, their webs made of string, as well as lawns covered with giant-sized blow up pumpkins and ghosts.

Rory nudged Teresa when she spotted a skeleton sporting sunglasses walking his dog at the end of a leash. "I've never seen an animal skeleton as a decoration before. That's really cute."

The group was talking to a man who was describing the Halloween-themed light and music display he put on every evening when they heard the faint sound of breaking glass. He stopped talking and turned his attention in the direction the sound came from, everyone in the painting group following suit. Two bicyclists rounded the corner toward them, aiming pellet guns at windows as they passed by. The sound of shattering glass followed them up the street.

Rory aimed her cell phone at the two riders and began recording. The homeowner they had been talking to ran out in the middle of the street and shouted while Penny called the police on her cell.

As soon as they saw the group, the bicyclists skidded to a halt, their green-masked faces momentarily turned toward them, then turned around and took off in the direction they came from. Everyone gaped at them as they rounded the corner out of view.

"In broad daylight too! Do they want to get caught?" Teresa looked over at Rory. "Did you get pictures?"

"Better than that. Video."

Everyone clustered behind Rory and watched the video on her phone. Although the bicyclist's faces were completely covered by the masks and there were no identifying marks on their clothing, one of the beach cruisers had decals on the frame and so many spoke lights Rory was sure she'd recognize it if she ever saw it again.

The vandals were long gone when a police car rounded the corner. While Rory gave her statement to the officers and handed over the video, all she could think about was how tired she was of pranks and green masks.

Chapter 25

"That didn't take long. Samantha sure had him pegged." Her gold and silver bracelets jingling, Liz held up her phone so Rory could see the screen.

On a break from working at the boutique house late that afternoon, the two sat on the bench in the backyard, scanning auction sites for items marked as being associated or belonging to Zelena Alvarez.

Rory read the entry. "Looks like something I saw in her place. I was really hoping Samantha was wrong about Tito." A few minutes later, she found an entry on a different auction site. "Here's another one. 'Original Bear used on *Mommy's Little Helper*. Includes three one-of-a-kind costumes.' This is the Bear I saw on Zelena's bed. It's still wearing the astronaut outfit."

Liz shook her head in disbelief. "What a lousy father. Didn't even wait until she was buried. His daughter's death certainly seems to have benefited him big time. If that's not motive for murder, I don't know what is."

"I can't see him actually killing her. He's more of an opportunist."

"Probably going to sell his story to the tabloids next. He should get gobs of money for it. Maybe he already has. That could be where that wad of cash you saw came from."

Rory looked up from her phone. "I hadn't thought of that. He was supposed to give an exclusive interview to Veronica. Wouldn't that prevent him from making another deal?"

"I haven't seen anything on *VBC* or in the paper. He probably reneged on the deal. He never actually signed a contract, right? Seems the type to me. He might even sell the tabloids those 'stalker' photos if he can get hold of them."

"They're only on the burner phone. The police have that now."

Liz looked up, a questioning expression on her face. "Didn't you find some in her email?"

"That's right. I forgot about that. I sent a copy to myself and one to the police, but I left the original in her inbox. I should get rid of it just in case he gets access to her account."

Rory logged into Zelena's email account on her phone and deleted the message containing the photos. She quickly checked the rest of the inbox to see if there was anything else Tito could profit from. The only thing she found of interest was a draft of the script Zelena had been trying to get funding for. Curious about its contents, Rory sent it to her own account in case it might prove useful to the investigation.

"At least now he won't be able to sell those photos." Rory thought about all the times she'd talked to Zelena's father. "He really loved his daughter. I can't see him killing her."

"Like I said before, they could have had a fight. Lots of pushing and shoving. Zelena could have fallen off the pier or a dock somewhere."

Rory tapped her phone against her hand. "You know, I never heard anything about the autopsy results. I don't think the coroner's office has made them public yet."

"Didn't she drown?"

"Remember what Martin said when he came to see us that night? It sounded like there was something else going on besides drowning."

"Go. Call Dashing D and find out. Maybe we've been looking at this all wrong."

Rory shook her head. "I'd rather not ask him. I wouldn't want to put him in an awkward position. He probably won't tell me, anyway. He doesn't want us investigating. You saw his reaction when we followed Mrs. Griswold."

"You mean you, he doesn't want *you* investigating. There must be some other way to find out."

"I probably shouldn't look into any of it. I don't want to risk my relationship with him."

"We're just looking at reports. No danger in that."

"I am curious. What about that client of yours who transcribes autopsy reports? She helped us once before."

"No dice. She moved out of state and I don't know anyone else who can give us that information."

Rory screwed up her face in concentration. "Veronica might know something. She's pretty persistent. If anybody could find out about the autopsy results before they're made public, it would be her."

"I don't remember seeing anything in the *View* last week."

"Let's see what she's been reporting." Rory checked out the most recent posts on *Vista Beach Confidential.* "Here's something. Drowning was definitely the cause of death. But it looks like someone tried to strangle her first. And there was a contusion on her head."

"She must have fought back."

Rory put her phone on the bench between them. "That's assuming Veronica's sources are accurate."

"No reason to think they're not."

"Doesn't really help us much, though, in finding her killer."

"We'll find out more tonight when we see Raven."

"I don't know why you think she's going to be helpful."

"Can't hurt."

"While she's at it, maybe she can tell us who shot out those windows today too," Rory said half seriously.

"These pranks are really getting out of hand. Bouillon cubes in shower heads and fake ghosts are one thing, but this is destruction of property."

"There's going to be lots of pressure on the police to find

them."

"As if there wasn't already enough of that." Liz shoved her phone in her pocket and nodded toward the back door of the house. "Here comes the Annoying One." She lowered her voice. "Has she said anything to you about the motel?"

"Not a word. I don't think she saw me there. If she had, I think she would have said something by now or at least tried to avoid me. She hasn't done either one of those things." Rory pocketed her own cell phone and stood up. "We'd better get back to work."

Jeanne crossed the lawn and clapped her hands when she got close to them. "Come on. Break's over. You've got customers waiting at the escape room."

Liz wrapped her scarf around her head and the two of them followed the woman back inside the house.

"I think this is going to be a complete waste of time." Rory settled into the passenger seat of Liz's Lexus sedan later that evening and fastened her seatbelt.

"I know you don't believe in psychics, but we're at a dead end. It can't hurt." Liz backed out of the boutique house's driveway and headed down the block. "Besides, Raven knew where we'd find Zelena's body and all about the RV park."

Rory folded her arms in front of her chest. "She never mentioned Zelena was dead. You'd think a psychic would know that. She could have known about the RV some other way."

"How?"

Rory shrugged. "I don't know, but she *must* have found out some other way. I can't believe it was a vision."

"Just keep an open mind. That's all I ask."

As Liz traversed the streets for the short drive to Raven Leek's office for their ten p.m. appointment, Rory wondered what the psychic would tell them. When Liz first told her about consulting Raven, Rory hadn't wanted to go along, but curiosity won out.

Liz pulled into a parking lot. "We're here."

Rory stared through the passenger window at the two-story building that was their destination. "Doesn't this look familiar?"

"This is where we followed Granny G to the other night. You don't suppose...?"

"I don't remember seeing anything with Raven's name on it when I looked online. Maybe the building's website isn't up to date. Let's find out."

In the lobby of the building, the two consulted the directory, but found no office space for Raven Leek or anything that sounded like it was remotely associated with a spiritualist or psychic.

"Are you sure this is the place? I don't see her name here."

Liz brought up a text on her cell phone. "This is the right address. Suite 205."

Rory looked at the directory once again. Her gaze zeroed in on the suite number. "That's a moving company."

"I don't know anything about that. Suite 205 is the number she gave in her text. Let's go up and see."

The two took the elevator to the second floor and knocked on the partially open door of the suite.

"Come in," Raven Leek called out.

Liz pushed the door open and entered, followed closely by Rory.

"Close the door behind you." Raven smiled at the two of them from her place behind a metal desk. Everything about the room seemed ordinary from the utilitarian desk to the row of filing cabinets to the stack of collapsed boxes in one corner. Nothing about it screamed spiritualism or the supernatural. Not exactly the environment Rory envisioned a professional psychic doing business in.

Raven gestured toward the two metal chairs facing the desk. "Please."

"The directory said this office belongs to a moving company," Rory said as they sat down.

"A friend lets me use this space after normal close of business. Many people I see prefer evening appointments, anyway."

"Why not use your own house?" Rory said curiously.

"I'd rather not have people know where I live. I've had...problems in the past."

"How late do you work?"

"Depends on the client. Midnight appointments aren't out of the question." Raven held out her hand. "Did you bring what I asked for?"

Liz pulled a wad of cash out of her purse and pushed it across the desk.

Rory's mouth gaped open. "That much?" she whispered to Liz as Raven silently counted the bills. "You didn't say it was going to be that much."

Liz waved her hand to silence Rory.

"And the rest?" Raven said.

"There's more?" Rory whispered.

Liz ignored her and pulled a bottle of pills and a scarf out of her purse. "I don't know if these will help. She held the bottle and painted the scarf."

Raven closed her eyes and fingered each of the items. She shoved the pills across the desk and kept the other. "This will do nicely."

"How does this work?" Rory asked. "Are we talking tarot cards, palm reading, crystal ball...?"

Raven looked at her with a pitying glance. "None of those things. I use objects owned by a person to connect with their spirits."

"I didn't realize we were going to a séance."

"I don't like using that word. It has too many bad connotations." Raven sat up straighter in her chair. "Let's get started. Is there anything specific you want to know?"

Rory and Liz exchanged glances.

"Just who killed her, really," Liz said.

"And where," Rory added.

"I thought Edgar Geller was in custody."

"We're not convinced he did it. Neither are the police," Rory said.

Raven nodded. "I'll try, but sometimes spirits get confused and don't remember the details of how they died." She held the scarf in her hands and closed her eyes. "Please don't say anything until the spirit speaks to you, no matter what happens."

The minutes ticked by while they silently watched the psychic intone in a quiet voice for Zelena's spirit to join them.

Rory had almost given up on anything happening when Raven's head slumped forward and a higher-pitched voice came out of her mouth and spoke Rory's name. If she didn't know better, she would have sworn Zelena was in the room with them.

Rory's eyes widened. "Does that...?"

"That sounds just like Zelena's voice," Liz whispered.

Either the woman was a great mimic or there was something to this psychic business after all, Rory thought. But as far as she knew, the two had never met. Chills ran up her spine as Zelena's voice called out once again, "Rory, are you there?"

"I'm here."

"Ask her who killed her," Liz mouthed.

Rory cleared her throat. "Zelena, can you tell us who killed you?"

"Killed?" the voice said.

"You were murdered," Rory said softly. "Do you remember who did it?"

"Confused."

"How about where you went after you left the RV park?" Liz said.

"Murdered."

"That's right, you were murdered. Do you remember where it happened?" Rory asked.

"Water."

"That's right. You were found in the water. You drowned."

"I feel seasick."

"Were you on a boat?" Liz said.

"Boat," the voice repeated.

Rory wasn't sure if that was confirmation or merely repeating what Liz asked. "So you were on a boat when you died?"

"Boat," the voice repeated with more confidence, then faded away. Moments later, Raven straightened up and opened her eyes. "Did you get what you needed?"

"We're not sure," Rory said. "All she said was *boat*. The voice sounded like Zelena's, though."

Raven handed back the scarf. "Sometimes the spirits are very cryptic. You're lucky I made contact at all. We can try again another time if you like."

Rory and Liz exchanged glances.

"We'll let you know," Liz said.

"Are all sessions like that?" Rory said curiously.

"You were lucky. I don't always make contact. Sometimes a spirit refuses to talk to the person who hires me. Sometimes all I get is a vision."

"Do people only consult you to talk to a loved one who's passed on?" Liz asked. "Or do they ask you to predict the future?"

"I give all sorts of advice, love, investment... Did you have something in mind?"

"My neighbor, Mrs. Griswold—"

Raven held up a hand. "I don't discuss my clients with anyone."

"So she is a client?" Liz said.

"I think you should leave now." Raven walked them to the door and firmly closed it behind them.

"Struck a nerve, didn't we?" Rory said when they were alone in the elevator. "That was a bit—"

"Creepy." Liz shuddered.

"You have to let me pay for half of it."

"Don't worry about it. It's on me. It was my idea in the first place. Not sure we got much out of it."

"She did talk about a boat."

"Do you think Zelena was trying to give us a clue?"

"You don't really think that was her, do you?" Rory said.

"How else do you explain the voice?"

"It did sound like her, didn't it? I'm sure there's a reasonable explanation. Do you know if she ever met Raven?"

"Not as far as I know." Liz took her car keys out of her purse as they exited the building.

Once they were on their way, Rory said, "Maybe there's something to that boat idea, though." She twisted in her seat to face Liz. "What if Zelena was on a boat right before she died?"

"Then the murderer dropped her overboard and her body washed ashore!" An excited gleam in her eyes, Liz pounded her hands on the steering wheel. The car careened down the street, occasionally drifting across the center line.

Rory clutched the armrest, only loosening her grip when the car was once again solidly in its lane and proceeding at a normal pace. "Her father said she was afraid of the ocean and couldn't swim. Do you know if anyone who knew Zelena has a boat?"

"Not offhand, but I'm sure I can find out. Leave it to me." Liz glanced over at Rory. "That bit about Granny G was interesting. What do you think she's consulting Raven about?"

"I don't know, but it worries me. At least now we know where she's been going so late at night. I wonder how long it's been going on."

On the rest of the drive home, Rory thought about her neighbor. If the fee Liz paid was any indication, all the sessions must be making a big dent in the woman's retirement income. No wonder she wanted a part-time job.

Rory made a mental note to talk to her neighbor and see if there was anything she could do to help. Mrs. Griswold had never struck Rory as someone who would consult psychics. She wondered what had changed in the woman's life to suddenly make her a believer.

Late that evening, Rory was getting ready for bed when she heard strange noises outside. She paused with her toothbrush in her hand

and listened intently. A series of thumps sounded, louder this time.

She walked into the kitchen and found Sekhmet perched on the table, her gaze riveted on something in the backyard. Rory peered out the window into the darkness. The lights from Mrs. Griswold's property were out, making it hard to see anything.

"What do you see?" Rory asked her cat who growled in response.

Moments later, what looked like disembodied glowing eyes crossed the lawn.

"Friend of yours? I bet it got into the trash can. I'd better go check."

Rory grabbed a flashlight and headed out the back door to see what damage had been done. She frowned when she rounded the corner and spotted her trash and recycling bins. Instead of sitting neatly against the detached garage, they were on their sides, garbage bags and recyclables spilling out onto the lawn.

She was bending down to right one of the bins when someone grabbed her from behind and placed a gloved hand over her mouth. Rory's brain screamed at her to fight back, but her body refused to respond. Moments later, something poked into the middle of her back and a computer-generated voice said, "I've got a gun. Don't try anything. Just listen. Forget about finding out what happened to your friend. If you don't, there will be consequences. This is your only warning. Count to one hundred before you turn around."

Moments later, the hand and pressure were gone and she heard footsteps fading into the distance. She started counting out loud. She'd barely gotten to thirty when she dared to turn around. No one was in sight.

Leaving the upended bins where they were, she raced inside to call Martin to tell him what happened.

Chapter 26

Rory slept fitfully that night, barely getting up in time for church the next morning. Right after the service, she headed straight to the police station. She'd just settled down at a desk when the phone rang. "Vista Beach Police Department tip line. Rory Anderson speaking."

She listened carefully and jotted down the information on her call sheet. Another spotting of Zelena in the days before her body washed up on the beach, this one in a bar in a neighboring city.

So far, all of these purported sightings had been cases of mistaken identity, but it wasn't her call to ignore it. Someone from the department would follow up on each and every tip just in case one of them could provide information that would lead to Zelena's killer.

Her stomach grumbled while she waited for the next call to come in. She'd been so out of sorts since the warning the previous evening, she'd skipped breakfast and forgotten to bring something to munch on.

As if reading her mind, Martin Green set a twenty ounce bottle of diet Coke and packages of vending machine size pretzels and chocolate chip cookies on the desk in front of her. "Thought you might be hungry."

"Thanks." Rory took a sip of the soda before opening the bag of pretzels.

He pulled a chair over and sat down beside her. "How are you doing?"

"Better. Last night seems like a dream. Thanks for staying over. I don't think I could have slept if I was alone in the house."

"You don't remember anything more?"

Rory shook her head. "It was dark and whoever it was came up behind me. I was bending down so I can't even tell you how tall they were."

"I can have an officer assigned to protect you, if you want."

After what happened last night, Rory thought how nice it would be to have someone keeping her safe. But, she knew she needed to be able to function on her own. She wouldn't let whoever confronted her force her to give up her independence. "Thanks, but I need to feel normal."

"Okay. Promise me you'll be extra careful, especially at night."

"I promise."

He looked at the pad of paper in front of her. "Anything interesting?"

She shoved the call log toward him. "Hard to say. Everyone who calls is adamant they saw Zelena. Some even saw a mysterious figure following her. No one could describe him, of course."

Martin studied the list. "We'll follow up. You never know where something might lead."

"I was thinking...what if Zelena was on a boat and she went overboard? Have you looked into that?"

"Interesting possibility. What made you think of that?"

"Oh, you know, something someone said."

"Uh-huh." A volunteer waved at the detective from across the room. "Gotta go. Let me know if anything promising crops up."

Rory polished off her snacks in record time. She'd barely sat back down in her chair after a short bathroom break when the phone rang once again. She glanced at the caller id, *Unknown Caller*, and jotted the information down in a slot on the call sheet.

After Rory identified herself, she waited for someone to speak, but all she heard was a faint rustling sound and someone breathing.

"Hello? Is anyone there?"

Eventually the caller responded to her repeated *hellos*. A muffled voice with a heavy accent said a few garbled words. The only thing Rory could make out was Zelena's name.

"I'm sorry. Could you speak up, please? I can barely hear you."

The caller spoke loudly and clearly this time, shedding all pretense of an accent. "I said, I saw that psychic, Raven something or other at Ocean View Rest Stop. You should look into her."

Rory's ears perked up. "The RV park? When was this?"

"The day before that woman's body was found, the famous one. This Raven person was hanging around the parking lot."

Rory furrowed her brow in thought. Something about the voice seemed familiar, but she couldn't quite place it. "Can I have your name?"

"I thought this was anonymous."

"It can be, if you like. Hold on, I'll get the detective on the case. He might have more questions for you." Rory waved her arm to get Martin's attention. As soon as she pointed to the phone, he headed in her direction. "I have someone for you to talk to." She handed the receiver to him. He identified himself and, seconds later, hung up the phone without saying another word.

"What happened?" Rory said.

"They hung up."

"She did sound a bit skittish."

"What did she tell you?"

Rory recounted what the caller had said about Raven Leek.

"Interesting. Did she give her name?"

"No. She wanted to remain anonymous. She tried to disguise her voice at first, but I'm sure I've heard it before."

"She mentioned the RV park. Could it have been someone you talked to there?"

Rory snapped her fingers. "Of course, the woman with the frying pan. Remember, I told you about her?"

"She was never around when we stopped by. I assumed she'd left. I'd better get over there and see if I can find out more. I'll make sure someone follows up on Raven too." He glanced at the clock on the wall. "I've got a few hours before the party tonight. Don't worry, I don't see any reason why I can't pick you up on time."

Rory spent the rest of her shift on the tip line itching to call Liz and tell her about Raven. She suppressed the urge until the next volunteer took over. She finally got hold of her friend when she was walking from her car to the boutique house.

"How'd your time on the tip line go? Anything good come in?" Liz said.

"That woman we met at the RV park called. She saw Raven in the parking lot when Zelena was still there."

"What?!"

Rory heard the "what" in stereo, through the phone and behind her. She turned around and found Liz, decked out for her time in the escape room, heading up the walkway toward her. They both hung up and moved to the side, leaving the path clear for people to enter the boutique house. Huddling next to the bushes, they talked in low tones so they wouldn't be overheard.

"Give me the blow-by-blow. What did the caller say?"

Rory tried as best she could to report the conversation word for word.

"And you're sure it was that woman from the RV park? The scary lady with the frying pan?"

"Pretty sure. Martin's checking it out now."

Liz put her finger to her lips and paced in front of the flowers. "She didn't say a lot, did she?"

"Maybe she'll tell Martin more when she talks to him face-to-face, though I wonder if she'll still be at the RV park. She's really distrustful of the police. I wonder why."

"Do you think Raven was following up on her premonition? The one she told Veronica about."

"Let's see. That article came out on Monday so Veronica interviewed Raven before that." Rory snapped her fingers. "I bet that's where she was going after we talked to Edgar on Sunday at the volleyball game."

"That was *after* Zelena's body was found."

"So much for her vision."

"That doesn't mean she's not legit," Liz said. "She could have had the vision and gone there to check it out. She just didn't tell anyone about it until after Zelena's body was found."

Rory looked around and lowered her voice. "Something else happened last night. Someone...visited me." Panic set in as memories of the warning flooded her brain. She took a few deep breaths. When she felt calmer, she told her friend what happened.

"A gun?" Liz's voice rose. "They had a gun?"

"Something poked me in the back. Couldn't tell you if it was a gun or not. I didn't really want to find out."

"You must have been so scared."

"I just froze."

"And you have no idea who it was?"

"It happened so fast and it was dark."

Liz hugged her. "I'm glad you're okay. And I'm glad Dashing D came to the rescue."

The curtains on the nearby window parted and eyes peered out at them. Moments later, the front door opened and Jeanne stepped out. "Are you two planning on working or are you just going to dilly dally all night?"

The two dutifully went inside and headed up the stairs to the escape room.

The sun had barely gone down Sunday evening when Rory stepped out of her car. Her next-door neighbor's motion sensor light came on, partially lighting up her driveway that was on the opposite side of her property from Mrs. Griswold's house. She looked around nervously.

A figure clothed in a hooded cape stepped out of the shadows and called her name.

Rory's heart leapt into her throat. She moved behind her open car door to shield herself from the mysterious figure. It stepped forward and lowered its hood, revealing silver blue hair.

"I didn't mean to startle you," Raven Leek said. "Could I talk to you?"

The pounding of Rory's heart lessened. "What about?"

"Zelena and the RV park."

Rory took her phone out of her pocket in case the conversation took an ugly turn and she needed to call for help. "Why did you come to see me? You're better off going to the police."

"The spirits sent me."

Rory cocked her head.

"Okay, fine. I thought you might help me with them. Put in a good word with that boyfriend of yours. I heard the police are looking for me. I gather someone called the tip line about my visit to Ocean View Rest Stop."

"How did you find out? And don't tell me the spirits told you."

"I have contacts at the station. Comes in handy sometimes."

I bet it does, Rory thought. Someone in the police department would have access to all kinds of information that a "psychic" could find useful. "Is it true? That you were at the RV park? Why did you go there?"

Raven looked around a little nervously. "Can we go inside and talk? I'll tell you anything you want, but I feel a little exposed out here."

As soon as they were inside, Raven took off her cape, revealing a black sweater and dress pants, and sat down on the sofa. "Could I bother you for a cup of tea before we start? Peppermint if you have it."

After the tea was served, Rory settled back in her chair. "You have your tea. What did you want to tell me? Start with why you went to the park."

Raven took a sip, then put her cup down on the coffee table in front of her. "I wanted to talk to Edgar."

"You knew he was there? How?"

"He hired me to go to the police and tell them about a vision I had of Zelena, the one I told you about. It wasn't a real one, but he was offering a lot of money for my help. He said he'd pay me in advance, but he didn't. When the police wouldn't let me tell them about the vision, he refused to see me or take my calls so I went to the RV park to see if I could find him. I'd overheard him talking about it one day."

So that's how she knew about the park, Rory thought. No psychic vision after all. "You knew about the publicity stunt and said nothing?"

"Psychic sessions don't pay all of the bills. I have to...improvise sometimes."

From the amount the woman charged, Rory figured she would have plenty of money, but who knew how much of a spendthrift she was. Maybe that was the real reason she didn't want clients coming to her house. She didn't want them seeing how much she owned. "Go on. You went to the park."

"When I got there, I looked around, but wasn't sure which RV Edgar was in. I was heading to my car when I saw Zelena storm out of one of them. She walked straight toward me and asked if I could give her a lift into town."

Rory sucked in her breath. This was it, the break they had been waiting for. "Did she know who you were?"

The psychic shook her head. "I don't think so. We never talked before and I'm pretty sure Edgar never told her about me. He likes to be the only one who knows the 'big picture.' Gives him complete control."

Rory's eyes narrowed. "So she just asked a stranger for a ride?" That didn't fit with the Zelena Rory knew who cautioned her students to not take rides from anyone they didn't know.

"People tell me I exude an aura of peacefulness and healing."

"Where did you take her?"

"I dropped her off at the edge of downtown near that gas station."

From there, Zelena could have walked anywhere, Rory thought. "Did you see what direction she went in?"

"She walked into an alley. I don't know what happened after that. She put up the hood of her sweatshirt and hunched over. I doubt anyone would recognize her."

"What time was this?"

"Not sure of the exact time, middle of the day, oneish, maybe a little later."

Not long after Zelena called me, Rory thought. That backed up what Edgar told them. "So that's how you know what Zelena's voice sounds like. You're a good mimic, by the way."

"You think I'm a fraud."

"Aren't you? Is that what Zelena thought too? Was she threatening to expose you?"

"Like I said, we'd never met before. She didn't know who I was when I drove her into town."

Rory studied the woman. "What about the vision you told us about at the silent movie theater? If Edgar didn't pay you, why did you go through with it?"

"After I finally got hold of him, we talked about Zelena. He said she was taking a break but would be back. Then he gave me some money so I figured I'd go ahead with the plan. Since the police wouldn't talk to me at the station, I decided I'd approach the detective on the case in a more casual setting. I didn't know she was dead. Look, I didn't have anything to do with her death. I have no motive. Besides, I had appointments right after I dropped her off. You'll put in a good word for me?"

"Just one more thing. When you picked Zelena up, did she have her purse with her?"

"Sure. Why wouldn't she?"

Rory picked up her cell phone. "You're going to tell all this to the police, okay?" After the woman nodded her agreement, Rory dialed Martin's number and explained the situation to him.

Chapter 27

At her place later that evening, Rory got ready for the party at the boutique house with Liz's help. She wrapped a corset around her body. Once it was in place, Liz grabbed the ends of the laces and pulled until Rory felt as if her ribs were in danger of cracking.

"Stop! Stop! Not so tight. I can't breathe."

Liz loosened the corset so Rory felt more comfortable. "Now you know what women in the 1800s had to deal with."

"I should have picked a costume that doesn't need a torture garment."

"You don't have to wear it."

"I'm not sure the dress will fit without it."

Liz helped her put on the rest of the outfit. Rory viewed herself in the mirror, turning so she could see the floor length red satin dress with black underskirt from several angles. With her hair up and neck exposed, she looked as if she'd just stepped out of the Victorian era. She tugged on the black ruffle on the front of the dress, trying to make the neckline a little higher.

Liz batted her hands. "Stop it."

"I don't usually wear anything this low cut. I should have gotten the one with the higher neckline."

"Wouldn't have worked as well as this one. Besides, you look great. Now for the finishing touches." Liz drew two large dots on Rory's neck with red blood trickling out of them. "Voila! You are now the victim of a vampire. You and Dashing D will be the hit of the party."

Rory gingerly sat down on her bed to make sure she could breathe in that position. "Thanks for your help. Are you wearing your Madame Elizabeth costume?"

"Yep. I volunteered to work the escape room during the party." Liz glanced at her watch. "Yikes, I'd better get moving."

Rory had barely closed the front door on Liz when a knock sounded. She opened it to find Martin Green standing on the porch, wearing a black T-shirt and jeans, the black cape with red lining draped around his shoulders. His eyes lit up when he saw her. He opened his mouth, exposing fangs. "What a lovely throat you have," he said in an accent reminiscent of Bela Lugosi playing Dracula.

"Ah, you say that to all the girls." Rory stepped aside so he could enter. "I'm almost ready. I just need to get my reticule."

Martin raised an eyebrow.

"Drawstring purse. I need somewhere to put my phone and keys. Can't leave the twenty-first century completely behind."

"Before we go, I need to talk to you about something."

Rory's heart raced at his words. Hoping they weren't a precursor to a breakup talk, she led the way into the living room and sat down on the edge of the couch. "What is it?"

Martin sank down onto the chair. "It's about Raven and Mrs. Griswold."

She breathed a sigh of relief. "Oh. What about them?"

"You don't seem surprised they know each other."

"I know Mrs. Griswold is seeing Raven in a psychic capacity."

"She told you that?"

Rory shook her head. "I heard about it...somewhere. Don't worry. I didn't follow her. How did you find out?"

"Raven gave me a list of the clients she saw after she dropped Zelena off in town. Mrs. Griswold was on it. I'd like to ask her about the visit."

Rory cocked her head, a puzzled expression on her face. "So ask her. You've talked to her many times."

"I feel like this one's a bit more...delicate. Would you go with me?"

"Sure. Just let me get something before we go next door."

When Mrs. Griswold opened her front door, Rory held out a plate of frosted sugar cookies. "We thought you might like some Halloween treats. I made them myself." She nudged Martin who said, "Happy Halloween."

Rory's neighbor raised an eyebrow at the couple in their costumes, but didn't say anything about how they were dressed. Her eyes lit up at the sight of the pumpkin-shaped cookies, then her expression quickly turned to one of suspicion. She took the plate and gestured for them to come inside.

After they were all settled down in the living room and the tea was poured, Mrs. Griswold leaned back in her recliner and said, "What's this really about?"

The detective put down his cup and pulled out his notebook. "I need your help."

Mrs. Griswold raised an eyebrow. "There haven't been any break-ins or other criminal activity on the block, as far as I know."

"That's not what I need your help with. It's about Raven Leek."

She glared at Rory. "Did you follow me again?"

Rory shrank back on the floral print sofa under the woman's angry gaze.

"No, ma'am," the detective said. "She didn't follow you. Ms. Leek told me about you herself. She said you could vouch for her whereabouts on Thursday evening, week before last. Said you were with her at..." he consulted his notebook and read out the address of the building the psychic used as her office.

"Why do you need to know?"

"It has to do with the murder of Zelena Alvarez." The detective let that sink in before continuing. "Ma'am, were you with Ms. Leek on the date she said?"

Mrs. Griswold stared off into the distance for a bit, then turned her attention back to them and slowly nodded. "Yes, I was with her that evening."

"What time?"

"Twelve thirty a.m. to about one thirty a.m."

"An odd time for an appointment, isn't it?"

Mrs. Griswold pursed her lips. "She said the spirits were more receptive then."

"So you're a client of her psychic services?"

"A gentleman friend of mine passed away recently. She's helping me contact him. That's all I'll say."

"How did she seem?"

"Her usual self. I didn't notice any difference from the other times I saw her."

"How often is that?"

"I have standing appointments on Wednesdays and Sundays."

"But this was a Thursday."

"We were making progress so I scheduled another appointment for the next day." Mrs. Griswold got up from her recliner, effectively ending the conversation. "I don't mean to be inhospitable, but I'm a little tired."

When they got to the door, Martin handed her his card. "If you ever need anything, give me a call. I don't like to see anyone being taken advantage of."

Mrs. Griswold seemed about to refuse, but she finally nodded and took the card. She was staring at it thoughtfully when Rory stepped outside.

"Rory, could you stay? I'd like to talk with you about something. It'll only take a few minutes."

"Just let me tell Martin what's going on." She headed down the walkway to where he was waiting for her.

He looked at her, a question in his eyes.

"She wants to talk to me. If I can, I'll let you know what she says. I shouldn't be too long. Wait for me."

"I'll be in the car."

When Rory sat down once again on the couch in Mrs. Griswold's living room, the woman said, "I need your advice."

Rory waited in silence for her to continue. She knew it wasn't easy for the fiercely independent woman to ask for help of any kind.

"I'm beginning to have my doubts about Raven Leek."

"Why?"

"You probably don't believe in all this psychic hoo-haw. Before my gentleman friend died, I'm not sure I did either. Maybe now I just want to believe."

"Why do you want to contact him?"

Mrs. Griswold looked out the window before replying. "The last time I saw him, we had a big argument. I said some horrible things. He died before I had a chance to apologize. That's all I want to do, to apologize and tell him I love him." She wiped a tear from the corner of her eye.

"That's why you contacted Raven?"

"She contacted me, actually. I bumped into her in the grocery store. She seemed to sense I had a problem. She said she could help me. I didn't realize it would cost so much."

"Tell me what happened."

"She seemed to understand me. Despite the difference in our ages, we had so much in common and I didn't have to tell her about my friend, she just knew." Mrs. Griswold took a sip of tea. "She got in touch with him, but he wouldn't talk to me. Said I was too attached to material things. That's what we argued about—money. She told me to give her some money and she'd put it in a jar. I could access it anytime. She said it was an exercise in letting go of wealth. It would help convince him to talk with me."

Rory stayed silent, but she didn't like where this story was going.

"It seemed to be working," Mrs. Griswold continued. "He gave me a few minutes, but he still refused to accept my apology. Raven said that would take more letting go. So I gave her a lot—more than I can afford, really. Now I'm not so sure about it."

"That's why you need a part-time job?"

"That's right. Your mother was nice enough to give me one. I know she probably doesn't need the help."

"Why don't you just ask for the money back? She said you could have it anytime."

"Do you think I should? What about my friend? I don't want to risk his being mad at me. He might never accept my apology then."

"I'm sure he wouldn't want you to be in bad shape financially because of him." Rory chose her next words carefully. "There may be real psychics out there. I'm open to the possibility, but I don't think Raven Leek is one of them."

"You think she's a fraud?"

"I don't know for sure, but I wouldn't be surprised. If she's sincere, she'll give you your money back. Go on, call her. I'll be right here."

Mrs. Griswold nodded and picked up her phone.

From what Rory heard of the conversation, she could tell it wasn't going well. When it was over, she said, "She refused?"

"I'm not sure what to do now."

"I think you should talk to Mart—Detective Green and lodge a complaint. He might be able to help you get your money back. He's right outside, waiting for me. I can go get him." She stood up.

"I don't want to appear like a gullible old woman." Mrs. Griswold eyed Rory's dress. "And it looks like you're on the way to a party."

"The party can wait. We don't have to be there at any particular time. He won't judge you. I'm sure something similar has happened to a lot of other people. It's her fault, not yours."

Mrs. Griswold nodded her head in agreement and Rory headed out the door to get the detective.

Chapter 28

"Get something to drink, everyone. I want to make a toast," Penny Worthington said to the group of painting chapter members, volunteers and guests gathered in the living room of the boutique house.

Partygoers hovered around the bar area, waiting for their drink orders to be filled. Martin joined them, fetching glasses of champagne for himself as well as Rory and Liz.

As soon as everyone had a glass in their hands, Penny continued. "I'd like to thank all of you for helping to make this such a successful event. We wouldn't have been able to do it without every single one of you." She raised her glass and they all followed suit. "To another successful year."

"And to Zelena," someone in the back of the room shouted. "Zelena," everyone said before they drank from their glasses.

No sooner had the woman's name been mentioned than her father entered the living room, glancing uneasily around him.

Penny looked momentarily startled when she saw him, then smiled and gestured for Tito to join her at the front of the crowd. "As you all so rightly pointed out, Zelena was an important part of the Halloween Holiday Boutique. She got the idea years ago before many of us became chapter members. I'm dedicating this year's event to her. She was and will continue to be missed. Let's have a moment of silence in appreciation for all of her hard work." She bowed her head and closed her eyes.

The crowd remained quiet, only an occasional sniffle or cough breaking the silence.

After an appropriate amount of time had passed, Penny continued, "I'd like to thank the following people in particular. Hold the applause until the end, please." She turned to look at each one as she called out their name. "Rory, for creating and maintaining our chapter website. Liz, for keeping track of sales and registrations. Teresa, for managing our funds and making sure we kept on budget. Arika, for providing sales support. And, of course, my husband Toby, for donating his time and talent to create a wonderful escape room experience."

An awkward silence filled the room as everyone waited for the chapter president to call out Jeanne's name, but Penny merely clapped her hands, indicating she was finished with her remarks. When no one followed her lead, she looked around, a puzzled expression on her face.

"Um, Penny." Rory looked over at Jeanne who stood to one side, a stiff smile on her face. "I think you forgot someone?"

"Oh, who?"

Rory darted another glance toward Jeanne, hoping Penny would get the hint.

Penny gave a nervous laugh. "Oh, of course. How stupid of me. My apologies. To Jeanne, for keeping us honest and running the whole show."

A smattering of applause broke out and everyone drank once again. While others proposed their own toasts, Liz whispered to Rory so only she could hear, "That was odd. Maybe Penny does know about the affair."

"Maybe," Rory whispered back.

Once all of those who wanted to talk had finished, Penny said, "Go, have fun, everyone. There's plenty to eat and drink and don't forget the escape room. It'll be open the rest of the night. Get a group together and try it out if you haven't already. I'd like to thank Liz and Teresa for giving up their party time and continuing to run the escape room experience for the staff. As a special treat, everyone can sign up to have your tarot cards read by a genuine psychic."

"It's not Raven Leek," Rory said when Martin raised an eyebrow at the mention of the tarot card reader. "Her name's Gayelette. She's a friend of one of our chapter members."

"Didn't realize there were so many psychics in the area."

The group dispersed, many of them heading straight for the dining room where Gayelette sat at a table waiting for her first customer.

Penny turned to Tito and held out her hand. "Mr. Alvarez, so good to see you here. I didn't realize you were joining us."

He glanced over at Jeanne who was heading down the hallway toward the kitchen. "Miss Cayce invited me."

"Of course. I'm sorry I didn't think of it myself. So much to do. You understand. I'm glad you could be here to see how much your daughter contributed to our chapter and how much we appreciated her. Enjoy the evening."

Penny moved around the room, greeting guests. Tito looked around as if unsure what to do next.

"Why don't you join us in the escape room, Mr. Alvarez?" Rory said.

"What's an escape room?"

"You're locked in a room with a group of people. You have an hour to solve puzzles and find the key to the door. Zelena was looking forward to trying it out. I wish she could have seen it in action."

"Thank you. I'd like to see it. It sounds interesting."

Liz slipped into her Madame Elizabeth persona, calling out for people to join her. She led the way upstairs with Martin, Rory and Tito following closely behind.

Rory and Liz entered the escape room to make sure it was ready while the others waited outside for a large enough group to gather. After they walked around the room, checking to make sure all of the clues were in place, Liz said, "I think we're ready. Let the first group in."

Half a dozen partygoers, including the detective and Zelena's father, entered the room while Teresa closed and locked the door behind them.

"You're staying?" Martin said to Rory.

"I want to see you in action. I can't participate, though, since I know all of the answers. Sorry, but I can't give you any hints, either."

While Madame Elizabeth began her spiel, Rory sat down on the trunk that stood against one wall and watched. Her gaze swept the room, taking in the decor once again. Liz was finishing up when Rory brought her attention back to the group.

"...called you in to help find her. You have one hour to save Endora. Search the room for clues, piece together the evidence and solve the mystery of the missing medium."

"Can we ask for help?" someone in the group asked.

"I can give you three hints, that's all. Begin." Liz waved her hand and stepped to the side where she sat down on the trunk beside Rory and waited for someone to ask for help.

Everyone seemed to defer to the detective who listened carefully to all of the suggestions before giving his own opinion. Tito soon lost interest and walked around the room, looking at the furniture and decorations, occasionally pausing to study the photos and paintings of the purported relatives of the missing Madame Endora. After he completed a circuit of the room, he joined the two women and leaned against the wall next to them.

"Who put this together?" he asked. "It's very detailed."

"Toby Worthington. He owns Escape Key, a business in town." Rory glanced around the room. "He did a good job, didn't he?"

"Where did he get all of it from?" Tito asked.

"He told me he rented most of it from one of those businesses that provides props for film and television," Rory said. "At least that's where the furniture came from. Not sure about the smaller items. He has a stash of things just like these at his business in town. They might have come from there. He's here at the party. You can ask him yourself."

The three of them watched the group follow clue after clue with the detective lending his expertise, but not dominating the experience. Less than forty-five minutes later, the group completed the task, finding the key to the door hidden in the backing of a painting that hung on the wall.

"That's a record." Rory clapped when the detective unlocked the door. She walked over and kissed him. "Well done. You didn't even have to ask for any clues."

He grinned. "It was a group effort, though I admit it would hurt my credibility and pride as a police detective if I needed too much help."

They exited the room and the next group moved inside with Liz and Teresa exchanging places.

Everyone in their group headed down the stairs, chatting about the escape room experience. Rory and Martin parted ways with Tito at the food table set up in the kitchen. Martin filled a plate with food while Rory walked over to Toby who was standing in front of the open refrigerator door, looking inside.

"Hiding out in the kitchen?" she said.

Toby took a plastic-wrapped platter of cut up veggies out of the refrigerator and placed it on the counter. "Just making sure everyone has enough food."

"I've been meaning to tell you how impressed everyone is with the escape room you put together for us. It's been a big hit."

Martin walked over to stand beside Rory. "I agree. Lots of fun puzzles. I liked all the details, especially all the photos of the relatives. Made me feel like Endora is a real person."

Rory nodded her head. "My favorite was the one of the biker and his mom."

"I'm glad you both liked it." He turned to the detective. "How's the murder investigation going? Any news?"

"We're following up on some leads."

"I hope you catch whoever did it soon. I'd better get these into the living room. I expect to see you two at Escape Key sometime." Toby picked up the vegetable platter and headed down the hall toward the front of the house.

After Rory filled her plate, they headed back toward the living room. As they walked past the dining room door, Martin glanced inside where Jeanne sat listening intently to what the tarot card reader was saying. "Are you going to get your cards read?"

Rory shook her head. "I've had enough of psychics. I'll leave it for everyone else."

Time flew by as they ate and listened to a variety of music piped through speakers placed throughout the house. Whenever they joined a group, talk inevitably turned to Zelena's death and the ongoing investigation. Martin simply smiled and steered the conversation away from the subject.

Rory was in the kitchen refilling her plate when she noticed Toby and Penny in the backyard, standing beside the bench. Moments later, he stormed off, heading down the side of the house toward the street instead of coming inside. Penny sat down on the bench and buried her head in her hands.

Rory left her plate in the kitchen and stepped outside. She stopped in front of Penny and gently said the woman's name. "Is there anything I can do?"

Penny lifted her head and gave a wan smile. "No, but thanks for asking."

Rory sank down onto the bench beside the woman. "I know why you're so upset."

"You do?"

"I saw them the other day at the Vista View Motel. It was an accident. I wasn't following Toby or Jeanne or anything. I just happened to be there."

Penny looked up, surprise written all over her face.

"I'm sorry, I shouldn't have said anything." Rory stood up. "Let me know if you need anything or you want to talk."

Penny laid a hand on Rory's arm. "It's okay. I've known about them for a while now. Thank you for your concern." She pushed back her shoulders and held her head high. "Let's go back inside and have some fun." She linked her arm in Rory's and chatted as if nothing were wrong as they made their way into the house.

Rory was heading back to join Martin when she stopped at the entrance to the dining room to watch the tarot card reader at work. To her surprise she found Tito Alvarez sitting across from Gayelette who was instructing him to cut the cards to get his energy on them. After she dealt them out, she glanced up and smiled.

Rory smiled uncertainly in return and continued toward the living room.

Right before they were going to leave, Rory headed upstairs looking for an open bathroom, finally finding the one sandwiched between two bedrooms empty. She closed and locked both doors. She was drying her hands when she heard a voice in one of the adjoining rooms. When Rory pressed her ear against the door, she heard someone speaking in accented English say, "If you don't want your secret to come out, you'll meet me. Midnight. Diner. Okay?" A pause where Rory couldn't hear anything followed by Tito saying, "That's right, midnight."

She exited the bathroom through the other bedroom and hurried into the hallway, hoping to catch whoever Tito had been talking with. But the only person around was Liz who was standing next to the escape room door.

Rory drew her friend aside. "Did you see who came out of that bedroom?" She pointed to the one down the hall she'd heard Tito in.

"Just Mr. Alvarez."

"No one else?"

"Not that I saw. Why?"

"I heard him in there talking to someone. Not sure who. I only heard his voice. I'm going to check to see if anyone's in there right now." Rory headed down the hall and peeked around the corner of the open door. As far as she could tell, no one was inside. When she rejoined Liz, she said, "It's empty. Is there any other exit from that bedroom? A balcony or something?"

"No balcony on that one. Anybody in there would have to enter this hall or go through the Jack and Jill bathroom."

"I was in that bathroom. That's how I heard him."

"Then he was in there by himself. Maybe he was on the phone. What did he say?"

As accurately as possible, Rory told her what she'd overheard.

Liz whistled. "Sounds like blackmail to me. I wonder where the meet is happening. All you heard was diner."

Rory furrowed her brow in thought. "There's only one restaurant in the area that's open at midnight that I'd call a diner. Buddy's."

"I wonder what he's got on someone."

"No clue, but maybe we should go and find out."

"Do you think we should? What about that warning you got?"

Rory considered the question. "We'll stick together. Nothing can happen then."

Wearing nondescript clothes with her hair concealed under a ball cap, Rory sat across from Liz in a booth in Buddy's Rockin' Diner. From their vantage point in the back of the restaurant, they could see both the front and side entrances. Even though it was almost midnight, half the booths and tables in the diner were occupied. The only twenty-four hour restaurant in town, it was the place to go for those late night cravings.

Rory glanced at the clock on the wall in front of her. She leaned forward and said in a low voice, "Ten minutes to midnight. Do you see anything yet?"

"Nothing so far. What's the plan?"

"See who Tito meets, that's all. I doubt we'll be able to overhear anything, but just knowing who he thinks he has dirt on could be useful."

"Does Dashing D know you're here?"

"I don't tell him every time I go out with friends for dessert." Rory took a bite of her chocolate pie. "Of course, this might not be the diner he meant, anyway."

"It has to be. Nothing else makes sense."

They waited in silence for Tito and his mystery appointment to appear.

"He's coming in the front door now." Liz gave an almost imperceptible nod toward the entrance.

Rory pulled her cap down and glanced over her shoulder. She breathed a sigh of relief when Tito settled into a booth on the other side of the restaurant. They waited on pins and needles to see who would join him. The minutes ticked by and nothing happened.

Rory looked over her shoulder once again. "He seems nervous."

"He keeps on looking at his watch." Liz sat up straighter. "This might be it. Is that the…tarot card reader from the party?"

"He couldn't have been talking to her on the phone. She was with people all night." Rory hazarded another glance over her shoulder. Gayelette stopped next to Tito's booth, her body shielding Rory from the man's view.

The psychic stood talking and gesturing to him for a few minutes. Rory strained to hear anything they said above the clatter of the diner, but they were too far away and the restaurant was too noisy. Moments later, Tito threw cash on the table and stormed out the side entrance.

"Is that it?" Liz leaned over and whispered.

Rory shrugged.

As soon as he left, Gayelette headed toward the front door. She paused as if she sensed them watching her. She turned around and met Rory's gaze.

Rory hunched over her plate, pulled down her cap and focused her attention on her food, willing the psychic to leave.

"She's coming this way," Liz whispered.

Moments later, Gayelette stood beside their table. "I didn't expect to see so many people from the party here." An amused expression lit up her face. "Before you say 'You're a psychic, you should have known', it doesn't work that way."

"So I've heard." Rory took off her cap, letting her hair fall down around her shoulders. "What brings you here?"

"A feeling. I came to warn Mr. Alvarez he's in danger. He didn't believe me, of course. Most people don't, but I had to try."

"Couldn't you have told him that when you were reading his cards earlier tonight?"

"The feeling came over me long after he left."

"How did you know where to find him?" Liz asked.

"I can't explain it. Something drew me here." A shudder ran through the woman's body and a far-off look came over her face. Moments later, the look was gone and she stared at them in concern. "You two need to be careful too. There's something...evil coming your way." Without saying another word, she turned on her heels and headed toward the entrance.

"She creeps me out," Liz said.

"No kidding. I wonder if she really came here to warn him because of a 'feeling'." Rory air quoted the last word.

"You think she's the person he arranged to meet? You said it couldn't have been her. I don't know what Tito would have on her, anyway." Liz stared thoughtfully off into the distance. "I don't know. I think she might be the real deal."

"Maybe he left her voicemail. We don't know he actually had a conversation with someone." Rory took a final sip of her soda and grabbed the bill off the table. "If you're done, let's get out of here. The show appears to be over."

After paying at the cash register, they walked out the side entrance into the alley next to the restaurant. They were heading toward the street where their car was parked when they saw a figure up ahead, bending down over something on the ground, arm raised as if to strike.

Rory's foot dislodged a rock, sending it skittering across the alley where it landed with a thud against a building.

The figure paused and glanced their way. As soon as it saw them, it ran in the opposite direction.

When Rory and Liz ran forward, they found Tito Alvarez lying still on the ground, his eyes closed. Rory bent down to check on him. "He's still breathing, but he looks pretty beat up. Call 911."

Chapter 29

"You didn't recognize the figure?" Officer Yamada asked Rory and Liz, his hand poised above a note pad to record their answers.

The three of them stood at the end of the alley, under a street lamp, talking while paramedics tended to Tito.

"It was dark, and whoever it was, was dressed in dark-colored clothes."

"A ski mask covered the face too," Liz added. "Or at least that's what it looked like to me."

"Do you think he's going to be okay?" Rory watched the paramedics place Zelena's father on a stretcher and take him to the ambulance parked in the alley.

"Hard to say, but you may have saved Mr. Alvarez's life," the officer said. "If you hadn't arrived when you did..."

"I'll take it from here," a deep voice said.

A sense of relief washed over Rory at the sight of the detective. He hugged her to his chest. "I'll be one moment," he said softly into her ear.

Martin consulted with the officer before returning to stand beside Rory and Liz. "Tell me what you saw."

They repeated their story while the detective took notes. He raised an eyebrow when they got to the part about seeing Tito and the tarot card reader in the diner.

"Interesting that you were all here tonight. I thought you promised to stop investigating on your own." He directed his attention at Rory, a stern expression on his face. "Is this why you refused police protection?"

"I wanted dessert," Liz said. "I dragged Rory along. She didn't think it was safe for me to go alone. They have the best pie here. You've really got to try it."

He raised an eyebrow. "You didn't get enough at the party?"

"Didn't have time to get anything, I was so busy working the escape room."

"Any idea what Mr. Alvarez was doing here?"

Rory glanced at Liz. "It looked like he was meeting someone."

"The psychic? Gayelette?"

"Not from what she told us." Rory paused. "He had a wad of cash on him the other day. Could it have been a robbery?"

"Maybe. His wallet's missing. When did you see the cash?"

"A couple days ago. He borrowed a twenty from me that day we saw him at the motel, remember?" After he nodded, she continued. "When I took Zelena's belongings from the school to him, he paid me back."

"Do you think it could have been the same person who warned Rory?" Liz asked.

"If it was, this was more than a warning. You two need to be more careful." Martin closed his notebook. "Okay, you've had enough excitement for one day. Go home." He looked meaningfully at Rory. "We'll talk more later."

Rory wasn't sure she liked the sound of that.

Rory woke up Monday morning to find a text from Jeanne sent in the wee hours of the morning: *Emergency meeting! 10 am at boutique house. Everyone MUST attend.* When she walked in the front door promptly at the scheduled time, Rory found half of the board members milling around in the entryway. She asked around, but no one knew why the impromptu meeting had been called.

"I don't have time for this. It better be important," Teresa said. "And it better be fast. I have a meeting with a client in less than an hour. Let me tell you, brides do not like to be kept waiting, especially this one."

Moments later, clipboard in hand, Jeanne walked down the stairs toward them. She stopped a few steps from the bottom and looked over the assembled group. "Where is everyone?"

"I think this is it." Teresa looked up from her phone. "We do have lives, you know. What's so urgent, anyway?"

"I guess this will have to do. I'll just have to rearrange some of your assignments. The house needs to be cleared out today. Toby will take care of the escape room tomorrow."

"But why?" Liz said. "The cleaners aren't coming until Wednesday and the owners are fine with us taking until the end of the week to put everything back in order."

"Because I say so. There's no reason to wait. It's better we take care of this now."

The board members looked at each other in confusion.

"Where's Penny?" Rory voiced the question running though everyone's mind. "She said we deserved a break. That we'd start closing everything down tomorrow."

"Change of plans. I'm in charge now. We're going to be doing things differently."

Teresa frowned. "What's there to change? We pack things up and move stuff out. Not that difficult."

"Did something happen to Penny?" Liz asked. "Does she know you changed the plan?"

"She's at the hospital. And, yes, she's on board with the change. Told me I could do whatever I wanted."

"The hospital?!" everyone shouted.

"Before you all get your knickers in a twist, there's nothing wrong with her. She's with Zelena's father. His wife's out of town. Penny seems to think a bedside vigil is appropriate." Jeanne rolled her eyes. "So I'm in charge now."

"What happened to Tito?" Teresa asked. "He was fine last night at the party."

"Maybe he had a heart attack," another board member

speculated. "He has been under a lot of stress lately. I'd have one too if my daughter had been murdered."

Jeanne sighed in resignation. "I can see no one's going to get any work done until everyone knows what happened. Rory, why don't you tell them."

Everyone turned to Rory expectantly. She explained how they had found Zelena's father in the alley behind the diner and interrupted an assault on him. She left out the part about his having a midnight assignation or why she and Liz had been there in the first place. After she was done, the two answered everyone's questions the best they could.

"I haven't checked on him this morning yet," Rory said. "I don't know his current condition."

When the conversation died down, Jeanne said, "If the gossip session's over now, let's get to work." She made some notes on her clipboard and started handing out assignments.

Not bothering to see what she was supposed to be doing, Teresa waved her hand and headed toward the front door. "I have an important appointment. Someone else will have to take over for me."

The other board members looked at each other. Someone said, "I thought this was just a meeting. I didn't expect it to take all day." Another said, "Count me out. I'll see you tomorrow."

One by one, the rest of the board members made their own excuses and headed outside until only Rory and Liz were left in the entryway.

"I guess you're the only ones who care."

"It's not that they don't care," Rory said. "It's just that everyone had plans. We thought we had the day off, that we didn't have to start clearing the house out until tomorrow."

Jeanne sat down on the stairs and stared gloomily at the floor. "I suppose we'll have to stick to the original plan." Without looking up, she waved her hand at the front door. "Go ahead, leave like everyone else."

Rory and Liz huddled in a corner and spoke in whispers so the other woman wouldn't hear them.

"I want to go to the hospital and check on Zelena's father, but I feel bad about leaving her here like this," Rory said.

Liz glanced over at Jeanne who was still sitting on the stairs. "I think I'll stay for a bit. Wouldn't hurt to go over the plans once again, make sure we've thought of everything. Plus, I think it's a little suspicious that she's in such a hurry to shut down the house today. If I stay, maybe I'll find out what's really going on."

"You don't think it's just her way of asserting control? You know how much she loves being in charge and having everything done her way."

"Maybe, but I want to be here just in case she lets something slip." Liz waved her hand at the door. "You go ahead and see how Tito's doing."

The last thing Rory heard when she walked out the door was Jeanne's strident voice explaining how she wanted things done.

When Rory walked down the hospital corridor a short time later, she found a uniformed officer guarding the door of Tito's room. Veronica Justice stood next to him, peppering him with questions, but he just stared at her with a blank expression on his face. Rory hung back and waited to see what would happen. When the officer denied Veronica access to the hospital room, the reporter headed down the hall toward the elevator. "Good luck getting inside," she said as she passed by.

Rory stopped in front of Tito's room. "Is it okay if I go inside? I'm a friend, not a reporter."

"I know who you are, Ms. Anderson." The officer glanced through the partially open door. "Someone's with him now. I suppose you can go in too. I need to leave the door open, though, so I can keep an eye on things. You understand." He angled his chair so he could see inside the room as well as down the hallway.

"Of course. Mr. Alvarez's safety is important." Rory thanked him and walked inside the room where she found Penny Worthington sitting beside an unconscious Tito's bed, her head bowed. Not wanting to interrupt the woman's prayers, Rory waited until she lifted her head before saying anything.

"Rory, I didn't expect to see you here. Jeanne told me everyone was going to be working at the house today."

"Things didn't go exactly as she planned."

Penny bit her lips as if suppressing a smile. "Ah, I see. A bit of a rebellion, was it?"

"You could say that."

"I told her no one would like it, but you know how everything has to be done her way."

"Any idea why she thinks it's so urgent?"

"She didn't tell me and I didn't bother asking."

Rory nodded at Tito. "Has he said anything?"

"Hasn't woken up yet, at least not as long as I've been here. They're keeping him sedated so he'll heal properly. That's what I understand, anyway."

"But they think he'll be okay?"

Penny shrugged. "They're not sure. I wish we knew more about what happened. Have the police caught the person who did this yet?"

"Not as far as I know. Liz and I couldn't give much of a description. The alley was dark and the attacker wore a ski mask."

"That's right, you were there." Penny stood up. "Why don't you take the chair. I've been sitting long enough."

Rory sat down gratefully. "Thanks. It's nice of you to stay with him."

"I thought someone should be here. Even if he's unconscious, there's a possibility he might be able to hear us. I want him to know someone is here for him and that people care."

"Do you know when his wife is supposed to arrive?"

"Not sure. Soon I hope." Penny paced the floor. "I used to think it was safe to walk around town at night. That we didn't have to worry about gangs and random attacks. I'm beginning to wonder."

"I'm not sure it was random. And it certainly wasn't gang-related."

Penny leaned against the wall and stared open-mouthed at Rory. "What do you mean?"

"I think he may have been meeting someone at the diner."

Penny sat down on the edge of the bed. "Why do you say that?"

"He kept on looking at his watch and..." Rory glanced toward the door and lowered her voice so the officer couldn't hear what she said next. "At the party, I overheard him talking to someone about a meeting. It sounded, well, like he was threatening someone."

Penny gasped. "Like blackmail? Do you know who?"

Rory shook her head. "I only heard part of the conversation."

Before she could say anything else, a loud ringing sounded from the direction of the hallway.

"What's that?" Rory said.

"Sounds like a fire alarm. I'll go see what's happening." Penny walked toward the open door.

"Pa haro," Tito muttered in his sleep. "Pa haro."

Rory directed her attention to the bed. Unsure she'd heard correctly, she leaned over and touched Tito's arm. "Did you say something, Mr. Alvarez?" He mumbled something she couldn't understand, then went silent once again.

"Did he just say something?" Penny asked.

"It sounded like pa haro, but I'm not sure. The alarm's pretty loud. Any idea what it means?"

She shook her head. "No clue."

Moments later, the uniformed officer poked his head inside the door. "I need you two to come out of the room now. I need to check this out and I don't want anyone inside while I'm gone."

When they were both in the hallway and Tito's door was closed, he said to them, "You can wait out here, but don't go back inside and make sure no one else does either."

They nodded their agreement. Rory and Penny leaned against the wall while the alarm continued to sound. Not long after the officer left, Toby rounded the corner. A momentary look of surprise came over his face when he spotted Rory standing beside his wife. "Oh, hi, Rory, I didn't realize you were here. I think they're evacuating. We should all leave."

"Do you know what's going on?" Rory said.

"Not sure, but it's better to be safe than sorry."

"But the officer told us to stay." Rory walked over and peeked inside the room where Tito still slept peacefully. "And what about Tito? We can't leave him alone. We have to protect him."

Toby nodded his head. "Hadn't thought of that. How about this, you ladies go and I'll stand outside and guard the door. I won't budge no matter what happens."

The two women were about to leave when the alarm stopped sounding and the officer returned.

"False alarm. No need to evacuate. Somebody tripped the fire alarm on purpose. Probably one of those punk kids who are pulling all those pranks around town."

"I should have known," Toby said. "They set one off in a building next to mine earlier this week."

The officer looked at the three of them. "I think you should go now. Mr. Alvarez has had enough excitement for one day."

Toby and Penny nodded and walked down the hall toward the elevator.

Before following them, Rory stopped to talk to the officer. "Are you sure it was a kid who pulled the alarm? It couldn't have been set off by someone trying to get at Mr. Alvarez?"

"Don't worry. We'll make sure nothing happens to him. It's our top priority."

While Rory waited for the elevator, she thought about Zelena. She owed it to her friend to help keep her father safe. She didn't know if what Tito had muttered was important, but she hoped he would wake up soon and tell them what it meant before someone tried to go after him again.

Chapter 30

Later that afternoon, when Rory couldn't deal with software bugs and clients any longer, she took a walk on the beach to clear her mind. She was sitting on a bench on the pier staring at the ocean when her phone rang.

"How did it go at the house? Did you and Jeanne work everything out?" she asked Liz.

"We're all set for tomorrow. I convinced her to stagger our arrival times. We should be able to work around everyone's schedules that way. Text her when you're available."

"Did she reveal any deep dark secrets or do anything suspicious?"

"Nothing at all. From what I can tell, she just has something she'd rather do tomorrow." Liz sounded disappointed. "How's Zelena's father doing?"

"Holding his own. They expect him to recover, but he's still unconscious. He did mumble something odd. 'Pa haro' or something like that. I think it's probably Spanish, but I have no idea how to spell it so I can't look it up. Any idea what he could be talking about?"

"Oh, you mean the Spanish word for bird, *pájaro*."

"That explains it. Tito told me once he used to call Zelena his little bird when she was young."

"Makes sense. His subconscious is probably occupied with thoughts of her. Was Penny still sitting vigil at the hospital?"

"She was. We had a bit of excitement." Rory told her friend about the fire alarm someone had tripped and how the officer had blamed a kid for it. "They didn't catch anyone, though."

"I wish these pranks would stop. Some of them were cute at first, but now they've just gotten annoying and destructive. I'm worried what's going to happen next."

"I know. I can't help wondering if the pranks and Zelena's murder are somehow related."

"Could be. Maybe we'll find out soon. But enough about that. We need to get down to business and figure out our next steps with the investigation."

Rory stared thoughtfully at the ocean where a sailboat was passing by. "What about the boat angle? Remember what Raven said? Zelena could have been on a boat when she died. We haven't looked into whether or not anyone she knew owns one. Do you know anyone who could help?"

"That's right. I completely forgot about that. One of my clients works in the harbor office. I helped him sell his grandfather's house recently. He might be willing to talk to us about the boats docked there. Let me call him and find out."

"Sounds good." After Rory hung up, she contemplated the water for a few more minutes, then headed down the pier toward the street. She was passing by a bike rack near the cafe next to the parking lot when she spotted a beach cruiser that looked vaguely familiar. After studying the decals on the bicycle and the LED lights on its wheels, she realized where she'd seen it before. She looked around to make sure no one was watching, then took a photo of the bicycle she was sure was ridden by one of the vandals who'd shot out the windows on Saturday.

A teenager walked over to her with a soda in his hand.

She looked at him and smiled. "Is this your bike? I'm looking to buy one for my brother, but I don't know anything about them. It looks nice. Do you like it?"

"That's not mine." He pointed to the beach cruiser next to it. "That one's mine."

"What about these lights? That looks like something my brother would like. Do you have them too?"

The teen's eyes lit up. "I wish. You should see these in action. The wheels look like they're on fire. Haven't saved up enough to get them yet, but I will."

They discussed the pros and cons of various kinds of bicycles. By the time the teen was done talking, Rory felt sure she knew more about customization of bikes than she ever wanted to know.

The teen gestured toward the stairs where Keith Halliwell was just stepping onto the pier. "It's his bike. I'm sure he'll be happy to answer any of your questions."

"That's all right," Rory said hurriedly. "I think I have all of the information I need. You've been very helpful."

Rory headed up the hill, waiting until she was several blocks away before calling Martin Green and telling him about the bicycle and its owner.

"That's all I need from you right now," Martin said to Rory who sat next to the detective's desk in the Vista Beach police station. He shut his notebook and leaned back in his chair. "It's fortunate you and your group saw the vandalism happening and you took that video. I don't know if we would have caught them otherwise."

Once Rory had sent Martin the photo of Keith Halliwell's bicycle, the police rounded him up and brought him down to the station. It didn't take long before Keith voluntarily gave up his accomplice in the shooting out of the windows.

"I don't understand why he'd do that in the middle of the day. He probably wouldn't have been caught if he'd done it after dark," Rory said.

"My opinion? He's getting back at his parents. They've really been pushing him to get good grades and get into a top-tier school."

"What do you think will happen to him?"

"Not up to me. That's the D.A.'s department, but I think they're both in big trouble."

"Did Keith confess to everything? All of the pranks?"

"He was involved in a lot of them. Turns out he was the one playing the 'ghost child' we saw on the beach. Not the one at the vigil, though."

"He was there when we found Zelena? Did he know anything about her death?"

Martin shook his head. "No. He was as surprised to find the body as we were. Though he did use it as 'inspiration' for the mannequin at the vigil."

"What else was he involved in?"

"He admitted to clogging up the toilets in the elementary school and causing all the damage. Some misguided attempt at getting back at Zelena for talking to his parents about her concerns. And the firework stunt on the pier, though he didn't do that one alone. The pranks he wasn't directly involved with he told us who did them. All friends of his from the high school. We'll be bringing them in soon."

"What about the alarm at the hospital?"

"He didn't mention that one. Doesn't mean it wasn't a prank. One of his friends could have done that and not bothered to tell him about it."

Before she could ask anything else, she heard a commotion coming from the station entrance.

"Where's my son?" Uri Halliwell stormed into the police station, his wife following closely behind. He looked around the room. When he spotted Detective Green and Rory, he marched over to them.

Martin stood up and moved away from his desk, shielding Rory from the angry man.

Uri poked a finger in the detective's chest. "What have you done with him?"

Two uniformed officers began walking toward them, but a slight nod of the detective's head stopped them in their tracks.

Martin motioned for Rory to move to the side, then stepped back so he was out of reach of Keith's father. "You are?"

"Uri Halliwell. Don't tell me you don't know who I am. I contribute enough to police department charities, you *should* know me. Now, where's my son?"

Tabitha plucked at her husband's sleeve and said in a quiet voice, "Uri."

He brushed her off without looking at her.

Martin gestured toward an interrogation room. "Let's sit down and I'll explain what's going on. Why don't we take this in here so we can talk in private?"

"I'm not going into one of your interrogation rooms. I've done nothing wrong and neither has Keith. This is harassment, plain and simple. I demand you release him now."

"Uri, perhaps we *should* talk in there." Tabitha started to walk toward the doorway, but Uri pulled her back.

"Your son is being booked. He and a friend were caught shooting out windows of several houses with pellet guns."

Uri shook his head. "You're mistaken. Keith would never do that. He's going to Harvard, for God's sake."

Martin gestured toward nearby chairs. "There are half a dozen witnesses who identified him and his friend plus we have video of them in action." He placed an evidence bag on the desk. Inside was a green mask. "We found this in his backpack."

"So he had a sinus mask in his backpack. Big deal! Anyone can buy that at the local drugstore."

"Keith has confessed to the vandalism as well as some of the other pranks around town. Did you know he was involved with them?"

Looking as if the fight had gone out of him, Uri sank down on the nearest chair. Tabitha sat down beside him while Detective Green leaned against the desk.

"We suspected," she said. "We thought he'd stopped. All of the pranks were just that, innocent pranks. We had no idea he was going to shoot out windows."

"Wasn't Keith's fault. Must be that friend of his. He's a bad influence," Uri said.

"I never told you who the other boy was."

Uri waved his hand in dismissal. "Doesn't matter. Keith wouldn't do this on his own."

Martin raised an eyebrow. "He said it was his idea."

Uri sat up straighter in his seat. "I'm a personal friend of Chief Marshall. Can't some...arrangement be made? His college career, his life is on the line here."

"We don't 'make arrangements' here." Martin crossed his arms in front of him. "Did Zelena Alvarez know about your son's activities?"

Uri looked startled at the sudden change in topic. Anger flashed across his face. "Dana's kindergarten teacher? Why would she know anything?" He stood up. "I think we're done here. Any more questions you can talk to our attorney. Can we see our son now?"

Martin motioned for a uniformed officer to come forward. After the officer led Uri away, the detective said to Rory, "I don't need anything else from you. You can go now."

"Can I wait here? Liz is picking me up in a few minutes."

He nodded and walked across the room toward Chief Marshall's office.

Tabitha hung back and walked over to where Rory sat. "I'm sorry about Uri. Sorry you had to see that. He gets like that sometimes. He just cares about his kids so much. You understand?"

Rory nodded. "I get it. But why are you telling me this?"

Tabitha looked earnestly at Rory. "You have some influence with the police. I thought you could put in a good word for my son. I'd do anything for him."

"I really don't think I can be of any help."

"Try, okay? I'll do anything you want." Tabitha started to turn away.

"What about that list of all the people who visited Edgar? The ones who might have planted that cell phone in his office. You said you'd give it to me the other day."

"Did I? Sorry, I forgot."

Rory studied Tabitha's face. "Did you?"

The woman's eyes opened wide. "Wait. You don't think *I* planted it, do you? That's preposterous. I'm sorry I asked for your help. I should have known better." She walked away, muttering angrily under her breath.

Rory was sitting beside Martin's desk, thinking about the possibility Tabitha had planted the phone herself, when she spotted a familiar photo on a nearby computer screen. She walked over to where a volunteer was updating the police department's Facebook page with people who were wanted. She pointed at the image on the screen. "I've seen her." After she told the volunteer how she'd seen the woman at the RV park, Rory sat back down and waited for her friend to arrive.

As soon as she spotted Liz entering the station, Rory hurried over to her. "Let's get out of here."

Liz flashed her a puzzled look and followed her out the door.

Once they were on the sidewalk next to Liz's car, a block away from the police station, Rory breathed a sigh of relief.

"Was it that bad?" Liz unlocked her car. "I thought you were just giving a statement. Did something else happen?"

Rory waited until she was sitting down inside the car before briefly describing what happened with Keith and his parents.

"Guess he's not getting into Harvard now. Shooting out windows is pretty serious."

"Uri seems to think Chief Marshall's going to play favorites and come to the rescue."

"Do you think he'd do that?"

Rory mulled over the possibility. "I don't know. The chief and I haven't always gotten along, but I think, deep down, he's pretty fair. I don't think he's likely to give into pressure from anyone, even a close friend."

"Is Uri Halliwell really a friend of his?"

"He seems to think so."

"I hope all of the pranksters have been caught now and things can get back to normal." Liz put the car in gear and pulled into traffic.

"There's something else," Rory said. "Guess whose picture I saw as being wanted by the police for identity theft?" Before Liz could guess, Rory continued. "That woman from the RV park. The one with the frying pan."

"At least we know why she's so skittish," Liz said. "Thanks for going with me to check on the boat angle. I'm hoping this guy I know at the harbor office can tell us whether anyone we know owns one. Maybe then we can figure out where Zelena was killed."

They were stopped at a light when Liz's phone rang. After a brief conversation in Japanese, Liz turned excited eyes to Rory. "That was one of my mom's cousins. They seem serious about one of the houses I showed them. I don't want to lose this opportunity. Who knows if they'll change their minds again."

"Go and take care of them. Drive me home. I'll go to the harbor and talk to your contact. Or we can reschedule for another time."

"Thank you for understanding. I think it's important one of us talks to him now. Will you be okay on your own, though? You know, after what happened."

"It's daytime and I'll be careful. I refuse to let anyone scare me away from getting justice for Zelena."

Liz made a U-turn and headed toward Seagull Lane. A few minutes later, she pulled into a spot in front of Rory's house. "I can't tell you how much I appreciate this. I'm sending you the guy's name."

Rory glanced at the text Liz had sent her. "Do you think he'll talk to me without you being there?"

"I'll make sure he does." She dialed a number and explained the situation to her contact. After she hung up, she turned to Rory. "I told him you're coming instead. He says that's no problem."

Rory nodded and headed toward her own car for the short drive to the harbor.

Chapter 31

"I'm sorry I couldn't be more help. But none of the people you mentioned own boats that are docked here," the man in the harbor office said.

Rory nodded, disappointed at the news. "Thanks for your time."

"Say hi to Liz for me."

Rory headed out the door onto a path that stretched around the harbor. She leaned against a railing and stared at row after row of sailboats, sport fishing vessels and yachts anchored nearby. She walked down the path until she found an empty bench with a view of the breakwater and harbor entrance where she sat down and stared at the sea of masts that stretched as far as she could see.

An older man with a cane walked down the path toward her and stopped in front of the bench. He pointed his cane at the seat next to her. "May I join you?"

She smiled and nodded. "Please."

The two sat in companionable silence for a few minutes, both staring at the boats going in and coming out of the harbor.

"I haven't seen you here before," he said. "Are you visiting?"

"I live pretty close to here. Just thought it would make a nice change to check out the harbor. I'm not that familiar with it. What about you? Are you here often?"

"Every day. I own one of those beauties. I've had it for years." He nodded toward the nearest row of boats. "Once upon a time I took it out as often as I could. Haven't been out in a while though."

"Why not?"

He patted her arm. "Not as spry as I once was. Nice of you to think an old man like me can still sail it. Truth be told, it's not as much fun since my wife passed." He touched his left leg. "Plus I have a bum knee. Not as easy to get around anymore."

"I'm sorry about your wife."

"Don't be. We had sixty wonderful years together. I don't regret a single minute of them."

"Which one's yours?"

He pointed toward a sailboat with *East of Eden* written on its side. "My wife's favorite book."

An idea forming in her mind, Rory stared thoughtfully out at the harbor. "Do you know any of the other boat owners?"

"A fair number of them. I may not get out on the boat much, but I still hang around and talk to people."

Rory pulled up the photos on her phone she'd gathered of friends and acquaintances of Zelena. "Could you tell me if any of these people own a boat?" She flipped through them, pausing at each one long enough he had a chance to study it.

He shook his head at picture after picture. Her hopes were dwindling when he said, "Wait, go back." He pointed at a photo of Jeanne. "I've seen her around."

"She owns a boat?"

"I don't know if she owns it, but she's here a lot. Thing is, I'm not sure she ever takes it out."

Rory's heart pounded at the news. "Which one is it?"

"I'm not sure, but she goes in this way." He pointed his cane at the white metal gate nearest them.

Rory settled back in her seat. She tried not to appear too eager as she said, "Tell me everything you remember about her visits to the harbor."

"I got your bat signal," Liz whispered as she slid into a crouched position next to Rory behind an equipment shed on the path that went around the harbor. "What did you find out?"

Her eyes trained on the gated entrance to the dock area, Rory whispered back, "A man I met said he's seen Jeanne here several times. He's pretty sure she gets on a boat, but he wasn't sure which one. Just that it's in this area." She pointed to the row of boats docked nearby. "She doesn't own it, or at least her name didn't ring a bell with your contact in the harbor office, but she's here fairly often around this time. We're going to see if she shows up and which boat she goes to."

Liz whistled softly. "That could be where Zelena was killed. Why don't we get closer? We can hide behind one of those really big yachts."

Rory nodded toward the white metal gate that separated the parking area from the boats. "See that gate? It's locked. Only people with the code can get past it. Besides, if we don't know which boat she visits, how are we going to know where to hide?"

"Good point. But how do you know Jeanne's not already on it?"

Rory felt a cramp in one of her legs. She moved it to a more comfortable position. "I've been here ever since I talked with your contact in the harbor office. I haven't seen her. Plus I checked in with my mom. Jeanne was at the store, going over receipts from the boutique house, half an hour ago. I also checked the parking lot. Her car's not here yet."

The two waited behind the shed, occasionally readjusting their position while watching boat owners come and go. Finally, a half hour later, Liz nodded toward a figure coming down the path. "Here she is now."

They tried to make themselves as small as possible to make sure Jeanne couldn't see them. She crossed the lot toward the metal gate. When she looked over her shoulder, they heard the faint click of a camera. Moments later, a woman with purple hair styled in a bubble cut crouched down beside them.

"Hello, ladies. I figured when you borrowed those binoculars you two were up to something, but I didn't expect to find you here," the woman said in a slight Boston accent. The private investigator who'd helped them discover the truth in a couple murder investigations lifted her camera and took a shot of Jeanne climbing onto a yacht docked nearby.

"Candy!" Liz said. "What are you doing here?"

"What else? Cheating spouse. How about you? Did you two get into the business?"

"Penny hired you?" Rory's mouth gaped open.

"Who's Penny?"

"The wife of the man who's having an affair with Jeanne, the one you just took pictures of."

"Don't know this Penny. That one has a husband." Candy pointed her camera at Jeanne who was now lounging on a chair on the deck of the boat.

"Jeanne's married?" Rory and Liz said in unison.

"Ssh! Keep it down. We don't want to spook her." Candy took several more shots of the boat and its occupant.

They waited in silence, all three staring at the nearby gate and the boats beyond. Every time someone passed through the gate, Candy lifted her camera and took a photo. None of the people they saw joined Jeanne on the yacht.

Half an hour later, Jeanne received a phone call on her cell. After she hung up, she gathered her things and left.

As soon as Jeanne was out of sight, Candy stood up. "I'm done. Too bad she didn't have any company. What about you two? Can I buy you ladies a cup of coffee? We need to talk."

Once the three settled down at a table in a coffee shop not far away, Candy took a sip of her pumpkin latte and said, "Okay, let's get down to business. You tell me what you know. I'll tell you want I know. Deal?"

Rory and Liz nodded their agreement.

"Let's talk about Jeanne first. Is she a friend of yours?"

They told the private investigator how Jeanne was a part of their painting group and what they had learned about her in the short time they had known her.

"We had no idea she was married. She never said a word," Liz said. "And she doesn't wear a ring."

"Who's this Penny you asked me about?"

"She's married to Tobias, Toby, Worthington," Rory said. "He owns an escape room business in downtown Vista Beach called Escape Key."

"He's having an affair with Jeanne," Liz added.

"Penny knows about it. They had a fight about the affair at the party yesterday. Or, at least, that's what it looked like to me."

"How did you two find out?" Candy said.

"It was an accident. I saw them together at the Vista View Motel when I was there visiting someone," Rory said.

Candy sipped her latte and digested the information. "I've followed her there. Saw her and a man go into the same motel room." She picked up her camera and brought up a photo on its display. "This him?"

"That's Toby, all right."

Candy put the camera back down on the table. "Other than them going into the same room, I haven't caught them in any compromising positions. They've been very careful. Wish I had something juicier. Without it, she could make up some excuse for being there."

"Jeanne's really married?" Rory said.

"Has a rich husband up north. What did she tell you two about where she gets the money to live on?"

"I never thought about it and I never asked. I don't even know if she works." Rory turned to Liz. "Do you know if she has a job?"

"I thought she was independently wealthy. She told me she moved down here after inheriting some money."

"That's one way to put it." Candy sipped her coffee. "She took off with that boat and a million dollars."

Rory almost choked on her peppermint tea. She coughed and the other two waited until she could talk again. "A million?"

"That's what I said."

"How did you track her down?"

"Wasn't hard. She hasn't made any secret about where she is. I've been following her for a while. That's what he wanted me to do, follow her and see what she's been up to."

"Are you going to call the police now?" Rory asked.

"Technically, she didn't break the law."

Rory and Liz exchanged puzzled glances.

"But you said she stole a million dollars."

"Not stole. Took off with. It was a joint account so the money belonged to both of them."

"What about the boat? That's got to be worth a pretty penny," Liz said.

"It belongs to a holding company that I'm not sure her husband wants anyone to know he's associated with."

Rory sat back in her chair. "What does he hope to get out of finding her, then?"

"He wants evidence she's having an affair so he doesn't have to part with even more money. Some pre-nup clause, I suppose. I just do what the clients ask and leave the rest up to them. Why were you following her? Did she steal some of the chapter's money or something?"

"We don't have much to steal. We think she might be involved in the death of a friend of ours," Rory said. "You've probably heard about the case, Zelena Alvarez."

Candy whistled. "Didn't see that coming. This puts a whole new wrinkle on the story. What makes you think she's involved?"

They told her what they had found out so far and why they thought Jeanne might have something to do with Zelena's death.

"So you think she took your friend out on the boat and pushed her overboard?"

Rory and Liz nodded.

"Interesting." Candy glanced at her watch. "Got another cheater to catch. Nice talking with you ladies. It's been enlightening." She took a final sip of her latte and headed out the door, a thoughtful expression on her face.

After she left, Rory and Liz stayed and finished their drinks. Between sips of peppermint tea and coffee, they talked about what they had learned.

"Sounds like Jeanne stands to lose a lot if her husband finds out about her affair with Toby," Rory said.

"Seems like motive for murder to me. Maybe Zelena knew and threatened to tell so Jeanne invited her on a little cruise and they got into a fight. Then she tried to strangle her and pushed her overboard."

"At least now we have the name of a boat the police can investigate. Maybe there'll be some evidence on it. I'll call Martin and tell him what we learned."

While she dialed his number, Rory hoped the search for Zelena's killer was finally over.

Chapter 32

Around lunch time the next day, Rory opened the refrigerator at the boutique house and stared at its contents. "I didn't realize so much food was left over from the party. What do you think we should do with it?"

Jeanne looked up from her spot at the kitchen table where she was checking over some notes. "Dump it."

"All of it? That seems wasteful. Some of it is still good." Rory took the containers out of the refrigerator and placed them on the nearby counter. She looked at the contents of each one, splitting everything into two piles, one for anything that couldn't be saved and one for the food she thought was edible. She pointed to the latter pile. "Let me take the sandwiches and the veggies to my church. We have a program where we feed the homeless."

Jeanne waved her hand in the air without looking up from her papers. "Do whatever you want with it. Just get it all out of here. You may as well take the cans of soda too."

Rory was putting the leftover food and drinks in a cardboard box when Martin Green walked into the room. She looked up and smiled. "Didn't expect to see you here."

Instead of an answering smile, he held up his hand, indicating she should stay where she was, and headed toward Jeanne. "Ms. Cayce. Could I have a word?"

Jeanne looked up and frowned. "What is it? Can't you see I'm busy?"

"I'd like to talk with you about your boat. Why don't you come down to the station with me where we can have a nice quiet conversation."

"What boat? I don't know anything about a boat. I don't have time for this. Go away." She flicked her hand at the detective and went back to her work.

He placed an evidence bag on the table. "What do you know about this?"

Trying to be as unobtrusive as possible, Rory quietly walked over to the table and looked at the plastic bag. Inside was a wooden earring in the shape of a tombstone, identical to those that made up part of Zelena's necklace. She suppressed a gasp.

Jeanne barely glanced at it. "It's an earring. Not mine. I don't wear them. Don't even have my ears pierced."

"We know it belonged to Zelena Alvarez."

Rory tried to stay quiet at the news, but couldn't. "Where did you find it?"

Martin ignored her and directed the answer to Jeanne. "It was on your boat, Ms. Cayce."

Jeanne slammed her pen down next to the papers. She stood up and leaned forward, her hands resting on the edge of the table, her face inches away from the detective's. "I told you, I don't own a boat. Aren't you listening?"

Martin leaned forward even further and stared at her with expressionless eyes. "Then it's your husband's. Doesn't really matter who owns it. You have control of it. Do you have an explanation of why Ms. Alvarez's earring was found on it?"

"My husband?" Jeanne turned pale and sat down. "Is he here?"

"Just answer the question."

Jeanne narrowed her eyes and looked at Rory. "You know something, don't you? What is it?"

Rory shrank at the woman's angry gaze. "Your husband hired a private detective to follow you. That's all I know."

"Why didn't you tell me?"

Rory started to respond, but Martin cut her off. "Can we get back to the boat? Was Ms. Alvarez ever on it?"

Jeanne gestured toward the evidence bag. "I don't know how that got there. She didn't even know I have a boat. As far as I know no one does."

"So you didn't take her out on it for a midnight cruise the Thursday before last?"

"I don't even know how to drive it."

"How'd you get it into the harbor, then?"

"Hired someone to move it for me. It's been in its slip ever since."

"That's not what the GPS on the boat tells us. Plus one of the other boat owners saw it leaving the harbor that night."

"I didn't kill her. What's my motive?"

"She knew about your affair with Toby," Rory said. "You do stand to lose a lot of money if she told your husband about it. And you were seen arguing with her."

Jeanne buried her face in her hands. "I knew I should have waited until the divorce was final, but our feelings were so strong. I didn't think that dud of a husband of mine would actually hire someone to follow me. I should have known better."

"You and Zelena fought about it?" Martin said.

Jeanne nodded. "We had words, but after I explained everything to her, she promised not to tell anyone." She looked him straight in the eyes. "I didn't kill her. I couldn't have. She was killed sometime that Thursday, right? Sometime after she called Rory during the board meeting?" She took a deep breath. "I can account for all of my time that day. After the meeting, I went on some errands for the house. Ask Penny, she'll tell you. I can give you a list of the places I visited."

"And in the evening?" Martin said.

"I had a dinner meeting with my divorce lawyer that lasted for several hours. By the time I got home, I was beat so I went straight to bed."

"Alone?"

"Alone."

"Why don't we head down to the station and talk more there."

Admitting defeat, Jeanne stood up and turned to Rory. "You'll call Penny and tell her what's happened? She needs to take over here. I'll leave my notes."

After Rory nodded her agreement, Jeanne grabbed her purse and led the way to the front door. As soon as they left the kitchen, Rory dialed Penny's number and let her know what was going on, agreeing to stay at the house until the chapter president could get there.

Rory itched to tell Liz how Jeanne's boat had been involved in Zelena's death, but every time she tried her number, the call went straight to voicemail.

Chapter 33

"What do you mean, she didn't show up?" Rory's voice rose to a squeak. She sat back in her desk chair and stared at the comings and goings on Seagull Lane while she took in what Martin Green had just told her about Liz. She took a deep breath and her voice returned to normal. "How late is she?"

"Her shift on the tip line started at two," Martin said.

Rory glanced at the time on her computer screen. "That's two hours ago. Something must have happened to her. She would have called. She always lets people know when she's going to be late. Did anyone try calling her?"

"Went straight to voicemail and, as far as I know, she didn't tell anyone she wouldn't be here. Any idea where she could be?"

"Maybe she's showing a house to a client and lost track of time. Are you sure she didn't leave a message? Someone could have forgotten to pass it on."

"You might be right. I'll double check."

"While you're doing that, I'll call around, see if anyone's heard from her today. Thanks for letting me know."

Anxiety built up inside Rory as her mind flashbacked to two weeks ago when she received the email from Beyond The Grave. Another friend missing under mysterious circumstances. She hoped this time things would turn out differently. Rory closed her eyes and said a silent prayer.

As if sensing she was in need of comfort, Sekhmet jumped up

on her lap and brushed against Rory's arm. She kissed the cat on the top of her head and, with Sekhmet curled up on her lap, picked up her phone and began making calls.

First she dialed the number for Vista Beach Realty where Liz worked. Soon she had the name and phone number of the client Liz was supposed to meet that morning. She hung up after the receptionist promised to call her if Liz checked in.

A quick call to the client and she was at a dead end once again.

Rory looked at her cat. "Liz met them at the house, but they didn't know where she was going after that. I think I'll call Liz's mom next. Maybe she's with the cousins."

Sekhmet meowed her encouragement.

When she talked to Mrs. Dexter, Rory put on her cheeriest voice, hoping her anxiety wouldn't show through. She didn't want to upset the woman unnecessarily. Disappointment surged through her when she learned no one in the family had heard from Liz that day.

Rory made call after call, but none of their friends had talked to her or seen her. Not until she spoke with Penny did she learn anything new about Liz's plans.

"She called me to check on Tito this morning when I was at the hospital," Penny said from the boutique house. "Said she'd be by to visit him later after she saw how everything was going here. I didn't see her at the hospital when I was there, but she could have stopped by after I left. That was about noon when you called, right? The officer who is guarding Tito's door would have seen her if she had. Or you could check with Jeanne to see if she came to the house this morning. Liz would have talked to her if she did." She paused. "I suppose that could be an issue seeing as how Jeanne's in custody. I'll ask around and see if anyone remembers seeing her."

Rory wrote down the information on a notepad and went on to her next call. After the last one was made, she put her phone down on her desk and rubbed her forehead. The anxiety she'd been suppressing for the last hour surfaced in the form of a pounding headache. She couldn't help wondering if this was her fault, if Liz's disappearance had something to do with the warning she'd received. If they hadn't kept on investigating, Liz might be here now, talking to her about the latest news.

Rory had her cell phone in her hand to call Martin back when she heard a soft knock on her front door. She flung it open, hoping to see her friend's smiling face. When she saw Martin instead, tears welled up in her eyes.

He took the phone from her hands, placed it on her desk and enveloped her in his strong arms. Rory buried her face in his shoulder and sobbed her heart out. He stroked her hair and said softly into her ear, "Don't worry, we'll find her."

After Rory had no tears left in her, they retired to the living room and sat down side by side on the sofa.

"Sorry about all the crying." Rory leaned against Martin and rested her head on his shoulder.

"No need to apologize. Your friend's missing and this hasn't been the easiest couple weeks. It's understandable. Everyone in the department is on the lookout for her or her car. They'll let me know if they see either one." He cleared his throat. "I checked the local hospitals. No one fitting her description was brought in. I also checked the accident reports. Nothing."

"What about...?" Rory didn't want to use the word "morgue" in case saying it made it become true.

"Nothing there, either."

Rory breathed a sigh of relief.

"I take it you didn't have any luck with your other calls."

"I've tried everyone I can think of, even Veronica and Candy, but no one knows much. I've been trying to trace her movements but haven't gotten very far."

"Tell me."

She went over the results of all the phone calls she made. When she got to the part about Liz planning on visiting Tito, he made a call of his own. He shook his head when he hung up. "She hasn't been at the hospital."

"I don't know where she went after she was with her client. My guess is she checked in at the boutique house. Jeanne would know. She might even be able to tell us where Liz went afterwards." Rory sat up and looked Martin squarely in the face, a determined look in her eyes. "I want to talk with Jeanne. Can you make that happen?"

"I'll question her myself, if it'll help. Are you sure you've thought of everything?"

"Let me think." Rory leaned back on the couch and closed her eyes. Moments later, she opened them again. "The tracking app! Remember the app Samantha used to find Zelena's phone? Liz and I put one like it on our own phones for emergencies."

Rory raced to her desk to get her cell. With trembling hands, she opened the app and stared at the screen. Her smile faded when no blinking dot appeared on it.

Martin leaned over and studied the screen. "I don't see anything. What does that mean?"

"Her phone must be turned off. Now I know something bad has happened to her. She might not always answer it, but she never turns it off. It's her lifeblood." Rory stood up. "We need to go to the station and talk to Jeanne."

"Let me talk to her alone." Rory stood beside Martin in front of an interrogation room door in the Vista Beach police station. "I think she'll tell me the truth."

He nodded and opened the door for her. When she stepped inside, Jeanne looked up from where she sat in a chair next to the table, confusion written all over her face.

"What are you doing here?"

Rory pushed a chair closer to Jeanne and sat down on it so her knees were inches away from the other woman's. She put her elbows on her own knees and leaned forward. "Where's Liz?"

"How should I know."

"You were the last one to see her. She's missing."

"That's got nothing to do with me." Jeanne inched her chair back and eyed Rory. "You think I did something to her? That's ridiculous."

"Penny said Liz was going to stop by the boutique house this morning. I didn't see her when I got there. Did she come by earlier?"

"She was there, checking to see if there were any problems with getting the house back in order. Wanted to see if she needed to do any paint touch ups or something like that. Didn't stay long. All I know is she was gone before you arrived. Teresa was there about the same time. Ask her, she'll tell you it's the truth."

"Liz didn't say where she was going?"

Jeanne shrugged. "She may have. I don't always listen when people prattle on." She leaned forward. "Listen, if I knew where she was, I'd tell you."

Rory studied the woman. Everything about her body language said she was telling the truth. When she left the room moments later, she walked over to where Martin was standing by the interrogation room monitor.

"At least we know she was at the boutique house this morning," he said. "Have you tried Teresa?"

"When I talked to her earlier, she hadn't seen Liz, but they could have just missed each other."

"Maybe you should try that app again."

Not expecting a positive result, Rory checked for Liz's phone once again. When a dot appeared on the screen, she stared at it in disbelief. "It's on again." She made a mental note of the location in case the dot disappeared.

After she showed him the screen, they headed out the door. When they arrived at the spot where the phone was supposed to be, a walk path on a stretch of beach in the northern end of the city, the area was almost deserted.

"You go north, I'll go south. It can't be far," Martin said.

Rory walked down the path, staring around her, stopping every few feet to look for someplace her friend or her phone could be hiding.

Before long, Martin shouted for her to join him. She ran to

where he stood next to a garbage can. As soon as she was close enough, he held up a purse by its strap.

"That's Liz's," she said.

He carefully opened it and examined its contents. "ID and credit cards are still here. And her phone."

"At least we know she wasn't mugged."

Rory examined the phone while Martin looked through the rest of the purse's contents. She scanned the recent texts and phone calls to see if any of them could tell her where her friend might be. "She didn't send any texts or make any calls after about eleven this morning."

"What about location data? Any idea where the phone's been?"

A few taps later, Rory had the answer. "Someone turned off location services and cleared the history." She handed the phone back to him, disappointed it couldn't tell them more.

Rory's legs wobbled. She leaned against the garbage can to steady herself. "This must have something to do with Zelena's death. Liz must have found out something important. But what?" She appealed to Martin with her eyes.

"It's time to talk to Liz's parents, let them know what's going on. Do you want to go with me?"

"I think it's better if I do. I'll give them a call and let them know we're coming." Rory took a deep breath and dialed the number.

Chapter 34

"Let's reason this out, okay?" Rory said as she walked back and forth across her living room floor. "Everything must be connected. Zelena's death. That warning. The assault on Tito. Liz's disappearance. But how?" She stopped and looked over at the window where Sekhmet was staring at the lawn outside. "Are you even listening?"

The cat turned her head, met Rory's gaze and meowed.

"I know, I know. I should let the police take care of this." Rory lay down on the couch and stared up at the ceiling. "You should have seen Liz's parents. They were so upset. Telling parents their child is missing isn't easy, no matter how old the kid is."

Rory glanced over at her cat who continued staring at her with unblinking eyes. "What? I didn't leave them alone. Mom and Dad are with them. I just couldn't stay there and stare at the walls, doing nothing." She sat up and reached for her phone to see if she'd somehow missed a call or text. She sighed and put it down again when nothing new appeared on the screen.

"Let's get back to work. Maybe it has something to do with Zelena's past." Rory looked excitedly at her cat. "The script she wrote. Samantha said it was loosely based on something that happened to Zelena. Maybe there's something in it that will help us." She walked over to her desk and opened the draft of the script she'd emailed to herself. She'd gotten through the description of the main character, a con artist with phoenix tattoos on his arms, when the phone rang. She snatched it up, hoping it was good news.

"Did you find her?"

"No, sorry." Martin Green's voice came over the line. "Just thought I'd check in, see how you're doing."

"Okay, I guess. Just wish I could do more to help."

"Do you want me to come over?"

"No, Sekhmet's keeping me company. I'd rather you continue looking for Liz. That's more important."

Martin told her he'd call her as soon as he had anything new to report and hung up.

Rory read more of the script but her eyes soon grew tired of staring at the screen and her brain could no longer make sense of the story. She closed her eyes, sifting through everything she'd learned so far. An image of a phoenix popped into her head. She'd seen it recently, but couldn't remember where. She gave up trying to force the information out of her brain and began pacing the floor once again.

"You know what I should do?" she said to Sekhmet. "I know it's late, but I should go where Liz was last seen, the boutique house. Maybe there'll be something there that I missed and that'll put me back on her trail."

Rory grabbed her keys and cell phone and headed out the door. When she got to the boutique house, none of the lights were on inside and the front door was locked. She walked around the outside of the house, stopping when she spotted the garbage cans stored behind the gate that led into the backyard. After taking all of the trash bags out and setting them on the pavement, she stood with her hands on her hips, deciding where to begin.

Four large black bags and one small white one lay on the ground before her. She dumped the contents of the white one on the ground and knelt down beside it. She sifted through the used napkins, empty toilet paper rolls and bits and pieces of discarded paper until she came across a photograph that someone had ripped into quarters. She pieced it back together on the ground, recognizing it as one she'd seen in the escape room. She brought out her cell phone and shone its light on the man in the picture. On his right arm she could barely make out a tattoo of a phoenix. Something about his face seemed familiar, but she couldn't immediately figure out who he reminded her of. After studying the photo for a few more minutes, the image of a man popped into her head. Subtract sixty pounds and shave off a beard and she was pretty sure she knew who it resembled. A quick call to Teresa to find out who she'd seen at the boutique house that morning confirmed her suspicions.

Rory pocketed the photo and replaced the garbage in the can. While she walked to her car, she called Martin's number, leaving a message explaining her theory when he didn't pick up. While she had a pretty good idea where Liz was being held, Rory had no idea how long she'd be there. She couldn't wait for the police. She only hoped she wasn't too late.

Rory parked on the street a couple blocks away from her destination and peered through the windshield. The area, full of auto repair businesses and repurposed warehouses, was deserted this late at night. No lights were on in any of the buildings. No cars moved down the out of the way street. No pedestrians passed by.

She walked down the sidewalk toward the building that housed Escape Key and tried the front door on the off chance it was open. As expected, she found it locked. She headed down the driveway as quietly as possible toward the garage she'd visited less than two weeks ago, figuring it was the most likely place Liz would be held.

At first glance, the property appeared deserted. No cars were parked in the lot and the roll-up door that covered the front of the garage was closed. Only a thin line of light coming from under the door indicated anyone was there.

Rory was about to try the side door of the garage to see if it was unlocked when she heard someone moving around inside. She flattened herself against the wall and waited until the sounds stopped. When everything once again appeared quiet, she opened the door and peeked inside. Spotting no one in the immediate vicinity, she slipped inside and hid behind one of the shelves filled with props while she surveyed the large open area before her.

Only a few feet away from her stood a large panel truck, its back open. Beyond that, a clearly agitated Toby paced the floor, mumbling to himself. She was trying to decide what to do next when she heard the sound of a telephone ringing in the distance. He stopped pacing and headed toward an office area toward the back of the garage.

As soon as he was out of sight, she peeked into the back of the truck, filled with the furniture from the boutique house's escape room. She hoisted herself inside and quietly called out Liz's name, hoping Toby wouldn't hear her. A faint banging and a muffled cry came from the back. She edged her way around the furniture until she came to a slightly battered trunk. Another bang, louder this time, seemed to come from inside it.

When Rory opened the trunk, she found Liz curled up inside, a blindfold over her eyes, duct tape across her mouth, and her hands and feet bound together.

"Liz, it's me," Rory whispered as she removed the blindfold. "I'm going to try to take the tape off now. I know it's going to hurt, but try not to make a sound." She yanked off the duct tape in one swift movement.

Liz whimpered in pain, but managed not to cry out. "I'm so glad to see you," she whispered between gasps of air. "I thought I was a goner. Not much air left in there. What time is it?" She drew in her breath when she heard how late it was. "I've been in there twelve hours?"

Rory helped her friend sit up. "Thank goodness it's an old trunk. Lots of cracks and crevices for air to get through."

Liz held out her hands. "Can you get these off me?"

Rory yanked on the plastic zip tie that bound Liz's hands, but it refused to budge. "Hold on, I've got an idea." She unlaced one of her tennis shoes and strung the shoelace through the zip tie.

Grabbing one end of the shoelace in each hand, she used a sawing motion, rubbing the string against the plastic. Ten seconds later, the zip tie snapped. She repeated the procedure on Liz's ankles and soon she was free.

"Where'd you learn to do that?" Liz sat up straighter and rubbed her wrists.

"You're not the only one who watches YouTube."

"Help me out of here."

Rory lifted her friend to her feet and helped her step out of the trunk. They huddled together in the corner while Liz slowly recovered. Rory massaged Liz's legs to help restore circulation while Liz rubbed her own wrists.

Liz looked around her, taking in her surroundings for the first time. "Where are we?"

"In the garage at Escape Key. Toby's out there. Not sure who else."

"Is that who took me?"

"I think so. What do you remember?"

"I went to the house to see how things were going. That was around ten this morning. I went up to the escape room. There was a mark on the baseboard near the trunk." Liz pointed toward the piece of furniture Rory had found her in. "I bent down to see if I'd have to get the baseboard repainted when I saw something tucked behind the trunk."

"What was it?"

"Zelena's purse. I'd just realized who it belonged to when someone came up behind me and knocked me out. Whoever it was must have tied me up and stuffed me in the trunk."

"Must have been Toby. I'm pretty sure he killed Zelena."

"That makes sense. I didn't see him at the house, but he'd be the one to oversee removal of the furniture from the escape room. What put you onto him?"

Rory dug the photo out of her pocket and pieced it together on the floor.

Liz peered at it in the dim light. "That's a photo from the

escape room."

"I found it like this in the garbage at the house. See the tattoo." Rory pointed at the photo. "Hold on, it's dark in here. You probably can't make it out." She shone the light from her cell phone on the picture and pointed at the phoenix on the man's forearm. "That must have been what Tito meant when he said 'bird'. He saw this and must have recognized the man in the photo as the person who took Zelena's money years ago."

"What makes you say that?"

"I read part of the script she wrote. Samantha told me it was supposed to be based on an event in Zelena's life. The main character is a con artist who specializes in financial scams. He has a tattoo just like this one on both of his arms."

"If Toby stole her money, why didn't Zelena recognize him?"

"She never met him. All her father told her about him was that he had a tattoo of a phoenix on one arm." Rory nodded toward the photo. "Look at it. I know he's quite a bit heavier and has a beard, but there is a resemblance. And Toby has a scar right where the tattoo would be. I saw it when I was here picking up that box the other day. He must have gotten the tattoo removed."

"I wonder if Penny knows." Liz looked pointedly at Rory's phone. "Have you called in the cavalry yet?"

"I called Martin before I came over. He didn't answer so I left a message. Let me try again." Rory went to dial his number, but there wasn't any service. "Shoot. No bars." She moved as close to the truck entrance as she dared. "No service here, either," she whispered and quietly returned to Liz's side. "We're on our own. Are you recovered enough so you can walk yet? We need to get out of here."

"My legs still feel a little tingly, but I think I can manage it. Help me stand up."

Rory helped her friend to her feet. Liz took a tentative step forward and wobbled. Another step and she collapsed onto the floor. "I don't know if I can make it. My head's all wonky. I need more time."

"I don't know if we have it." Rory cocked her head, listening for any sounds coming from the garage. "It's quiet out there. Let me see what's going on." She edged her way around the furniture, trying not to make any noise, and stopped at the entrance. When she looked around the corner, she spotted Toby and Penny only a few feet away. "Penny's here."

"Maybe she can help us."

"What if she's in on it?"

"Hadn't thought of that." With great effort, Liz crawled across the floor toward Rory. "If she is, that's two against one since I won't be much help right now. Go. Get help. I'll be okay."

"I'm not leaving you. You can't defend yourself."

They settled down on the floor and braced themselves for what would come next.

Chapter 35

While Rory and Liz waited in tense silence to see what would happen next, Rory looked around the truck to see if there was anything they could use to defend themselves. From a nearby box, she pulled out a crystal ball and the velvet tablecloth from the escape room.

"We can use these as weapons, just in case," she whispered to Liz who gave her a thumbs up.

Before long, they heard angry voices.

"What did you do?"

Rory mouthed Penny's name to Liz who nodded her head in agreement.

"She had Zelena's purse in her hand. What was I supposed to do?" Toby said.

"You didn't have to hit her on the head. What happened to the smooth talker I married? You've lost your touch since you retired. You could have convinced her you knew nothing. You've been doing that for years. What was so different now?"

The sound of footsteps became louder then faded away. Rory hazarded a peek at the room outside the truck. Toby paced the floor while Penny stood nearby, her arms crossed in front of her chest. Rory ducked her head back inside the truck so they wouldn't see her.

"Those were all financial scams, not murder," Toby said. The pacing stopped. "I should have checked the escape room before this to make sure nothing was left behind. Zelena must have come to and stuffed her purse behind something. Liz was standing beside the trunk when I saw her."

"Doesn't matter now. Between this and your attack on Tito Alvarez, you've ruined it for both of us. I knew we should have left town as soon as we realized one of your marks lived here."

"She hadn't seen her father in years. How was I to know he'd come sniffing around again?"

"You didn't have to hurt him."

"He was trying to blackmail me."

"He was the one in the alley," Rory whispered to Liz.

"I would have taken care of him if those two hadn't interfered. I tried warning Rory, but they wouldn't stop," Toby continued.

"Those two are friends of mine. I didn't appreciate that warning of yours."

"I wasn't going to hurt her. I didn't even have a gun. If we'd been able to convince everyone Edgar was responsible for Zelena's death, none of this would have happened," Toby said.

"We hinted around enough and you planted the phone you found on Zelena in his office. What more could we do?" A short pause was followed by the sound of glass smashing against a wall. "I like it here. I like being Penny Worthington. This has been the best year of my life. I have friends, real friends. I don't even care about your little affair. I don't want to have to move and start all over again."

"Neither do I, but the ship's sailed on that, hasn't it?"

"Not my fault. You're the one who's made it impossible for us to stay."

"I can't do anything about that now. We have to get rid of her. Can't use the boat again. The police are swarming all over it."

"I didn't sign up for this," Penny said in an angry voice. "I was willing to help you with Zelena because I thought she was already dead. This is different. Liz is my friend. I won't let you hurt her."

Rory peeked around the corner again to see Penny heading toward the truck. She was halfway across the floor when Toby grabbed her and spun her around. The couple started to argue once again.

"Now's our chance. Quick, let's get out of here," Rory said.

She eased herself to the ground, landing as softly as possible on the garage floor. She helped Liz down, then grabbed the crystal ball and, with her arms around her friend's waist, slowly headed toward the side door. They were almost there when she glanced back to see Toby within striking distance, brandishing a piece of wood.

"Run!" Penny shouted at them before she launched herself at Toby, pummeling him in the back with her fists. Toby turned and pushed his wife away, giving Rory enough time to place herself between him and Liz. When he charged toward her, she threw the crystal ball at him, hitting him squarely in the middle. He lost his grip on the two-by-four and clutched his stomach with both hands. Before he could recover, Rory ran over to the truck, grabbed the tablecloth and threw it over his head.

While Toby thrashed around, trying to free himself from the entangling cloth, Rory helped Liz out the side door. They'd barely made it outside when police cars screeched to a halt in the driveway in front of them.

"Toby's inside with Penny. He killed Zelena," she told the first officer who reached her.

While the police went inside, Rory led Liz down the driveway as far away from the action as possible. She'd just settled her friend against one of the police cars when Martin drove up. After making sure Liz was okay, he hugged Rory to his chest and said, "I got here as soon as I could. Thank God you're both okay. Don't worry. No one will hurt you anymore. We've got this."

Chapter 36

The sun sparkled on the ocean and warmed the crowd gathered near the Vista Beach pier on Halloween. That afternoon the block down to the pier was closed to traffic and an area cordoned off. A line of people, many of them dressed in costumes, held brightly decorated pumpkins, patiently waiting for their turn to race. Five entrants were lined up on the starting line, ready for the next heat to begin.

Decked out in a black and white striped shirt and black pants, the race official went down the line, inspecting each one of the entrants. He stopped by the fifth and final racer, brought out his tape measure and measured the distance between axles. Satisfied with the results, he continued his inspection. Bending closer to the miniature witch painted a bright green, he knocked gently on it. After listening closely, he brought out a knife and cut out a piece of the witch, revealing the red flesh inside.

He raised the hand containing the bit of watermelon above his head and addressed the crowd. "We have a cheater pumpkin!"

Rory and Liz laughed and booed along with the rest of the crowd. The woman who'd entered the faux pumpkin in the race put both hands to the sides of her cheeks, feigning shock. "I'm soooo embarrassed."

"What do we do with cheater pumpkins?" the official shouted.

The crowd erupted into cries of "Smash it, smash it!"

After an assistant spread a plastic sheet on the street and the offending watermelon was placed on top of it, the official raised a large mallet above his head and brought it down on the melon, smashing it into smithereens.

Once the remains were cleared off the course, the next contestant placed a pumpkin decorated like BB-8, one of the droids from the *Star Wars* movies, on the starting line. After a quick inspection, the race began. The pumpkins barreled down the incline, most hitting the blocks at the end, a few veering off course and running into the side.

"The key is to get the axles on straight," a man beside Rory said.

As soon as the race was over and the winner of the heat crowned, Rory and Liz headed toward the nearby parking lot where some of the prize-winning pumpkins were on display.

"That one's cute." Liz pointed toward a pumpkin painted like the pigs in the Angry Birds app, the winner of the Most Creative award in the children's department.

"I like that one." Rory nodded toward a pumpkin with bandages wrapped around it like a mummy. She gave her friend a quick hug. "I'm so glad you could make it today. I wasn't sure you would after your ordeal."

"I had a whole day to recover. I'm still a little stiff, but I wouldn't miss this for the world. It's my favorite time of year." Liz spread her arms wide and spun around. She stopped abruptly and leaned against Rory for a moment. "Guess I wasn't quite ready for that. Just a little dizzy."

"What's going on with your cousins? With all of the recent excitement, I forgot to ask."

"I finally found them a house. Turns out they really liked all of the ones I showed them. They planned on putting in a cash offer for one of them, but the stock market took a dive and they couldn't come up with the entire amount. They were trying to finance part of it, but that can be hard for foreigners."

"Why didn't they tell you about it? Couldn't you have helped them with the financing?"

"They were too embarrassed. Anyway, everything's fine now. They're in escrow on a place a street over from my parents' house."

They were walking back toward the race course when Candy waved at them from her place in line. "Yoo hoo, ladies, over here!"

They waved and headed toward her, stopping on the other side of the metal barrier that separated the contestants from the spectators.

Candy put down her pumpkin with hair styled in a bubble cut similar to her own and hugged each of them in turn.

"I heard about what happened," she said. "So glad to hear you're both okay."

"I wouldn't have been without Rory." Liz's eyes glistened with unshed tears.

"You would have done the same for me," Rory said.

When the line moved forward, Candy picked up her pumpkin and moved with it.

"So Toby killed Zelena, right? What happened there? I've heard a number of versions."

"You know about her deal with Edgar Geller, right?" Rory said.

"The CEO of Beyond The Grave? Sure. She was staying in that RV park, pretending to be kidnapped. I heard she decided not to go through with it."

"That's right. After Raven dropped her off on the edge of town, Zelena walked over to the boutique house to ask Penny for advice on what to do next. She'd forgotten our board meeting was still going on at my mom's store. Toby was at the house by himself setting up the escape room so she talked to him instead. She was helping unpack a box and spotted the phoenix tattoo in the photo. When he admitted it was an old picture of him and his mother, she put two and two together and realized who he was."

"So she accused him of stealing her money?" Candy said.

Rory nodded her head. "She was heading out the door to phone the police when he grabbed her and covered her mouth so she wouldn't scream. Before he knew it, his hands had tightened around her neck and she passed out. He thought he'd killed her. He locked the escape room door and called Penny."

"But Zelena came to long enough to stuff her purse behind the trunk. That's where I found it," Liz said.

"So Penny helped him get her out of the house that evening and onto Jeanne's boat?" Candy said.

"Only she came to again when they were about to throw her overboard and she fought back." Rory touched a spot on her own head. "That's where the contusion came from. Toby threw her overboard and jumped in after her, making sure she drowned. Probably wasn't hard since she didn't know how to swim."

"Then they left her and her body drifted away." Candy shook her head. "That's some story." She moved to the front of the line. "Looks like I'm up next. Wish me luck, ladies."

After watching Candy come in third in her heat, Rory and Liz headed toward the area set aside for putting together the pumpkin racers. They joined Teresa who was putting the final touches on the painting chapter's entry.

"What do you think?" Teresa waved her hand at the pumpkin painted with a floral pattern in bright colors, topped with a beret.

"Looks great," Rory said. "Where are its wheels?"

"Right here." Jeanne hurried over with a race kit and, between the four of them, they quickly attached the axles and wheels to the pumpkin.

"Who's going to race it?" Teresa said. "As chapter president, Penny was supposed to have the honors."

The four fell silent while they thought about the woman they had thought of as a friend and the recent events that led to her arrest.

"What about you, Jeanne?" Rory asked. "Aren't you next in line?"

"Rather not. I've had enough of publicity. I have to leave, anyway."

"I'll do it," Liz said.

Everyone nodded their agreement. Rory watched Jeanne as she made her way up the hill away from the race area until her figure was no longer visible. "Things didn't work out exactly like she planned. I'm sure she didn't expect her boyfriend to be a retired con artist as well as a murderer and end up in jail."

"Don't feel too sorry for her," Teresa said. "She's not exactly innocent herself. Though she does seem to have bad taste in men."

"There's one thing I don't understand," Liz said. "How did Toby plant the phone in Edgar's office?"

"He dressed up like a food delivery man and put it in the office when he was out." Veronica walked up to the group clustered around the pumpkin. "He knew about the deal Zelena had with Edgar, remember."

"How'd they get by Tabitha?"

"Penny called her on the phone and kept her busy. She just waved Toby through into the office. He had lunch delivered every day so she didn't think anything of it. Edgar was out at a meeting."

"Must have paid the usual delivery man to let him do that," Rory said.

"That's what I heard. Let me get a picture of you and your entry." After everyone arranged themselves behind the pumpkin that sat on the table, the reporter snapped a few photos. "Great."

Liz scooped up their entry and headed to the back of the line, Teresa trailing behind her.

"Where's that boyfriend of yours?" Veronica said to Rory.

"Should be here soon. He's getting the police department racer ready."

Veronica brought out a copy of the newspaper from her tote bag. "There are a couple articles in today's *View* I think you might find interesting." She pointed to one on the front page about the arrest of Toby and Penny Worthington for Zelena Alvarez's murder as well as one on an inside page regarding the pranksters.

Rory read the inside article first. In it, Detective Green was quoted as saying "We're confident we've apprehended all of the people responsible for the pranks around the city." The only one of the group mentioned by name was Keith Halliwell.

Rory looked at the reporter. "I only see Keith's name here."

"All of the others are under eighteen. We don't publish the names of juvenile offenders."

"His father claimed he'd get the chief to let him off easy."

Veronica snorted. "He should have known better. Chief Marshall doesn't let people off. Ever."

"I didn't think so." Rory directed her attention to the front page article on the murder. "Tito's awake?"

"And talking." Martin Green walked up to them, holding a pumpkin painted black and white with blue and red lights attached to its top. "Seems he recognized Toby from an old photo in the escape room. Even though he'd changed his appearance, Tito realized he was the one who had stolen his daughter's money once he spotted the phoenix tattoo in the picture. It didn't take him long to put two and two together and realize Toby was the man in the photo. He threatened to tell the police unless Toby gave him some money."

"So Toby tried to kill him. I don't understand why Tito would resort to blackmail. Why didn't he just tell the police?"

"And publicly admit that it was his fault he'd lost the money in the first place? You told me yourself he blamed his daughter's manager for that."

"But everyone knew it was true."

"Except he'd never admitted it. There's a big difference."

Rory nodded toward his pumpkin. "Nice racer. Do the lights work?"

"Yep. Sirens too."

After taking a photo of the detective with the racer, Veronica drifted off.

Teresa gestured at them from a spot against the railing. "Hurry up. We're up next."

Rory and Martin joined the group lined up against the waist high railing and cheered on the racers. Rory watched while her painting chapter's pumpkin sailed down the hill, groaning when it crashed into the side and failed to make it to the bottom.

"Guess we didn't get those axles on right," she said.

"It was a valiant effort. Join me in line?" Martin said.

While they waited for their turn to race, Rory said, "What's going on with Raven?"

"She's out of business."

"What about—" she mouthed Mrs. Griswold's name, not wanting to say it aloud in the crowd.

"Our...mutual friend got her money back. Raven's being charged with multiple counts of fraud."

"Good. She won't be able to con anyone else out of their hard-earned money." Rory craned her neck to see how close they were to the front of the line. "Almost there."

"Are you taking over as Neighborhood Watch block captain?"

"Mrs. Griswold stopped asking me. I think she's going to continue in her role. She enjoys it too much to quit."

Martin handed her a check. "Edgar Geller wanted me to give this to you."

Rory's eyes opened wide when she saw the amount written on it. "Ten thousand! He's giving me the reward money?"

"He thinks you deserve it and so do I. What are you going to do with it?"

Rory stared thoughtfully into the distance. "I think I'm going to donate it to Zelena's favorite charity."

"Seems fitting."

Rory stuffed the check in her pocket. She looked over at Martin and said hesitantly, "Are we okay?"

"I won't lie. I thought about giving up on us, but I can't. You're the best thing that's happened to me in a long time." He took a deep breath. "I do wish you'd stop taking chances, but I know you do it because you care about people. That's one of the things I love about you, how much you care about others."

Rory breathed a sigh of relief. "I'll be more careful. I promise."

For the next few minutes, they stood silently and soaked in the festive atmosphere. When their turn came to race, Martin put his entry on the starting line, then enveloped Rory in his strong arms as his pumpkin, lights flashing and sirens blaring, raced to victory.

Sybil Johnson

Sybil Johnson's love affair with reading began in kindergarten with "The Three Little Pigs." Visits to the library introduced her to Encyclopedia Brown, Mrs. Piggle-Wiggle and a host of other characters. Fast forward to college where she continued reading while studying Computer Science. After a rewarding career in the computer industry, Sybil decided to try her hand at writing mysteries. Her short fiction has appeared in *Mysterical-E* and *Spinetingler Magazine*, among others. Originally from the Pacific Northwest, she now lives in Southern California where she enjoys tole painting, studying ancient languages and spending time with friends and family.

**The Aurora Anderson Mystery Series
by Sybil Johnson**

FATAL BRUSHSTROKE (#1)
PAINT THE TOWN DEAD (#2)
A PALETTE FOR MURDER (#3)
DESIGNED FOR HAUNTING (#4)

Henery Press Mystery Books

And finally, before you go...
Here are a few other mysteries
you might enjoy:

CROPPED TO DEATH

Christina Freeburn

A Faith Hunter Scrap This Mystery (#1)

Former US Army JAG specialist, Faith Hunter, returns to her West Virginia home to work in her grandmothers' scrapbooking store determined to lead an unassuming life after her adventure abroad turned disaster. But her quiet life unravels when her friend is charged with murder – and Faith inadvertently supplied the evidence. So Faith decides to cut through the scrap and piece together what really happened.

With a sexy prosecutor, a determined homicide detective, a handful of sticky suspects and a crop contest gone bad, Faith quickly realizes if she's not careful, she'll be the next one cropped.

Available at booksellers nationwide and online

Visit www.henerypress.com for details

SECRETS, LIES, & CRAWFISH PIES

Abby L. Vandiver

A Romaine Wilder Mystery (#1)

Romaine Wilder, big-city medical examiner with a small-town past, has been downsized and evicted. She's forced to return to her hometown of Robel in East Texas, leaving behind the man she's dating and the life she's worked hard to build.

Suzanne Babet Derbinay, Romaine's Auntie Zanne and proprietor of the Ball Funeral Home, has long since traded her French Creole upbringing for Big Texas attitude. Hanging on to the magic of her Louisiana roots, she's cooked up a love potion—if she could only get Romaine to drink it. But when the Ball Funeral Home, bursting at the seams with dead bodies, has a squatter stiff, Romaine and Auntie Zanne set off to find out who is responsible for the murder.

Available at booksellers nationwide and online

Visit www.henerypress.com for details

I SCREAM, YOU SCREAM

Wendy Lyn Watson

A Mystery A-la-mode (#1)

Tallulah Jones's whole world is melting. Her ice cream parlor, Remember the A-la-mode, is struggling, and she's stooped to catering a party for her sleezeball ex-husband Wayne and his arm candy girlfriend Brittany. Worst of all? Her dreamy high school sweetheart shows up on her front porch, swirling up feelings Tally doesn't have time to deal with.

Things go from ugly to plain old awful when Brittany turns up dead and all eyes turn to Tally as the murderer. With the help of her hell-raising cousin Bree, her precocious niece Alice, and her long-lost-super-confusing love Finn, Tally has to dip into the heart of Dalliance, Texas's most scandalous secrets to catch a murderer...before someone puts Tally and her dreams on ice for good.

Available at booksellers nationwide and online

Visit www.henerypress.com for details

A MUDDIED MURDER

Wendy Tyson

A Greenhouse Mystery (#1)

When Megan Sawyer gives up her big-city law career to care for her grandmother and run the family's organic farm and café, she expects to find peace and tranquility in her scenic hometown of Winsome, Pennsylvania. Instead, her goat goes missing, rain muddies her fields, the town denies her business permits, and her family's Colonial-era farm sucks up the remains of her savings.

Just when she thinks she's reached the bottom of the rain barrel, Megan and the town's hunky veterinarian discover the local zoning commissioner's battered body in her barn. Now Megan's thrust into the middle of a murder investigation—and she's the chief suspect. Can Megan dig through small-town secrets, local politics, and old grievances in time to find a killer before that killer strikes again?

Available at booksellers nationwide and online

Visit www.henerypress.com for details

Made in the USA
Coppell, TX
30 October 2020

40505215R00154